Simon Raven was born in London in 1927. He was educated at Charterhouse and King's College, Cambridge where he read Classics. After university, he joined the army as a regular officer in the King's Shropshire Light Infantry and saw service in Germany and Kenya where he commanded a Rifle Company. In 1957 he resigned his commission and took up book reviewing. His first novel, *The Feathers of Death*, was published in 1959. Since then he has written many reviews, general essays, plays for radio and television as well as the scripts for a number of successful television series including *Edward and Mrs Simpson* and *Love in a Cold Climate* plus a host of novels. The highly acclaimed ALMS FOR OBLIVION sequence is published for the first time in this Panther edition in chronological order. The sequence takes its title from a passage in Shakespeare's *Troilus and Cressida*, has been referred to as 'a latter-day Waugh report on another generation of Bright Young Things', and has been compared favourably with the *romans fleuves* of Anthony Powell and C. P. Snow. With the publication in 1984 of *Morning Star* he began a new novel series under the title THE FIRST BORN OF EGYPT. It is a sequel to ALMS FOR OBLIVION. Simon Raven lives and works in Deal, Kent.

D1280729

By the same author

Novels

The Feathers of Death
Brother Cain
Doctors Wear Scarlet
Close of Play
The Fortunes of Fingel

The ALMS FOR OBLIVION sequence,
in chronological order:

Fielding Gray
Sound the Retreat
The Sabre Squadron
The Rich Pay Late
Friends in Low Places
The Judas Boy
Places Where They Sing
Come Like Shadows
Bring Forth the Body
The Survivors

Essays

The English Gentleman
Boys Will Be Boys

Plays

Royal Foundation and Other Plays

SIMON RAVEN

Friends in Low Places

PANTHER
Granada Publishing

Panther Books
Granada Publishing Ltd
8 Grafton Street, London W1X 3LA

Published by Panther Books 1967
Reprinted 1967, 1968, 1972, 1979, 1984

First published in Great Britain by
Anthony Blond Ltd 1965

Copyright © Simon Raven 1965

ISBN 0-586-02190-6

Printed and bound in Great Britain by
Collins, Glasgow

Set in Monotype Garamond

ALMS FOR OBLIVION *is a series of ten novels (of which* Friends in Low Places *is the fifth) covering the English upper-middle-class scene since the war. The series is not planned as one long saga; each volume presents an independent story. But the ten major characters are all loosely connected with one another by birth or upbringing. If there is one theme which dominates the series it is that human effort and goodwill are persistently vulnerable to the malice of time, chance, and the rest of the human race.*

A GAME OF CHANCE

"JESUS CHRIST," said Mark Lewson: "what a bloody boring place this is."

"You don't have to stay," said Angela Tuck.

They were sitting on the promenade at Menton, drinking champagne cocktails at half past noon on a Sunday in the April of 1959.

"I like being with *you*, dear. It's so suitable. We can console each other in our grief."

"Tuck was killed nearly three years ago," said Angela Tuck. "Neither then nor later have I needed consolation."

"You're heartless, that's your trouble. *I* need consoling. It's only a few weeks since my beloved wife passed away to the happy land, leaving me desolate in more senses than on."

"How did she die, Mark? You've been a little vague."

"Drink, dear. Even the coffin smelt of gin. It caused a great scandal among her dreary relations."

"They came all the way to England for the funeral?"

"The two sisters. To see if there was any money left."

"Which there wasn't?"

"There never had been very much. When the old Count Monteverdi died, having spent most of his life in England, he left about a hundred thou. in the funds, as they say, a few valuable paintings, and a little property in Rome. Felicity's share after duties was twenty-odd thou., one small Sisley and three Dalis, and a flat in the Piazza Navona."

"Enough to be going on with," Angela said.

"As it happened, not." Mark giggled. "The two sisters went

home to Tivoli and interested themselves in pious works. Felicity stayed in England and interested herself in me. She was fifteen years older, of course, but I thought, what the hell, she's a good-natured cow and they say she'd got a lot of cash. As usual, 'they' had exaggerated. We'd barely finished with the honeymoon before she announced that the crinkle had run out."

"Twenty thousand?"

"I'd bought a small yacht. You see, no one," Mark said petulantly, "had told me that twenty thou. was all there was."

"She must have been mad."

"Right, dear. Mad about me."

I'm not surprised, Angela thought. She surveyed the cherubic face with the weak, vicious chin; the dark wavy hair; the torso, thin but tough under the flowery shirt; the Botticelli legs under the white flannel shorts. She surveyed all these, and thought of other things, and decided that a woman fifteen years his senior might well have been mad about Mark Lewson, so mad as to spend her entire fortune buying him a yacht. But I, she thought, am not fifteen years his senior, only five; he'll get little enough out of me and what he gets he'll earn. In fact, I'm not sure that he hasn't already had his ration.

"What happened to the yacht?" she said.

"Sold at a loss when things began to get difficult."

"Rotten luck."

You mean sow, Mark Lewson thought. *I* know all this chat about Felicity's money is just a way of telling me that I'll get none from you. You'd hang on to the little bit Tuck left you if they tried to drag it out of you on the rack. And you'd better hang on, dear, because there's not going to be much left of *you* in another five years. You're all crows' feet and flab as it is, and teeth awash in cheap brandy nine nights out of ten. You're jolly lucky to get me, simply because I'm having a bad patch, for bed, board and pin money. But I'm only passing through. Something will turn up, it always does, and then it's toodle-ooh to you, Angela Tuck, you and your sagging tits.

Meanwhile, however, make the best of the bed and board. "Let's have another drink," he said.

"You've already had three."

"I'll do my stuff after lunch, if that's what's worrying you."

The narrow eyes glinted and the weak chin twitched with simulated lust. The Botticelli legs straddled. Sweating with the sudden excitement of it, Angela decided that she was not yet quite finished with him after all.

"All right," she said, as Lewson beckoned a waiter and gestured at the empty glasses, "but only one. They're expensive." She passed him two notes over the table, each for a thousand old francs. "What happened," she said, "after you sold the yacht?"

"We got along for a while. Then the Dalis went. Then the Sisley. Finally the flat. After that, we'd only got her family name and the title. *Née* Monteverdi. Contessa – or contessina for sentimental old men. This was a help in cashing cheques."

"Not for long, I bet."

"Longer than you'd think. We kept moving."

"And in the end?"

"In the end she died."

"Just when she'd ceased to be useful."

Mark grinned.

"She died of drink, dear. Drink and the English winter."

"I'll buy it . . . as you've been so frank about the rest."

"I wouldn't try it on with you, dear. You're up to everything."

The compliment was sincere. Mark Lewson was telling the truth, and finding it a great relief to be free, just for once, from the Jacobean complexities of his own invention. Not that he was consciously seeking relief in this unaccustomed candour; it was just that Angela – he felt it in his bones – would neither believe his lies, brilliant as they often were, nor, if she did believe, be impressed. This was still not to say that he told her the truth out of respect: there was just no point in telling her anything else.

"You're up to everything," he repeated. "You've got a kind of genius for being a slut."

And after three and a half champagne cocktails, he thought, you don't look too bad at that. So he leaned over to whisper in her ear, and she squirmed with pleasure in her seat.

"After lunch," she said with an effort. "So she left you with nothing?"

"Except a bad name in half the hotels in Europe."

"So what are you going to do now?" she asked him, not unkindly.

"Have some lunch and a lot of fun after it."

"And then?"

"Sufficient unto the day. . . ."

"But not unto the morrow."

"Since you ask me," he said, "I need an *angle*. Something I can *work*, like I worked the Contessa's name for cheques. Something to go on. That's why I get so fed up with Menton. There's nothing here, never could be."

"There's peace. And economy."

"Not what I need."

"We'll have to see what we can find for you," Angela said.

Angela had enjoyed her last fortnight with Mark Lewson and, other things being strictly equal, she wished him well. But with Mark other things, so far from being equal, were not even commensurate; and despite the manifest and mounting excitement of the present moment Angela knew, for she was an experienced woman, that in a few days time at most she must get him out of the way. He represented menace: to her, to her money, to her little house in the town. So rid of him she must be; but if she could only do him a service at the same time, so much better for both of them, as they could part in kindness and no harm done. She wouldn't, couldn't pay him off in cash; she must find him what he called his "angle". She might think, for a start, about that story she had heard from Max. . . . Angle, not Angela, she said to herself, and giggled.

"What's so funny then?"

"I'll maybe tell you later. Lunch."

Behind the closed shutters the bedroom, which faced north, was cool and reassuring. Angela, fed and pleasured, slept, pinching the nipple of her left breast between the first two fingers of her right hand, for all the world like a Rubens goddess about to squirt milk into the open mouth of a cherub. Mark Lewson's mouth was open, but not in expectation of Angela's milk: he always gaped when he was thoughtful. He was thoughtful just now because he was wondering whether he could open Angela's bag on the dressing table, remove two of the four ten thousand franc notes which he had seen in it before lunch, and then get out of the bedroom and out of the house without waking Angela, who, however well pleasured, was a light sleeper. Although this plan, which would conclude with a visit to the afternoon session in the Casino, offered action of a kind, something to offset the stagnation of Sunday in Menton, it had several disadvantages. First, Mark did not care for gambling and usually lost; and secondly, even if he returned the money later, Angela would almost certainly find out that it had been taken. She would turn nasty, she would probably turn him out. This danger, however, was the less deterrent as it had become increasingly plain, from Angela's demeanour over the last few days, that she was going to turn him out in any case. Before marrying the Contessa, Mark had had much experience of this kind of sojourn: he could read the signs as a poacher can read the weather, and they heralded the rapidly approaching end of this particular idyll. So what the hell, he thought: nothing to lose.

Stage one: to ease himself off the bed, inch by inch, so that it did not give out a tell-tale creak. This was easier said than done, for the bed, a huge and ancient *letto matrimoniale* from over the border, was much given to creaks, and indeed making love on it to Angela always sounded like being in the bowels of a wind-jammer which was running before a gale. But Mark was an agile mover and had devoted much of his life to studying such skills; after a few discreet wriggles of his delicate buttocks, he had both feet hanging over the side of the bed, and with a final slow roll of his upper body he was safely and silently off. Angela, still posed as some goddess of peace and plenty, slept on.

Stage two: to open the bag and take the money. While he was about it he might as well take the lot. (Nothing to lose.)

Stage three: to open the door, which was almost as rackety an apparatus as the bed. Here luck was with him: Angela, frantic with post-prandial lust, had left it ajar.

Stage four: to creep to the dressing-room down the little passage and get suitably togged up. (The Casino, while small and friendly, did not encourage informality of *tenu*.) Thank God he didn't keep his clothes in the bedroom. Now then: the light grey suit, pink shirt, old Etonian tie (a falsity which he had sported for so long that he now almost believed that he had been at Eton), and the dark suède shoes. Hair: eau de cologne: mouth wash. (Since one of the troubles about this kind of life was that one was never in the same place long enough to take a proper course with a dentist, his teeth and gums were bad and he had, as he well knew, atrocious breath.) Cigarettes. Passport. And that (with Angela's forty thousand francs) was the lot.

Stage five: to go back past the bedroom, down the stairs and out. She could hardly stop him now, but he might as well keep up the charade. After all, if he could get out, make a profit, return the forty thousand, all without her knowing, so much the better. He might be able to hang on here as long as another week. He tip-toed past the bedroom, was pleased to hear a gross snore, slid down the short banister, opened the front door, left the latch up in order to re-admit himself (Angela refused to allow him a key), and emerged into the blue and sticky afternoon.

Angela Tuck dreamt that she was back in India again, up in the hills near Oute, that day they came to arrest her father nearly fifteen years ago. They were sitting, she and her father, drinking gin before lunch. Since she had been playing golf and was very thirsty, she was having hers with lime juice and a lot of soda. Just as she was about to drink, her father said:

"Make the best of it, girlie. There may not be many more where that came from."

She raised her glass again but now it was empty, except for a small cube of ice which slid along the tilted tumbler to burn her lips.

"All gone," her father said, in the tones he had once used in the nursery. He leaned forward and started tickling her, a favourite game when she was little. But then there was a curt, loud knock on the door of the bungalow; her father's hands fell away from her; and in the moment before she awoke Angela knew that at long last they had found him out and had come to take him away.

As indeed they had, she thought to herself, sweaty, dry-mouthed, wide awake. Cooking the Pay Rolls; a wonder he'd got away with it for so long. But never mind him, dead and unlamented in his Hongkong grave. That knock on the door. The empty half of the bed.

"Mark?" she called.

It was obvious what had happened. He had slipped out and woken her as he left. She rose from the bed to check her handbag. Forty thousand, the little rat. But never mind: if he'd gone for good, forty thousand was not too disastrous a price; and if he came back and tried to brazen it out, she'd have a good excuse for giving him notice to quit. Thinking of him without rancour she returned, with the handbag, to bed, lit a cigarette, crushed it out, thought of her father in Oute again, thought wistfully of the pretty race meetings and the green fairways on the golf course, and fell into a light doze from which she awoke without difficulty when, ten minutes later, the door bell rang downstairs.

The patrons of the Casino at Menton have always been a predictable bunch. Since the stakes are low and the furnishings shabby, since the croupiers are for the most part ageing and kindly men who, too wise to aspire higher, too honest to sink lower, have spent a placid lifetime here, the place has acquired a "family" atmosphere in which even the Casino detective behaves with prim geniality, like nanny supervising a tea party of well conducted children. These latter are the regulars, expatriate ladies and gentlemen of the English upper-middle class with an addition of tight-faced French women of the indigenous commercial bourgeoisie, all of whom, English or French, are as well known to each other as they are to the management and staff.

If we leave aside the ethnical division, the regulars fall into two groups: those who come when the Casino opens at two in the afternoon and those, more resourceful, who do not arrive until after an early dinner. Both groups, as soon as they enter, seat themselves at the double-ended roulette table and stay there until it closes down at two in the morning, those who have exhausted the funds set aside for the day being quite happy to sit and watch, and not dreaming of giving up their seats to any more serious players who may (even in Menton) occasionally appear.

"Routine", then, is the Casino motto, and right loyally both staff and clients live up to it. The only variation is itself routine: every Sunday afternoon both groups, instead of arriving at two and eight-thirty respectively, arrive at half past four to take tea and anticipate the grand treat of the week – a two-hour game of chemin-de-fer which runs from five till seven and is never prolonged, no matter how earnestly the players may implore, for fear, no doubt, of over-exciting the children and disturbing the wholesome discipline which must rule the remainder of the week. But from the given hours of five to seven something near anarchy is permitted: some six of the regulars, who are rich enough to afford the higher stakes, will be joined at the Chemmy table by two or three outsiders (a sensitive Italian, perhaps, sickened by the noise and crowding in the rooms at San Remo, and a local embezzler or two, anxious to risk their loot in the most discreet *venue* available); while the rest of the regulars, enjoying brief freedom from the tyrannous wheel, will stand round and *kibbitz*, occasionally soliciting a good-natured banker to take bets of a few hundred francs from the floor.

It was just as this weekly period of licence was about to begin that Mark Lewson entered the Salon. The *chef du parti*, who was, as tradition prescribed, the most benign and atrophied of all the croupiers, retained enough professional instinct to sniff money in Mark's demeanour; and since there was still one vacant seat, he smiled and beckoned, with both coquetry and command, like a worldly uncle who is just about to put one on to "a good thing" – a quicker cure for clap or advance intelligence of a new issue of stock. Mark, while he was not impressed by this *bonhomie*, recognised the convenience of the empty chair and the necessity of starting at once if he was to have any chance of getting back before Angela awoke. He grinned like a juvenile vampire, passed Angela's forty thousand to the croupier, received plaques and counters in exchange, ordered himself a bottle of champagne from a rusty waiter, lit a cheroot, and sat.

The empty place which he had filled was place five, dead opposite the croupier. To his left was an ample French woman who had crumbs of icing in her moustache; to his right an ageing and *distingué* Englishman (writer? poet? don?) with long and obscenely youthful hair, Marlborough suit buttoned high, wing collar and bow. The French woman looked at him as though judging, objectively, whether or not he might be edible; the Englishman smiled, very sweetly, and murmured something about the spring weather. The game began. The first three bankers lost at the first *coup*, and the shoe was with the French woman, who put down an opening bank of ten thousand francs – rather more than this table normally ran to.

"*Banco*," said Mark, and lost to a natural eight.

"*Banco*," he said again, and again lost to a natural eight.

"Bad luck, dear boy," said the writer-don, sentimentally patting Mark's hair. "If you're not going to follow again, I'll take it myself."

Mark was not going to follow again. He had already lost three quarters of his capital and must use his remaining 10,000 with care if he was to survive at all.

"You're more than welcome," he said.

"Banco," chirped his neighbour, dewlaps foaming over the wing collar.

The French woman emitted four words, like a sharp burst of bren-gun fire aimed straight at the croupier's false teeth. No, he replied, Madame could not garage any of her winnings, under the house rules, until after the third *coup* of her bank. Madame, who knew this as well as she knew her married name, announced that it was "*effroyable*" and that the bank would nevertheless continue.

"Banco," repeated the Marlborough suit, and eventually won with a two to Madame's baccarat.

The bank now passed to Mark, who put down the minimum starter of 2,000, immediately lost it with a natural eight to the Marlborough suit's natural nine, and received another pat of sympathy on the hair. He was about to retaliate with the burning end of his cheroot, when he remembered that he now had only 8,000 francs left and had better preserve good relations. In return for the right to pat away for the rest of the session, wing collar might perhaps "do" him a small loan or a cheque.

This question became pressingly pertinent after the bank had passed rapidly round the table, arrived at Mark once more, and cost him immediately the 5,000 francs which he rashly put up for it. Only 3,000 to go (and the champagne to be paid for).

Wing collar's frail hand now pushed 5,000 forward to start his new bank. The old idiot was in luck: cash in on it.

"Can I come in with you?" asked Mark. "Half shares?"

Hopefully he proferred 2,500, leaving himself only a miserable lozenge, of what looked like hotel soap, worth 500.

"Couldn't do that, dearest boy. Never play with other people's money. Makes for nasty quarrels, don't you know."

The Marlborough suit then won ten times running and received, when he finally went down, the better part of 200,000 francs from the croupier. If the old Yid had let me share, thought Mark viciously, I'd have been up, off and clear. And now the old bugger's got the cheek to pat my hair again.

"I've got my cheque book here," he began casually: "as one Englishman to another. . . ."

The hand was unhurriedly removed from Mark's head.

"Try the Caisse." The dewlaps wobbled like two buttocks parted by a crack in the chin. "They know all about that. Classical man myself – get confused by figures."

Deftly the pale hands sorted and counted the glittering *bijoux* delivered by the croupier's rake. Mark began to sweat in the crutch. Only 3,000 left. Stuck. Back to Angela? *Peccavi?* God, you look so sexy I can't wait? How bored he was with being tied to that bloody woman; if she wasn't so mean, none of this would have happened.

Meanwhile, another large bank was running. The hair-patter's right-hand neighbour, as often happens, was repeating his predecessor's luck. After his sixth win the new banker consulted with the croupier; a large pile of chips was placed to one side, a second, even larger, left in the middle.

"*Cent milles pour la banque.*"

"Banco," said Mark on impulse. They *might* let him play

without seeing the money; in which case the penalty for loss
would probably be gaol. That was what it said in one of
Fleming's novels, but of course they might just turn him out
and leave it at that. In any case this was *action*.

"Banco," he said again.

The kibbitzers muttered blithely: banco on 100,000 was a
rare treat. The hair-patter looked bland, the female cake-eater
sceptical, the rest of the players expectant. The atrophied
croupier's mind began to click over. The residual instinct
which had led him to beckon Mark to the table had told him
that the young man was worth perhaps 60,000. Not more.
But the champagne, the carelessness over what he had lost....?
On the other hand, the rather worn suit, the placatory whispering to the English professor. . . . What was one to think?
No, he decided, one must see the money first.

"*M'sieur . . . l'argent?*"

"Up to your old tricks, Lewson?" said a soft voice in
Mark's ear. "I'll stand you this one, provided you give me
your seat when it's over. Win or lose."

A chunk of mauve plastic proclaiming 100,000 francs
landed by Mark's right hand. The professor smiled genially.
The cake-woman fingered her moustache with the practised
effrontery of a colonel of dragoons. Two cards were passed
to Mark: a ten and a king – makes nought. "*Carte, s'il vous
plaît.*" The banker turned up his own to reveal a seven and a
knave, and flicked Mark an eight. "*Je reste.*" "*Sept pour la
banque et*" – turning over Mark's two openers – "*huit pour
m'sieur.*" All over. Mark received a second mauve plaque for
his winnings and turned to his benefactor.

Even though he had only met him once, three years ago
and briefly, he could not have failed to recognise, from the
numerous photographs which had since appeared in the press,
the gambling impressario, Max de Freville. The furrows
arching down from the base of the nose were quite unmistakable. But what was de Freville doing at a seedy little game

in Menton? De Freville, who was worth half a million (so they said), who no longer gambled himself, who merely organised discreet games for the big money and took his cut on the turnover?

"De Freville?"

"I'll have the stake money back, if you don't mind. And my seat."

Mark rose, passed one mauve plaque to de Freville and put the other in his pocket. Clear, out and up – by 60,000. Time to get back to Angela, replace the money he had borrowed. But curiosity held him. It wasn't every Sunday afternoon that one encountered as notable a figure as Max de Freville, whose presence here certainly needed explanation. Furthermore, he was impressed that de Freville should have remembered so clearly his own name and reputation although they had done no more than pass in (literally) the night. Having waited until de Freville lost his bank on the second *coup*, Mark ventured:

"Haven't seen you in three years odd. Not since that dance of Donald Salinger's. What are you doing in Menton of all places?"

"I come here when I can. There's a smell of middle-class mortality which I find pleasing. And of course there's some good stuff to be seen inland."

He gestured out of the Casino and over the hills, away into Provence.

"They said you'd given up playing."

"I have." The voice was slightly blurred, as though coming from a great distance, from under many layers, formed by the inexorable years, of ennui and regret. "I'm only sitting here to keep you out of trouble and give them a sporting chance to get their money back. My professional conscience. I can't allow a seat to be vacated without warning. But we'll leave when the shoe's over. I don't think they can reasonably ask more."

"You came here because of me?"

"Because of Angela. I dropped in just now and I've been hearing about you. *Banco*. It seems she wants you out of the way, and so, since I'm to be here a few days, do I. She thought you might have gone for good, but I said, not you, your type never go until they've squeezed the last drop. So I volunteered to take a look around. And since you are still here – "

" – You know what to do about it."

"*Carte*. . . . I've already done it. You can cash in that mauve plaque, give Angie her 40,000 and keep the balance. For the rest, if it were up to me, I'd kick you out and leave it at that." He pushed over a pile of chips which he had just lost. "But Angie reckons she owes you a bit more for her good time. She wants to see you in business, as she puts it. Luckily we can give you a start."

"In your organisation?" said Mark eagerly.

"I wouldn't employ you, Lewson, to clean my lavatory floors. No. Last time I was here I heard an interesting story which may add up to occupation for you. If I give you the right introduction."

The tin rattled out of the shoe. De Freville rose, bowed to the French woman, and nodded to the Marlborough suit on his right.

"Come on," he said to Mark: "cash that plaque, pay for your fizz, and back to Angie's."

While Mark and de Freville walked back to Angela's villa, she was preparing with love and happiness an enormous English tea – this meal, as she knew, being de Freville's favourite.

The relationship between Angela and de Freville, now of two years' duration, was curious. It had started with a chance meeting on the promenade of Menton, when Angela had tripped over an Algerian carpet on display at the side of the pavement. She had fallen full length, badly grazed both her knees, suffered minor shock and major humiliation, and had been very relieved when a tall, taciturn and tactful Englishman had picked her up, brushed her down and settled her in a chair for a drink. Unsettled by the childish nature of her performance and slightly loosened by alcohol, she had treated him, as a kind of smoke-screen for her embarrassment, to an account of her recent widowhood and of the motives (love of peace induced by a rackety and uncertain youth, together with the residual need to know that racket was still readily available in her neighbourhood) which had brought her to harbour in Menton. Since de Freville's motives for frequenting the place were similar, a provisional sympathy had immediately grown between them. Later they had walked, dined, talked of local and domestic life, discussed the price of fish and the insolence of cashiers in French banks, danced together closely but without excitement, and had finally, sympathy being by this time absolute, gone to bed together without passion and without any attempt at consummation.

For although de Freville shared Angela's *letto matrimonale* for companionship, their relations remained entirely platonic. The one thing of which each had always been deprived and which each now found in the other was tranquillity – the placid expectation of an unhurried, unworried and common progress from day's beginning through day's triviality to day's end, when they would retire to lie side by side, just touching, as innocent and easily lulled as two children to whom the morrow could only bring sound nourishment and loving care. After five days of this, when de Freville had to return to his affairs, they both resumed their normal manner of life: de Freville the restless and ever more tedious supervision of his gambling tables in London, Angela the daily search for the nightly master of her flesh. Both knew what the other would do in his absence; both pitied and acquiesced; both waited eagerly, but without amendment of life, until they could meet again in Menton and once more be together and at peace. Although they had friends in villas up and down the coast, they visited them seldom, for the spell only worked, it seemed, in Menton, and a journey of even a few miles made them wary of each other and ill at ease. By the same token there could be no question of marriage, of a continuous life together where-ever fortune might take them: their association could be no more than a periodic rest-cure, therapy which could be taken quite often but could not be indulged in permanently without abdication from life itself.

De Freville's unexpected arrival during the Lewson regime did not cause embarrassment either to himself or to Angela: it simply meant that Lewson must go straight away in order to make place. Since such an outcome was in any case desirable, and since de Freville could now lend assistance should Mark prove obdurate, the arrival of the former was doubly oppor-tune. Indeed trebly so; for de Freville knew much more than Angela did about the bit of "business" which she was hoping to put in Mark's way to ease his predicament when he departed. So now, she thought, as she stood at her kitchen window watching them approach, we can discuss the whole matter sensibly and pack him off before night. I wonder where Max found him. . . .

When this had been explained to her and her 40,000 francs had been returned, they all sat down to tea.

"Right," said Angela. "Owing to Max's help you've got 60,000 francs in your pocket, so from now on you're on your own. But there's one more thing we can do for you. Tell him, Max."

She busied herself conscientiously about the teapot, with the air of a housemaster's wife giving a farewell tea to a boy who was leaving suddenly because his father had gone bank-rupt to prison. Max, cast for the part of the housemaster, leaned forward, took his tea with a grave nod of thanks, and began to speak carefully and even sympathetically of his plan for Mark's future.

"I have a friend," Max said, "a Greek gambler called

Stratis Lykiadopoulos, who is much in demand, because of his cool head and dignified presence, to play as banker for the big baccarat syndicates. With everything else, he is also supposed to be lucky, and the big money boys are nothing if not superstitious."

"Like Napoleon with his Marshals?"

"Something of the kind. But like even the luckiest of the Marshals, Lykiadopoulos is not immune from errors of judgment. Two years ago he accepted, in the course of play, a cheque for three million old francs from a Frenchman called Jacques des Moulins. By the time the cheque bounced, des Moulins was far away; and my friend, since he had acted on his own responsibility, had to make up the three million for the syndicate – which, however, allowed him the use of its extensive agencies in an effort to trace the defaulter. Des Moulins was finally run to ground, in a pretty bad way, in Beirut. Although there was clearly no question of getting money from him, Lykiadopoulos, who is an amateur of human vagaries, went to see the man and enquired into his story. It seemed that he had been a professional diplomat of some promise, but had been dismissed the service, or rather, eased out of it, as the result of seducing the seventeen year old son of a certain Minister, to whom he had been acting as what we would call Private Secretary. Deprived both of livelihood and occupation, he had commenced gambling, run through his savings, and had then tried the *coup de dishoneur* on Lykiadopoulos in a final attempt to restore his position. When that failed, all had failed, and the poor wretch had fled East to hide his disgrace in the classical manner of his forefathers."

"Why didn't he join the Legion?" Mark said facetiously.

"For the same reason as you don't. Because he was too lazy. And less concerned to redeem his past than simply to live safe from its consequences. He had managed to blackmail an aunt into sending him just enough money every month to drag out a miserable living in the brothel quarter near the Place des

Cannons, where he was attended by an idiot Arab boy, of hideous appearance, to whom he was passionately devoted and who returned his devotion. Indeed, as Lykiadopoulos remarked to me later, here was an important lesson about human love: it is not directed towards a particular person, it is *projected* out of circumstance or need and will embrace the first attainable object in its path. The Titania story, you see."

He glanced quickly at Angela to see whether she had drawn the inference. If she had, she ignored it, placidly pouring and distributing fresh cups of tea.

"It so happened," Max went on, "that Lykiadopoulos was detained in Beirut for several weeks, there being some delicate negotiation about foreign currencies with which his syndicate had charged him. One of the more amusing results of this intrigue was that Beirut was swamped with Egyptian pounds going at one and sixpence each, but that need not concern us now. What you should know is that Lykiadopoulos, part from kindness and part from interest, went two or three times more to see des Moulins in his hovel and was able to do him several small kindnesses. And when Lykiadopoulos came for the last time to say good-bye, des Moulins did his best to show his gratitude. In settlement of the debt of three million, he handed him the only thing of value that he had: a letter. A letter which was the property of the French Minister he had served before his dismissal and which he had stolen on impulse when he left the Minister's house for the last time."

"If the letter was valuable, why didn't des Moulins cash in on it himself?"

"He had kept it as a last resort, but when the time came to use it he had given up hope. He no longer had either the energy or the desire to change what he now regarded as his fate. When he called his bet of three million against Lykiadopoulos and supported it with a worthless cheque, he was asking God to tell him whether he should continue to live in the old way or resign himself, virtually, to death. God decided for the latter course and des Moulins accepted the decision. He would bury himself in Beirut with his pittance of income and his idiot boy until God disposed of him altogether. He was not unhappy, just numb; and he had, after all, someone even lower than himself to care for. As for the letter, it was no longer of any significance within his scheme of things: let Lykiadopoulos turn it into money if he could – for himself, he would stay at peace, lying down for ever in the dirt and darkness to his beloved idiot's embrace."

"I see," said Mark. "And what was in the letter?"

"The letter," said Max, in a bored, objective tone which he might have used to recite figures from an account book, "was from an Israeli businessman of German birth, now called Yahel. It had been entrusted to the Minister's son – the one des Moulins later seduced – when he was on holiday in Israel with a school party in 1956. Indeed, there is reason to suppose that the whole expedition to Israel was arranged simply and solely so that a secret message might be delivered back to the Minister in France."

"Rather cumbrous?"

"It is only in spy stories that things can be arranged slickly. In real life the wheels are all jagged and rusty from long exposure, and the grooves are invariably the wrong gauge ... Cumbrous or not, the scheme worked. As soon as the boy returned, in mid-September of '56, he delivered the letter to his father, and what it said was this. One: the Israeli Army had prepared a plan for the invasion of Egypt which could be implemented at twenty-four hours' notice. Two: the feeling of Ben Gurion's Cabinet was definitely in favour of 'close understanding' with France as to common motives and 'compatible lines of action'; the moment the French gave the least indication that they were prepared for discussion, the Israelis would meet them in a spirit of 'total co-operation'."

"Nothing much more than is already known or suspected."

"Ah. Yahel's third point was this. He had been in touch,

through his agents in London, with a senior member of the British Cabinet, who had been charged by certain of his colleagues with the top secret conveyance of their – top secret – policy. Names, I should add, are firmly named. From what Yahel then says, it is absolutely plain, not only that a section of the British Cabinet was ready and eager to join in the fun, but the whole idea of tri-partite collusion – Britain, France, Israel – had originated in London and was the brainchild of the senior Cabinet Minister aforesaid. No question of just drifting in through force of circumstance, of tagging on to the column at the last minute. The guilt for the whole affair lies with one man, who deliberately and at an early date conceived the course of action, canvassed it among chosen friends, and conspired with foreign agents to promote all the necessary preliminaries. It was only after, *and because*, Israel had received the green light from London that the Israelis, speaking through Yahel, thought fit to approach the French."

"In other words," said Mark slowly, "the whole crisis was engineered by a handful of Cabinet Ministers – regardless, one imagines, of the wishes of the rest of the Cabinet."

" And *without the knowledge* of the rest of the Cabinet. Which explains why some departments, notably those responsible for the armed forces, were so badly caught out when the balloon went up. Nobody had warned the warlords."

"But surely . . . the guilty Ministers would have made the perfect scapegoats when the whole thing turned out such a disastrous flop?"

"Not on your life. Could the Prime Minister get up and say that unknown to himself and most of his advisers a small body of men had successfully conspired to bring the country into what might have been total war? No. The whole affair had to be explained away as a well-meant response to a difficult situation, or excused as the dutiful support of a misguided ally, or even admitted as downright muddle – *anything you like* rather than revealed as a pre-concerted plan. And this involved keeping quiet about the guilty ministers . . . most of whom, I grant you, have since been edged out of the way. But three at least are too talented, too necessary, to be got rid of, and are riding high at this very moment. That letter, Lewson, not only discredits some leading members of today's government, it could destroy the country's confidence, for many years to come, in the entire image of Conservative rule."

"Valuable, as you say."

"Worth more than three million francs. Especially in an election year."

"And Lykiadopoulos?"

"Simply does not know what to do. Out of his sphere, he says. He doesn't want trouble, he says: he has an inbred Balkan fear that he'll be knifed or blown up the minute he comes within a hundred miles of politics. Unfair, he says, to the French Minister's son: to be compromised at the beginning of his career for having acted as go-between when still an innocent boy."

"So he is a sentimental man."

"All gamblers are. A compensation for their way of life. But the real trouble with Lykiadopoulos is that he is being inept. He is so conditioned to dealing with short-term issues at the gaming table that he cannot think straight through when it comes to the longer distance. He cannot even distinguish clearly between the two kinds of market: between buyers who would pay for the letter in order to cry scandal and those who would pay, even more heavily perhaps, in order to ensure silence. He will not understand that a sale on the latter terms would guarantee, among other things, that there could never again be any risk of anyone getting at that wretched boy."

"Greeks don't think in such terms. They are inured to a tradition of regurgitating personal honour, of vendetta, which ensures that no issue ever dies. Take the fortunes of the House of Atreus. . . ."

"Retribution inspired by a primitive religion," said Max crossly. "There is no reason why this letter should cause any unpleasantness at all. All he has to do is negotiate its sale, for a large sum of money, into safety and oblivion."

"For a treasury cheque, you think?"

"There are special funds for this kind of thing."

"Why not leave Lykiadopoulos to do as he likes? It's his letter."

Angela collected the tea things on to a tray.

"Since Lykiadopoulos has no use for the letter," she said demurely, "I . . . we . . . thought it might come in handy for you."

"I see. I just march up to him and ask for it."

"Listen to Max," she said, as if encouraging a petulant child to pay attention to paternal homily.

Max grunted and heaved himself out of his chair to hold the door open. Angela passed out with the tray.

"You can finish your little talk while I do the washing up," she said. "Then we might all go for a nice walk."

Really, thought Mark, if I see much more of this "little woman" pose, I shall scream. Aloud he said.

"Well? How do I get hold of it?"

"You don't sound grateful."

"I'll be grateful all right . . . if you've got any kind of feasible suggestion."

"It's very simple," said Max. "I'll give you a note of introduction. As I've told you, he's a sentimental man. So you then take advantage of your opportunities to find out where the letter is and steal it."

"Very simple, I'm sure."

"You can't expect the whole thing on a plate."

"Supposing I'm not his type?"

"Anybody as young as you is his type."

"Supposing there's someone else?"

"He's not one to refuse a little extra."

"Where is he then?"

"In Venice. Hotel Danieli. He's to run a big bank out on the Lido in about ten days' time. You'd better do your stuff before it starts – he'll be rather pre-occupied when it does."

"Just tell me this," said Mark: "why are you so keen to have your own chum robbed?"

"I'm keen, or rather Angie's keen, to get rid of you on fair terms. As for my chum, the letter's not doing him any good. Last and by no means least, I shall be interested to hear what you do with it."

"I'm not quite with you."

"Corruption in high places," said Max patiently, "is a hobby of mine. I don't exploit it, because I've already got my own little corner in human weakness, but I enjoy collecting instances. I told you just now that gamblers were sentimental. They are also desperately in need of reassurance. I'm not a gambler any more, but I live through gambling, and I too require constant reassurance."

"Reassurance about what, for Christ's sake?"

"I like to be reminded that the world is run, even at the highest level, by petty-minded and venal men. It makes me feel more secure – that I'm inside the regular pattern, that I'm conforming with an important human norm. You let me know how you dispose of that letter, what people say, what they want it for, and I assure you you'll find me generous. Just a straight-forward account of the facts, that's all. And don't amuse yourself with sending me lies, Lewson. Because sooner or later I'd find out, and then God help you."

"And what will you do with this information?"

"Hoard it like a miser's gold. Take it out, during the long winter nights, and gloat over it. Compare it with the pompous speeches, the unctuous voices on television, then laugh myself silly and go contented to bed."

Angela came in.

"I've done your packing," she said to Mark meekly.

"There's a train at six. You can be in Milan by mid-night and go on to Venice tomorrow."

"And we can all come down to the station," said Max happily, "to see you off."

"Don't worry. I shan't hang around."

"My dear chap, a pleasure. I shall enjoy the walk, and Angie's a great one for stations."

"Stations are such fun," she murmured.

So a little while later they all left the house and walked down the road, Mark Lewson carrying the single grip that contained all his movables, Max and Angela arm in arm like a married couple of long standing.

2

A GAME OF CHESS

ABOUT THE same time as Mark Lewson was taking his seat at the chemin-de-fer table in Menton, two elderly gentlemen sat down on a terrace in Somersetshire. Although a chess board was set ready for play on a table between them, and although they went through the formality of moving the pieces, their attention to the game was cursory; which was not surprising, as they had both played much the same match together, down to the last tactic and almost to the last move, many times before. For the most part they looked neither at the board nor at each other, but gazed over the lawn beneath the terrace and the valley beneath the lawn and then away to the distant line of the Quantock Hills. When they spoke, it was as though they were taking part in a play and were addressing their words, quietly but firmly, to an audience on the grass below.

"One of these days," said Alastair Dixon, his bald head gleaming in the April sun, "I shall work out a new opening."

"It would make a change," said Rupert Percival, who was slightly the older of the two but still had a full head of glossy hair: "and of course you will have plenty of time for the game in your retirement."

"I'm not so sure. Remember my *magnum opus: Forty Years in the House of Commons.*"

"I should have thought," said Percival, "that it would have been enough to live through them without spending the rest of your life writing about it."

"The House is an addiction. Once it gets into your system you never get it out again. I shall need my book as a substitute."

"What it is to have a vocation." Percival shifted a knight to complete the first stage of his own laborious version of the King's Indian defence. "When I give up practice, I shall feel nothing but relief."

"You've virtually given up practice already. How many times a week do you go to that office of yours?"

"I keep an eye on things. The young men handle the wills and the tax-returns. I reserve anything juicy for myself."

"*Juicy?*" said Dixon. "In Bishop's Cross?"

"You don't know your constituents. We've had two divorces this last winter. And an amusing row with a headmaster about allegedly wrongful expulsion, which the headmaster quite rightly won. And a venomous to-do about the rough shooting rights at Thyme. So you see, I'm kept quite busy. And what with the Hunt and the Conservative Association. . . ."

"That reminds me," Dixon said. He took Percival's knight with his bishop and then, to save his friend the trouble, took his own bishop with Percival's pawn.

"How do you know I want to do that? There's such a thing as refusing an exchange."

"Not at your level there isn't."

"I suppose not. . . . *What* reminds you?"

"The Conservative Association. What are you doing about my replacement in the House this autumn?"

"Ah," said Percival, leaning back and taking out his snuff box, "I wondered when you'd get interested in that."

"Edwin Turbot wants to know."

"I don't see that it's his business. He'd better employed paying proper attention to his Ministry."

"He sees himself not only as a Minister but as a kind of Grand Vizier to the Party. And since the old man plays along with him, he has to be humoured."

"All the same, you might remind him that local associations are strictly independent."

"He only wants to know what's going on," said Dixon rather huffily: "after all, this is the safest seat in Wessex."

"The less need for Edwin Turbot to bother himself."

"He's interested in what he calls the Party's Overall Image for the General Election."

"Well," said Percival between prodigious sniffs of snuff, "there's an official short list of five names. But all you need to worry about is my personal short list, on which there are only two: Somerset Lloyd-James, whose father, you'll remember, lives just over the border in Devonshire, and –"

" – Shagger Lloyd-James? Roman Catholic?"

"That's right. Distinguished recusant family. Well, Shagger's son, Somerset, edits that beastly paper, *Strix*. You know, a sort of heavy journal of commerce which invents plausible reasons for money-grabbers to think themselves high-minded. But the boy's got his head screwed right down to his neck, and he does know a great deal about money. Practice as well as theory."

"That will please Edwin. Modern commercial image with no intellectual frills."

"On the contrary. Somerset Lloyd-James is bristling with intellectual frills. He won the Lauderdale at Cambridge in '48. But he knows when they're not needed."

"I never met an intellectual who knew that," said Dixon patronisingly. "And the other horse?"

"Peter Morrison. . . . Formerly member for Whereham."

Alastair Dixon castled on the queen's side, took out his cigar case, lit a cigar with avid concentration, and at last said:

"So they're bringing him back already?"

"*We* in Bishop's Cross," said Percival firmly, "are *considering* whether to adopt him as *our* candidate. One of the reasons being that he has a wife and two children, which goes down well with the women."

"Central Office had nothing to say about it?"

"Certainly not. He's on their list of course – they kept his name there when he resigned in case he might want to come back. I gather, despite appearances at the time, that his resignation was entirely to his credit?"

"Yes," said Dixon. "There was some sort of family scandal, but he only used that as a smoke-screen. His real reason seems to have been that he didn't want any part of Suez."

"Then why didn't he say so? That Young England Group which he started – they've always been against antics like Suez and pretty plain about it."

"It seems," said Dixon, with a mixture of admiration and bewilderment, "that this Mr Morrison has a very nice sense of honour. He felt that to speak against Suez, as was his duty if he stayed in the House, would be to stab the Army in the back. And to resign, giving Suez as a pretext, would have been just as bad. So since there was a story going about just then that he'd got some girl in trouble, he let it be known that he was resigning because of that."

"*That* won't go down well with the women."

"There was never anything in it. . . . But I'm surprised he's coming back quite so soon."

"He came to see me about that," Percival said. "He told me – entirely off the record of course – that several of his friends in the Young England Group are anxious to have him back because they don't much care for Carton Weir, who's running it at present."

"I like Carton Weir," said Dixon. "He's a very civil . . . and civilised young man."

"You're not in the Young England Group. They want Morrison, who, come to that, could have Whereham back by lifting his little finger."

Underneath the table Dixon's short legs frisked in irritation.

"Then why had he come here?" he said.

"He doesn't want to unseat the chap who took over Where-

ham in '56. Unfair, he says. And since we've got a vacancy.
. . . Whose turn is it to win this game?"

"Mine," said Dixon, untruthfully. "You might as well
resign anyway. . . . And which of the two do you really want?
Lloyd-James or Morrison?"

"That," said Percival, po-faced, "will be for the selection
committee to decide."

"Suppose they pick one of the other three on the official
short list?"

"For someone who has spent forty years in the House, and
boasts about it, you understand very little of politics."

"I understand enough to know that Edwin Turbot's not
going to be keen about Morrison, whatever your committee
decides. He's respected, Morrison, but he's apt to be a
nuisance. The Young Englanders have settled down nicely,
under Weir, as a harmless prestige group. No one wants
Morrison stirring them up again."

"Apparently *they* do," said Percival. "And Sir Edwin can
hardly complain about that."

"He won't. He'll just say that it's too soon after the scandal
for Morrison to come back."

"You said there was nothing in the scandal."

"Who's being naïve about politics now? Check mate," said
Dixon, spitefully plonking down his queen.

"Don't thump the pieces about," said Percival placidly.
"They're expensive. Whatever Edwin Turbot may think or
feel, Minister or not, Grand Vizier or not, there's no way he
can bully a local association."

"Isn't there just?" said Alastair Dixon. "You wait and see."

On this same April evening, some three miles from the East
Anglian market town of Whereham, Peter Morrison was
bowling to his eight-year-old son in a net which he had put
up on his abundant lawn.

"One more over, Nickie," he called. "This one will be well

up and outside the off stump. Left foot well over now. . . . ."

Six foot two inches tall, broad both at chest and waist but giving no impression of overweight, carrying his huge round head thrown back like a guardsman's, he lumbered easily to the bowling crease and placed the ball just where he had told his son, who hit it back hard over his head and laughed aloud with pleasure.

"Not bad, but your foot wasn't there. That one should have gone through the covers, not straight back. After it, Jeremy."

Five-year-old Jeremy, younger brother and ball-boy, scampered down the lawn and returned his father a chest-high catch.

"Nice throw, my dear. . . . Now then, Nickie. Good length outside the leg stump. Don't hit too hard and aim at mid-wicket."

From a central door in the long, low house of stone, stepping (like a goddess) just a little larger than life, came Helen Morrison. She stood quietly behind Nickie, appraised his next stroke, murmured something through the netting, then moved to her husband and took the ball from his hand.

"Telephone call from the West country," she said.

"Hell. . . . Give him four balls, darling. Then pack it in."

"And Jeremy?"

"His turn tomorrow. Younger sons must learn their place early."

Leaving his wife to work out for herself how seriously she should take this remark (his tone had been light but without irony), Peter ambled away towards the house, like a comfortable monk strolling in a cloister. Never, in his sons' presence, would he betray any sense of urgency. For two pins, he told himself, he would have finished the over; but that might have smacked of discourtesy to his caller. As he stepped off the lawn and through the door, he heard with satisfaction the level tones of his wife:

". . . No, just some old friend of Daddy's he hasn't heard from for a time. . . ."

Later that evening, Peter said to Helen (who had not enquired):

"That telephone call was about the seat for Bishop's Cross."

"So I imagined."

"I gather my closest rival for the candidature will be Somerset Lloyd-James, of all people."

"Will that embarrass you? After that business three years ago?"

"No . . . though of course he'll need watching. Somerset's devious by nature, that's all. It's no good blaming him. He's always been like that, and in other ways he's a lot of fun. I remember when he stayed here once, just after the war. . . .'

He fell into a silence which Helen did not attempt to break.

"There's another slight worry," Peter said at length. "Rupert Percival said that Alastair Dixon, the retiring member, reckons Edwin Turbot won't like me coming forward just now."

"There's nothing he can do to stop you."

"Officially, no. Although Edwin Turbot's a kind of Provost Marshal inside the Party he still can't dictate to local branches. Not openly, that is; but he can make himself felt in other ways."

"What sort of man is Rupert Percival?"

"A strong man and an honest one."

"Then there is nothing to worry about."

"I don't know. Percival may be strong, but he is not one for superfluous exhibitions of strength. Somerset is in every way as proper a candidate as I am, and if Percival understood that senior men, in Central Office perhaps, had good reason for preferring him, he might just accept this and follow suit. His honesty would not be compromised. He is under no moral obligation to support me."

"But suppose," said Helen, "that Central Office's reasons for preferring Somerset Lloyd-James are *not* good? Did Percival say what they might be?"

"No. He didn't even mention Central Office. He just said that *Turbot* might not want *me*."

"And Turbot's reasons?"

"Percival could only go on what Alastair Dixon had said, which was all conjecture anyhow, and he was kind enough to indicate that he didn't think much of it. But one thing you can be quite sure of: if Turbot has reasons, good or bad, for wanting me out of the way, they will be framed and presented as speciously as the Sermon on the Mount."

The next morning just before ten a.m. Somerset Lloyd-James shuffled into Gower Street from his lodging in Russell Square, paused to examine the weekly bill outside the offices of the *Spectator* ("Levin on Working-Class Fascism"), leered knowingly, and slouched on up the street to Philby House (so called since 1958) from which he edited *Strix*. Since only three out of the four electric fires in his office were switched on, he rang for his secretary to require an explanation, was reminded of a directive issued by Lord Philby, the Proprietor, who enjoyed economy in such matters (it was, after all a delicious April morning), personally switched on the fourth electric fire and the second bars of the other three, and called for the mail.

"There is a gentleman," his secretary said, "waiting to see you."

"A gentleman?"

"I use the term advisedly. He has been here since half past nine, and claims to be an old friend of yours."

"Name?"

"Major Gray. A retired rank, I gather."

"*De profundis*," said Somerset, mildly shaken. "Bring in the mail, and then, in exactly five minutes, bring in Major Gray."

When his secretary had set the mail on his desk, Somerset,

having established in thirty seconds that what was not routine was merely trivial, selected from the pile of letters the one typed on the most imposing note-paper and placed it dead in front of him, side by side with a sheet of blank foolscap. On the latter he wrote carefully as follows:

FIELDING GRAY.

Left school Autumn 1945.

Father (died '45) well off; but (? ?) something odd thought to have happened to the money.

Anyhow, F.G. in smart cavalry regiment from '46 onward. Last heard of in '55, when seen by Peter Morrison, who was on Parliamentary tour, on small island off Malta. At that time responsibly employed (? Officer Commanding a Squadron on detachment) and apparently resigned to his lot, though still bitter (in theory, so to speak, rather than practice).

Questions:

(1) Why has he left the Army?

(2) What does he want of me?

(3) Am I under any enforceable obligation to him?

Answers:

(1 and 2): To be presently resolved.

(3) No. But prudence directs that his claim of friendship, since he sees fit to call it so, be honoured, and any reasonable request considered.

Under these notes, which took up about a third of the page, he ruled two lines in red ink; the rest of the page could now be used for recording further information, under the pretext of drafting an answer to the important letter before him at the same time as he was conducting the interview. A corny technique, which seldom failed to unnerve his visitors. Since his secretary was now twenty seconds late in producing Gray, he reached forward with irritation to press the buzzer; but before his finger reached it the side door opened from the secretary's

office and he found himself rigid in his chair, his hand arrested
two inches short of the button, his every muscle paralysed by
the horror of what he now saw.

Fielding Gray had been, when Somerset last saw him, a
lithe and beautiful boy of seventeen. From Peter Morrison's
description, given four years back, Somerset gathered that
he had thickened somewhat, and that drink was already beginning to show in his cheeks, but that he still retained poise
and even distinction. As indeed he did now. His figure, correctly adorned as for an officer on leave in London (well cut
dark suit with waistcoat, white shirt with stiff collar and
regimental tie, bowler hat and gloves carried in the left hand),
did him no discredit for a man in the early thirties, while his
movements were easy and precise. The only trouble was his
face. It was impossible to tell now whether Peter had been
right or wrong about the burst veins in the cheeks, because
the cheeks, like everything else except a thin, twisted line of
mouth and one red, bald, tiny eye, were coated with a mottled
surface of shining pink like icing clumsily spread upon a cake.

Gray moved calmly up to Somerset's desk, as though about
to report to his Commanding Officer on a semi-formal occasion. A foot from the desk he halted and then, looking
Somerset straight in the face with his one little eye, held out
his hand.

"It is kind of you to see me," he said.

The voice was normal but the mouth writhed with every
syllable. Somerset, who was already so far in control of himself as to have recovered his powers of motion, rose to shake
hands. A prompt enough answer to question (1), he thought.

"Fielding," he said, his voice soft yet grating, like a mixture
of powdered ash and clinkers being raked from a dead hearth,
"what a long time it has been."

He gestured to a chair, then sat down again himself; he
took up a pen, glanced down at the letter and the sheet of
notes in front of him. No, he thought, you can't do it, not

now, not with him. *Yes*, he answered himself, you must; you must do everything as you always do – the more pitiable Fielding, the more steadfast your routine. Slowly he retrieved and straightened the two sheets of paper, which he had already begun to brush to one side.

"Well, my dear?" he said, and the words whispered back down the years, with echo upon tiny echo, so that it seemed nearly a minute before there was silence between them once more.

"As you see," said Gray in matter-of-fact tones, "I've been badly injured and have left the Army. An explosion in Cyprus," he added, almost apologetically, in answer to the question that glinted behind Somerset's thick lenses. "A local truce had been declared, you see, but the Cypriots neither understand nor respect the nature of contract. Any form of treaty with them will be meaningless. . . . But I don't suppose you need my opinions about that."

He glanced up at a shelf which held the bound volumes of *Strix*, as though to imply, if not without polite irony, that all knowledge and all wisdom reposed between their covers.

"I'm very sorry – "

Gray held up his hand.

"No need to be. It was time I had a change in my life. You may remember that I once had ambitions . . . of a non-military kind."

Somerset twitched slightly in assent. Answer to question (2) coming up.

"Well," proceeded Gray, "I have a pension and a gratuity which between them will keep me fed and watered. But little more. I could probably apply for a University Grant, but it's a little late in the day for that. I must do as best I can with what I know already."

"The Army . . . ?"

"The Army. Most of Europe and the Near East. East Africa. Hongkong. Extensive reading for the last thirteen years – soldiers have a lot of leisure, you see. It all adds up to a body of knowledge."

"Certainly," said Somerset; and then, amiably, "unspecialised knowledge."

"If you like. Wide but unspecialised knowledge of men, places and events. Not to mention books. The equipment of a general commentator."

Gray's tone was still steady, but Somerset could detect a thin, ghostly plea for encouragement, for one word to show that he understood and might approve. Well, perhaps he would give that word. But not yet.

"And so?" he said.

For the first time since Gray had been in the room Somerset now started adding to his notes. "Not broke," he wrote: "wants work and is convinced that he can do it. (?Ambitious?) But uncertain whether he can get anyone to share his faith in himself."

"I hope I'm not interrupting you in anything important," said Gray politely when Somerset raised his head again.

"Not really. . . . Just a point to be made in a letter. I didn't want to forget it. I find my memory slips more and more as I grow older."

"I know what you mean. Life is so complex. There are so many threads to be sorted and kept straight. That is why I have tried to keep my hand in all these years."

"Keep your hand in?"

"As a writer. You may remember that my little efforts were well regarded when we were still at school. But of course everything was very simple then; every day was either wet or fine, so to speak. It has grown more complicated since; so I have tried to develop my talent – such as it is – accordingly. To use it to sort the threads and keep them straight. For my own satisfaction . . . for my own mental safety."

Somerset considered this.

"By which you mean you've kept a journal," he asserted at last.

"Yes. Dating right back to the time when things first started to get complicated. To that last summer at school. You remember, Somerset?"

Somerset remembered. On the foolscap sheet in front of him he sketched a Maltese cross, his personal symbol for danger.

"But of course," said Gray indifferently, "I've no intention of trying to publish it. The journal was for myself, so that I might understand who I was. What I had hoped," and now the faint note of supplication was back in his voice again, "was that I might be able to do something about publishing a couple of novels which I have also written."

"Based on the journal?" said Somerset heavily.

"No," said Gray. His mouth flickered briefly in what might have been either a smile or a sneer; there was no way of telling. "The journal is an attempt to analyse the characters and explain the actions of myself and people I have known well – you among them. The novels are also analytic, but of situations rather than people. They deal with technical problems, not moral ones. The first of them turns on a vexed point of military law; the other on the necessity to make a starving tribe eat food forbidden by its faith."

"A moral problem, surely."

"Perhaps, but in no sense individual and therefore not concerned with subtleties of human character. As you may see from the solution, which is merely administrative: you deceive them into thinking that the forbidden food is in fact something else, veal, say, and not pork."

All this he offered poker-faced. Somerset drew a small fish, which meant "danger passed", but qualified it with two question marks.

"Let the dead bury their dead," said Gray, as though reading his thoughts; "it was all too long ago. Things are as they are; and as they are, Somerset, I want your help."

Somerset excised the question marks. Before looking up he wrote: "A curious example of God's Grace. By his own endeavours alone, apparently by the simple effort of keeping a journal, Fielding has come to understanding and forgiveness. Even so, he could be troublesome if he chose. Therefore help him; but also make difficulties, so that the help may appear the more valuable. A.M.D.G. "

"I'm sorry," he said, and pushed the papers away from him: "I just wanted to get that finally out of the way. I'm all yours, Fielding."

"I have come to you because you are the only person I know in this line. You presumably know a bit about publishers, and of papers, like this one, which might be prepared to give me a trial."

Gray had tried to speak bravely but there was in what he said the pathetic eagerness of a small boy on the beach claiming his turn to bat.

"This kind of work is sought after," Somerset said. "It is held to carry prestige."

His hair, he thought, is still as beautiful as ever. Ample, auburn, with the same gentle wave. Above such a face it is incongruous, obscene.

"But," Somerset said, "I can certainly offer you something. This paper deals mainly with economics and industry, but in the review section we often take on books which are on the margin of these subjects. Well documented travel books, for example. They should be within your compass. Or books on military organisation and supply – logistics, I think you call it."

Gray nodded enthusiastically.

"I'll give you two books to do during the next month," Somerset went on. "If I like what you write, I'll give you more, and perhaps commission a straight essay from you. If your work for *Strix* is any good, you'll find you get enquiries from other quarters soon enough."

Gray's one eye blinked. He's moved, Somerset thought he's moved because after all these years I'm going to help him. He was always a sentimental boy. . . . But this train of thought was interrupted by his secretary, whose voice now crackled at him from his desk.

"Tom Llewyllyn here to see you."

"Ask him to wait a few – No," said Somerset, "send him straight in. Tom Llewyllyn's publisher," he said to Gray, "has a reputation for helping new writers. Even aspirant novelists, God help him."

"Gregory Stern."

"You keep abreast."

"I told you. Soldiers have a lot of leisure. Particularly wounded ones."

Yes, thought Somerset, a great part of whose motive for admitting Llewyllyn so promptly was to see how he reacted to Gray's disfigurement.

"I want you to meet an old friend of mine," he said as Llewyllyn came through the side door; "Major Fielding Gray."

Gray rose and confronted Llewyllyn, who merely held out his hand and nodded with visible annoyance, for he had been hoping to find Somerset alone.

"Fielding's just going," Somerset said, reading Llewyllyn's mind at once and reflecting that had the devil himself been present Tom's only reaction would have been to indicate his superfluity. Not that Tom was insensitive to other people; but when he had something on his mind, as clearly he had now, his anxiety to discharge it precluded any other emotion, whether of sympathy, curiosity or fear.

"Fielding," said Somerset, "should meet your publisher. He has written some novels."

"So have five thousand other people," said Tom grumpily. But then he seemed to remember something, and looked Gray straight in the face with candid interest. "I heard about you," he said, "after that wretched business in Cyprus. Your regiment . . . didn't a Captain Detterling belong to it? The M.P.?"

"Yes. He retired a long time ago, but he rejoined us from the reserve for Suez. As it happens it was Detterling, back in '45, who persuaded me to become a regular."

"He is an interesting man," said Tom, "of a type I cannot approve. Nor do I approve of the old boy net. But I'm going to let you in on it now. . . . Christ, it's hot in here," he said, switched off the nearest electric fire.

Success, reflected Somerset as he switched the fire on again, had given Tom the habit of airing rather pompous ethical judgments – without, however, affecting the essential kindness of his heart. Although Tom might moralise adversely for an hour together, it did not in the least detract from his practical good-will.

"The thing is," Tom was saying, "that my publisher, Gregory Stern, wants to expand, so he has been looking about for partners who will bring some cash with them. One day this chap Detterling turned up and offered ten thousand in exchange for a nominal directorship, a proportionate share in the profits, and the right to interest himself, anywhere short of actual interference, in what went on. Stern liked the look of him – he said he reminded him of a Trollope character called Dolly Longstaffe – and jumped at him. Come to that, I like him myself."

"Then why do you disapprove?" asked Somerset.

"He's too blatant a member of the old gang. He not only takes his privileges for granted – White's, M.C.C., chambers in Albany – but he expects everything to operate in that particular medium. It's to his advantage, you see, that it should. Because although he's a shrewd man, his shrewdness doesn't extend beyond his own world. For example, when Peter Morrison left Parliament three years back" – Tom glanced furtively at Somerset – "Detterling dropped out of the Young England Group simply because he couldn't understand the new leader

Carton Weir – who's built on a more contemporary pattern."

"I thought," said Somerset, "that he just *disliked* Carton."

"Same thing. Detterling disliked Carton because he was incapable of understanding him in Detterling's terms."

Major Grey was beginning to fidget.

"Sorry," said Tom, turning back to him abruptly. "What I was thinking was this. If you know Detterling, he should be able to help you with Gregory Stern. As I say, he doesn't interfere, but if he makes a suggestion, Gregory will listen."

"Odd," said Gray: "that Detterling should take to publishing. And with this sort of firm."

"You mean a firm owned by a Jew?" said Tom sharply.

"No," said Gray unperturbed. "Detterling always admired Jews. He used to say that Jewish blood gave a spice to personality, though like all spices it was perhaps better . . . diffused. What surprises me is that he should have chosen a small firm of recent origin. Something outside what you just called his 'medium'."

"Gregory Stern," volunteered Somerset, "is very much of Detterling's medium. Eton and the House; his father the first Jew ever to serve as an officer in the Household Brigade; a massive merchant bank in the background. Cream of the establishment – with Jewish blood to lend spice, as you say."

Somerset seemed about to add something more, but then sat back in silence. The question was closed; so was Fielding Gray's interview.

"Thank you both," said the latter as he rose. "You've been very kind." And then, with his earlier hint of boyish eagerness, "You'll send those books, Somerset? Care of the Cavalry Club, until I'm settled."

Somerset nodded and rose. Tom Llewyllyn smiled and waved his hand but did not rise. Major Gray turned about smartly and marched out.

"Now," said Tom, the smile fading from his face, "what's the game?"

"Fielding's an old friend – "

" – Never mind Major Gray. Bishop's Cross, Somerset. I hear you've offered yourself for the seat."

"And why not?"

"Well. . . . Let's say that I thought you had your hands full already."

"I can always resign this editorship."

"Somerset. You are, in your own terms, a good editor. In no terms will you be a good politician. You have what the Americans call an unfortunate personality – for public life, that is."

"That is why," said Somerset, "I have chosen Bishop's Cross. The Tory candidate there cannot fail, not even if they adopt a barbary ape."

"You think they will adopt you?"

"To be candid," said Somerset, "no. I think they will adopt Peter Morrison. But there's just a chance, and it's worth taking. Why are you so keen to stop me?"

As someone had once observed of Somerset, he derived much of his massive self-confidence from a poker-face which he thought he possessed but didn't. When Somerset was bluffing his eyes glazed over, and they were rapidly glazing over now. It was clear, Tom thought, that Somerset's genial and modest disclaimer was not sincere: he had reasons for thinking he had a very good chance, and if Somerset had reasons they would be sound. Meanwhile, his attitude must be accepted, for the purposes of discussion, at face value.

"I wonder you bother, that's all," Tom said. "Years ago you told me to stick to what I was good at. It turned out to be excellent advice. Now I'm offering it back."

"Let me refer you," said Somerset, "to your own work." He went to a bookcase and took out a copious volume, the mauve cover of which proclaimed *An Analysis of Practical Politics*, by Tom Llewyllyn (Gregory Stern, 35s.). "Page 113. I quote. 'As with literature, so with politics: if a Party these days is determined to sell a policy, or a man, the merit of the man or the policy is a secondary consideration. The sale can be effected by high pressure methods which ignore or obscure the real issues and insist on others which, while irrelevant, are plausible and attractive. This has always been true, but never so true as now, when techniques of publicity are quicker and slicker than ever before. Just as a book may be made into a best seller by the announcement, at the right time and in the right tone, that the author keeps a canary or lost a leg at Anzio, so a hack politician, however disagreeable, or discredited, may be transformed overnight into a potential Prime Minister – if only his sponsors can hit on the right image.' In other words," said Somerset, "there's hope for all of us. Once we get a footing, that is."

"For God's sake," said Tom. "You are now a successful, even a powerful man, who need depend only on his own undoubted abilities. What can you possibly want in Parliament? Your abilities will go for nothing there. You'll have to spend your odd time grovelling for the good-will of second-rate men and learning confidence tricks from television interviewers."

"But it is of our age. The power of the written word is declining, Tom. What counts is the personal appeal, the appearance on the silver screen."

"All I can say," said Tom, "is that it will take one hell of an image to make you acceptable on the silver screen."

"I am an ugly man," said Somerset calmly, "bald, liable to acne, prematurely aged, and long since deprived of my own teeth. I am, in fact, the very symbol of under-privileged humanity. To look at, I am the archetypal underdog in an era of underdogs. So my appeal to a large section of our industrialised and physically degraded community will be immense."

"Until you open your mouth and start in with your posh, clever talk."

"I shall affect the simplicity of Socrates – who was also, you will remember, an ugly man."

"Ugly or not, Socrates had charm."

"So have I."

This was undeniably true. Leave aside his ability to amuse and interest other men, Somerset had a distinct if possibly perverse appeal to women. This he seldom exploited, as he held that women made irrational demands on one's time and purse. But Tom could remember at least one notable conquest: Lady Susan Grange, now Lady Philby and wife of Somerset's Proprietor. It was whispered that Lady Philby still had a kindness for Somerset and was not above indulging it during Philby's frequent business trips. From his knowledge of Lady P's character, Tom doubted this; but the very existence of the story paid its own tribute to Somerset.

"So," said Tom, "you see yourself as a sort of . . . anti-celebrity. But first you've got to reach Parliament."

"Hence my application to Bishop's Cross."

"Where you nevertheless think they will prefer Peter Morrison."

"It'll be experience," said Somerset smoothly. "Local associations, selection committees, chairmen. . . . It'll be useful practice for next time."

His eyes were glazed to the point of opacity. I wonder whether he can see out of them, Tom thought.

"What does Alastair Dixon say?" he enquired. "As retiring member he'll be listened to, I suppose?"

"Alastair Dixon likes Carton Weir, and Carton Weir wants me. Again: Carton leads the Young England Group – which has behaved discreetly under his leadership but which will cease to be so obliging should Peter return to take over. In sum: Alastair Dixon has a personal reason for wanting me to come in, and a political reason, which he shares with the rest of the Party, for wanting Peter to stay out."

This was the strongest point in Somerset's favour, and he

saw no reason to conceal it from Tom, who was certainly shrewd enough to have hit on it for himself.

"Fair enough," muttered Tom. But this was not the whole story, he thought. There was something else behind those glazed irises. Something only embryonic as yet, a mere seed, perhaps not even a fertilised one. But a seed there was, needing only some chance spermatozoon to quicken it, to set the foetus swelling. Which must be as may be, Tom thought; there was nothing more to be discovered just now.

"Why are you so concerned in this?" Somerset was saying. "You'll forgive me, Tom, but a Labour sympathiser has enough . . . interfering to do . . . on his own side of the fence."

"My interest is personal. A Tory will sit for Bishop's Cross whatever happens. My hope is – you'll forgive me, Somerset – that it will be a decent Tory. Not, as you yourself put it, a barbary ape, but someone like Peter Morrison. . . . I've brought you the copy you asked for." He slapped an envelope down on the desk. "Don't try to underpay me like last time, Somerset. Three guineas a hundred is the rate we agreed."

"That was a try-on by Accounts. Mistaken zeal after Philby's call for economy."

"Just put them right then, dear."

Tom shook his curls reprovingly at Somerset and skipped to the outer door, where he paused to perform a brief tap-dance.

"I shall be following what happens at Bishop's Cross, dear," he said. "You know how interested I am in everything you do."

When Fielding Gray left Gower Street, he took a taxi to the Regent's Park and sat down on a seat by the lake.

So Somerset would try him, it seemed; and Captain Detterling, one time comrade in arms, might be approached to help over the publication of his books. At least he should be able to ensure that they were properly read, not just tossed on one side and returned without comment six months later. And since Fielding knew that he had had something real if limited to say, and since he was confident that in his two novels he had said it with style and precision, he could reasonably hope for a fair outcome.

But what then? Suppose his work found favour with Somerset and his novels were published by Gregory Stern, suppose, even, that they achieved some measure of public esteem, what was to follow? Would there be anything more to say? Could he face the prospect of carrying on indefinitely with such a career? For did not even the two existing manuscripts pose the question, "While this is quite well done, was there ever, in truth, any real reason for doing it?" Works of supererogation . . . and of course that was how ninety-nine writers in a hundred made a living: producing work, conscientious in its kind, modestly saleable, worthy of some small critical attention, but work which, in the end of all, added not one jot to the human experience. Was consciousness of this essential sterility made bearable, he wondered, by the photographs, the occasional notoriety, the literary luncheons? Was it obliterated altogether, perhaps, by the women who wished to sleep, not indeed with the man, but with his books? (Would anyone wish to sleep with *his* books?) Or did authors suffer torment, in the reaches of the night, when faced with the inexorable fact that an entire *oeuvre* was little more than an elaborate tautology?

But then again, an author's occupation, by comparison with those of most citizens, could hardly be called sterile. At least he gave pleasure (a condition of earning his bread), did not spend his days persuading fools to buy rubbish or twisting regulations so that crooked little men might ride with their whores in Bentleys. The writer's avocation was decent, civilised. . . . Yes; but this was not why he had chosen it. He had chosen it because it was work he could do (or thought he could), work which might bring him reputation and money, and work – one of the very few kinds – the bare notion of which did not fill him with boredom or snobbish contempt. In other words, he was in it for the *cachet*; which brought him round again to the question with which he had started: would his proposed career be founded, so to speak, *in the truth*, or would it be one long vanity and vexation of spirit?

But of course, he reminded himself, he was taking much too much for granted. He had not so much as started on this career: time enough to pose superior moral questions when he was properly established in it. The error of equating aspiration with fulfilment was a dangerous one which had taken toll of him before now; this time there must be no dream before there was substance. There were, he told himself, only two things he had to do for the present: to get on with his work with as much professional competence as he could muster; and to come to terms with his deformity.

Or rather, to persuade other people to come to terms. Physical terms. For the most part, as he had already found, his appearance, after giving rise to brief shock as it had in Somerset that morning, was merely ignored. A very few seconds sufficed to reconcile people to his presence. But what, if anything, would suffice to reconcile people to his touch, to his bodily love? Since he required no one to kiss his hideous face, and since the rest of his body was wholesome enough for anybody's kisses, in logic there should be no difficulty. But in the eye of the beholder, he knew, the part would infect the whole: because his face was an obscenity, his body would be deemed untouchable; and Fielding, now as ever, required urgently and often to be touched.

He rose to leave the park. Nothing would be achieved by sitting here brooding; he would go and check through his novels, and that afternoon, perhaps, he would walk down Curzon Street and see if one of the girls would take him for ready cash. That would be a start. . . . There was a small, choking cry, and a little girl landed almost at his feet. Since no one came to her aid, Fielding knelt, helped her up, and started to wipe the dirt from her bleeding knees while she blubbered quietly into his shoulder. Eventually she drew back her face and regarded him with care.

"One eye?" she said, with curiosity but without censure.

"I mislaid the other."

The child accepted this explanation without further comment and allowed him to proceed with her knee. She at any rate did not resent his touch.

"Where's your mother?" Fielding said.

The child pointed to a bench a hundred yards away, where a large sluttish woman was talking with animation to a small wizened one.

"Run back to her, then, and ask her to bandage you up."

But the child lingered, then leered into his face.

"Pink," she said, "lovely and pink."

Her hands came towards him in order to feel.

"Nice, nice," she cried, as her fingers passed over the smooth surface of his cheeks. "Not rough, like Dadda. Nice."

Fielding rose unsteadily to his full height and gave the child a gentle shove in the direction of her mother. Then he walked away trembling violently in every muscle, as he had not trembled since they brought him a looking glass for the first time.

When Tom Llewyllyn left Gower Street he took the Underground to South Kensington, whence he walked to Buttock's Private Hotel in the Cromwell Road. In the hall was Tessie Buttock, who was busy gluing up letters she had just steamed open and placing them in the letter rack.

"Censoring the mail now?" said Tom.

"Only the old ones, dear. They've been hanging about for weeks, waiting for people who haven't come."

"Then why are you putting them in the rack?"

"Makes a bit of a show, dear. Which is about all they're

good for. It's been a dull old morning I've had reading them."

Albert Edward, Tessie's terrier, lifted his leg against the grandfather clock. Really, thought Tom, it was high time for a change. And a change there was now to be. But what should he tell Tessie? After all these years.

"Tessie," he said hesitantly. "I'm going away for a couple of nights. Down to the country."

"Very nice too, dear. . . . It's not that Albert Edward doesn't know better, but he never cared for that clock. Woozums, woozums," she intoned; "woozums widdle on horrid clock."

"Tessie. . . ."

"Yes, dear?"

"I'm engaged. You'll see it tomorrow in *The Times*. That's why I'm going to the country, to stay with my fiancée's parents. . . . She'll be there too, of course."

"Well, don't go overdoing it, dearie," said Tessie, as if he were going round the corner for a drink. "Leave a little something to look forward to. That's what I always told Buttock."

"And did he?"

"Not so's you'd have noticed, no. Real horny, Buttock was. Until he went on the booze, and even then he could do as well for himself as most men between here and Highgate Hill. I remember one Sunday afternoon, just before the war – "

" – Tessie," said Tom, sadly but firmly. "When I get married I'll have to leave you."

"So I supposed, dear. Though you can have one of the back rooms for two quid a week. *Pied-à-terre*, if you take my meaning."

"Tessie. I am very much in love with my future wife."

"Of course you are, dear. But it never did no harm to have a *pied-à-terre*. You can come and do your writing when she starts throwing the pots about."

"She's a lady, Tessie."

"Go on? Starts breaking up the mirrors, then, since she's

a *lady*." Tessie paused to quiz him with something as near affection as her bleak and greedy eyes could convey. "You've really come on these last few years, haven't you, love? Those books and all, and now this. What's she called?"

"Patricia. . . . Patricia Turbot."

"Turbot. . . . Anything to do with that bossing minister man? The one that's always telling us to work harder and save our money."

"Daughter," said Tom reluctantly. "Oldest daughter."

"My, my. You *have* come on. But all the same, dear," Tessie said, scooping up Albert Edward and tickling his groin, "I should think hard about that *pied-à-terre* if I was you."

"Like to look at some pictures, dear?" said plump, kind Maisie to Fielding Gray.

"I don't think that will be necessary."

"No," said Maisie, looking down at him rather apprehensively, "I can see that. But they're rather fun all the same. There's this photograph of two girl guides and a scoutmaster, and – "

" – No pictures, thank you. . . . What did you say your name was?"

"Maisie."

"Well then, Maisie. Like this. . . ."

About thirty seconds later, Maisie said,

"Don't go away at once, love. Stay and talk a little."

"I thought . . . you'd want to go out again."

"No, love. I don't usually go out in the afternoon. Or at all, for the matter of that."

"Then why were you out this afternoon?" said Fielding peevishly.

"Lovely spring day. A girl gets restless. But what I really do, dear, is to have regular gentlemen. They come here for appointments, or I go to them. Lucky for me, really, now this new law's going to come."

"Regular gentlemen?"

"Ones who want something special. Or ones like you who might find it awkward getting a girl of their own."

It was so easily and pleasantly said that it was impossible to take offence.

"You see," Maisie went on, "even the girls on the line might not be too keen. They're an ignorant lot, and some of them think that an injured face means – well – an injured mind."

"They could be right."

"Not with you, dear. Not yet, anyway. I spotted that quick enough when I saw you coming along just now – it was the easy way you walked. You'll be all right if you have someone regular, someone who understands. . . ."

"You think you understand?"

"Not everything, love. But quite a lot. For instance, I know why you were so quick just now."

"It's been a long time."

"Not only that," Maisie said. "You wanted to get it over quick for my sake . . . and for yours, in case I said anything."

There was so much in this now he came to think of it, that Fielding, who had been on the point of leaving, sat down again on Maisie's bed.

"That's right," she said. "Now we can relax. Spend the afternoon, if you like. It'll only be another five quid if you're going to visit regular. And you may as well look at these pictures, now we know each other. They're all good for a laugh."

When Fielding left Maisie at half past five that evening, they had arranged regular appointments for two afternoons a week until further notice on either side.

Ever since Tom Llewyllyn had left his office that morning, Somerset Lloyd-James had entertained vague feelings of unrest and dissatisfaction. The unrest he attributed to the surprise, by no means unpleasant but still unnerving, of seeing Fielding Gray again. The dissatisfaction he blamed on Tom. Why was Tom interesting himself in the Bishop's Cross candidature? To what extent would he, could he, interfere?

If Somerset had known about Tom's engagement to Patricia Turbot and his consequent visit to Sir Edwin in the country, he would have been very put out indeed. Even as it was, past experience told him that Tom, if so minded, could do a lot of damage. For Tom, despite tendencies to dissipation, combined energy, integrity and intelligence; as he had shown more than once, if he undertook something he saw it through. It was plain from what had passed that morning that he wished Peter Morrison, whom he had always admired, back in Parliament, and that for this reason among others he resented Somerset's application to Bishop's Cross. If Tom had nothing much else on for the summer, thought Somerset crossly, he would make every difficulty he could.

But what difficulties could he make? Tom was a "heavy" journalist of some reputation, and he had also published three books: an early and striking political novel, then, in 1956, a brilliant assessment of Russian cold-war strategy since 1945, and finally, in the Autumn of 1958, his *Analysis of Practical Politics*, which had enjoyed even greater critical esteem than its much acclaimed predecessors. All this added up to authority, to waxing authority at that; as things now stood, Tom might request and receive space from almost any prestige journal in the kingdom; the question was, how much of it would he care to devote to so trivial a matter as the candidature at Bishop's Cross?

Very little, Somerset decided. Editors wouldn't like it; the Bishop's Cross selectors wouldn't heed it; and in any case the only really damaging material Tom had against him was quite unprintable. It followed that Tom's activities must take another form, that of personal intrigue or canvass; and while Tom, as he acknowledged, was a tried performer in *that* genre,

Somerset was no novice himself. It would be a fair match, one to which in other circumstances he would have looked forward with some relish. The trouble was that he would have so much else to do this summer that he was not anxious to open up a special new front for Tom.

But that, he thought, must be as it may be. Leave Tom aside for the moment, and how did things look? *Pro*: his family had a good name in the country round Bishop's Cross; Alastair Dixon was on his side; Carton Weir, a rising M.P. who was privileged to whisper in important ears, would whisper in his favour; and last, least but not negligible, his own brand of conservatism was less flexible than Morrison's and might therefore find the more favour with Bishop's Cross. So far, so good. But . . . *Contra*; Rupert Percival, the local chairman, did not like him; Carton Weir's support was only valid in the House itself and might at any moment be rendered useless and even dangerous by grave scandal, for Carton persisted in playing with private fire of a kind liable to cause public conflagration; Morrison was, quite simply, a more attractive man and – what would undoubtedly operate to his advantage – a far less able one; and to top everything, Somerset's long association with *Strix*, though it would commend him in many quarters, would arouse distaste in the leaders of a rural and agricultural community – who would instantly recognise in Morrison the farmer a kindred spirit, albeit from a distant land.

All in all, the odds were unpromising, and there was no reason why Somerset should not have been speaking the truth when he told Tom that he did not give a lot for his chance. But he was not speaking the truth, as Tom had perceived, and he *did* give a lot for his chance. He gave a lot for his chance because (as Tom had also more or less perceived) he had one impalpable but very powerful advantage: he was prepared, indeed determined, to fight dirty if he saw his way. He had yet to see it (here too Tom was right); but his spies were posted and his aircraft hovered, and any day now he might hope for the intelligence he needed to mount his subtle and treacherous campaign.

Meanwhile it was important, with all that lay before him, that he should not neglect his health; so he had made an appointment with Maisie for half past six. Maisie, so lust-making yet always (any time these four years) so soothing and understanding; Maisie, mistress and mother, aphrodisiac yet anodyne, the prostitute-priestess who incited frenzy and then extended pity. Our Lady of the Red Lamp. (Steady now: God be merciful to me a sinner.) And tonight, she had promised him, a new consignment of photographs would be in: a brilliant series of permutations of boy scouts with girl guides. With any luck, this should help them to construct a whole new fantasy, for the present one was wearing rather thin. Maisie could be a cub-mistress and he would be a wolf cub, who had wetted his camp bed . . . Jubilantly Somerset lurched down Gower Street, barely restrained himself from the expense of a taxi, and stuck out his tongue at the *Spectator* bill ("Gilmour on God") as he passed.

3

CUPID AND PSYCHE

"Tell me," said Patricia Turbot: "who else?"

"No one of importance," Tom said.

"Nevertheless I must know."

Patricia Turbot was a girl of spirit in more senses than one. To start with, as her father never tired of saying, she had a lot of spunk, and she was also endowed with a high moral and spiritual sense. It was her habit to employ the "spunk" in the propagation of the morality; and now, as she walked across the Wiltshire Downs with Tom, she was conducting an inquisition into his past. Her spiritual sense, to say nothing of female possessiveness, had told her that such an enquiry ought really to be conducted before they became engaged; but she had been afraid lest this might deter Tom from proposing at all, and had restrained both conscience and curiosity until he was safely in the bag. Since in the bag he certainly now was, with all the authority of that morning's *Times* to prove it, she felt safe at last to obey her spiritual promptings and was more than making up for the delay.

"It's a question of truth," she was saying. "I quite see that you may have had adventures – Daddy says most men do – and I promise I won't be angry. But I must know, in order. . . . How can I put it? . . . In order to exorcise the past."

"The past," said Tom, "is not exorcisable."

"All evil can be exorcised."

"So you assume my past *was* evil?"

Patricia flushed. Although she was eager to go into things, she did not want to be caught out, just yet, making overt judgments.

"Well," Tom went on, "in your terms you are quite right. Though perhaps sinful would be a better word. But there is nothing to be done about it now. One can exorcise ghosts, I dare say, but not the actions or events in which one joined with them. Past actions are immutable; the only thing to do about them, if they are inconvenient, is to forget."

"You can atone," Patricia said. "You can ask forgiveness."

"Why should I? Many of my worst actions have in the end proved mentally – even morally – enriching."

Patricia pondered this remark with peevishness and anxiety. Truth to tell, she was out of her depth. Brought up in confinement, her only close companions a younger sister and a faithful but stupid nurse, she had been able to take her intellectual pre-eminence for granted ever since she could remember. There had been no possible rival: her mother had bolted when her sister was ten months old; while her father, a stern and able man before the world, yet encouraged and indulged Patricia in a manner which implied that even he had nothing to teach her. Apart from outlining the basic rules of social practice, he had abrogated his role as tutor and deferred to what he called "the inborn feminine wisdom" of his daughter to the extent that she firmly believed this quality to be equivalent, if not superior, to intellect. Since she had been confirmed in this fallacy by the doting of her foolish nurse, by the subservience of her young sister, and by the Platonic attentions of an evangelical governess, Patricia Turbot had grown up a prim, priggish, spoiled, ignorant and not unkindly girl, whose substantial intelligence was badly stunted from lack of the need to exert it and whose assumption of superiority had yet to meet its check.

And now here was Tom, the man to whom she was to give herself, questioning her edicts, disputing the moral and religious truths on which they were based, and, worst of all, advancing propositions which she could neither understand nor confute. It was not to be borne.

"You're evading the issue," she told him. "I have to know about the other women, and you have to tell me, so that we can start fresh. With everything clear between us."

"There are no fresh starts in life," said Tom, who was enjoying teasing her, "and you can never get anything clear. But I'll tell you about my sex life, since that's what you want, provided you'll tell me about yours."

"I've had no sex life," said Patricia smugly.

"What? No crushes on the girls at school? But of course, you had a governess. . . . Odd of your father, that."

"Daddy doesn't believe in boarding-schools for girls."

"He sent your sister to one."

"She was getting out of hand. And when she went, it was more important than ever that I should stay at home to be with him."

"So no sex life. No games of doctor with visiting cousins? No hot, straying little hands during the Christmas game of Sardines? And what about that governess? From what you say, she was rather keen."

"No gentleman would talk like that."

She really meant it too, thought Tom. But she'd started it all and she could jolly well take what was coming to her. It would be useful practice for marriage.

"Who's evading the issue now?" he said cheerfully. "I'm going to tell you something, my sweet. One of the conditions of marriage, or of any relationship between two people, is that neither must try to see too much. You can look as hard as you like at what is shown you; don't ask to see what isn't."

"But two people in love should share everything."

"Only what they both understand. If you are shown what you don't understand, you will resent it, and there will be the first breach in love. That's where the Greeks were so sensible. They did not consult their women on important matters because they knew that lack of understanding would result in jealousy."

"We were talking of something quite different," she snapped.

"Of my sexual past. It is rather squalid, though no worse than a lot of other people's, and you would not understand it. You may be able to when you are older, in which case I will tell you about it. Meanwhile, you must take my word for it that nothing which happened was important or need in any way call in question my love for you."

He turned towards her and kissed her on the forehead, then on the eyes, then on the mouth. Although she made no response, she pulled him back when he began to draw away.

"Tell me why you love me," she said.

"Because you are beautiful and good. . . . Another Greek speciality. Because you are true. And because you will be worth teaching."

"What must I learn?"

"Almost everything. When I first saw you at that party in London, I said, 'There is the beautiful princess, sleeping the sleep of ignorance. When the prince comes to wake her, kissing won't be enough: she'll need a damned good shake'."

"She had one this afternoon."

"I know and I'm sorry. But there will be kisses too."

They walked over a meadow towards a sloping croquet lawn and a large, smug, square red house beyond it. Tom opened a door in a brick wall and stood aside for Patricia to pass. As they stepped on to the lawn, they saw Isobel Turbot, Patricia's eighteen-year-old sister, come dancing out of the shrubbery towards them, her big breasts flapping, her thin legs (so unlike Patricia's strongly fleshed ones) back-heeling sexily under her bottom, on the verge of a Charleston.

"Lovely day for snogging," she yelled.

Her respect for her elder sister had declined since nursery days; low cunning and a boarding school education had supplied her with some dubious mental acquirements, on the strength of which she had set up as the sophisticated member of the household.

"Heavy petting," she said, giggling wildly, and Charlestoned off towards the stables which adjoined the east side of the house.

"I can't think," said Patricia, "where she gets her frivolity."

"I can," said Tom, remembering mama the bolter.

"I hope there's not to be trouble," Patricia said.

"She'll sober up."

"Some of the young men she sees in London. . . . The ones that take her to those cellar places. . . .'

"She also had some more suitable friends," said Tom dryly. "That guardee she produced the other day – "

"I'm so afraid she leads them on. And the way she keeps running off to the stable to see Wilkes. . . ."

There was in her eye a fierce, prurient look, combining acute distaste with speculation and even with yearning. Quite what it boded Tom did not know, and would not until their wedding night: because this time, he had told himself, he was going to wait; it might not be wise, but it would be a novel experiment – and not the only one which he proposed. For he had noticed with interest that he was still capable of such detachment, of loving Patricia with all his heart and yet of making cynical evaluations, about how to get the best value out of her, on the side.

"Do you think she – ?"

"Forget it," Tom interrupted her; "Isobel won't come to any harm. She's indestructible."

Although he could not be sure, he fancied he caught a gleam in her eye which hinted at a wish for a very different answer: she wants me to cry lechery, he thought, because her conventions forbid her to give tongue herself; there's strong magic bottled up there, and I'm the one that's fated to remove the cork and release the djinn. This prospect he found, exciting, yet also remote, unreal, like the dreams he sometimes had of being in bed with the Queen.

They moved into the drawing-room for tea.

Sir Edwin Turbot placed his buttocks before the fire and then stuck them insolently out at it. He held one crumpet in the flat of his left hand while he used the right to feed another into his mouth. He did not take separate bites; he placed it between his teeth and then slowly absorbed it, like a snake with its prey. When the first crumpet had been engulfed, he surveyed the second cannily, as though he half thought it might try to escape, and said:

"Bad business about Bishop's Cross. Why does Morrison want to stick his nose in?"

"I gather," said Tom, "that he has quite a following at Bishop's Cross. Enough to put him on the short list."

"Rupert Percival should never have allowed it," said the Minister peevishly. He looked sharply at his crumpet, then whisked it to his mouth with a glint of revenge.

"They say that Percival rather likes Morrison."

Sir Edwin, mouth full, acknowledged this by raising the toe of his left shoe and rapping smartly on the stone hearth. Patricia, who knew this indicated a sense of deprivation, poured her father an out-size cup of tea with seven lumps of sugar and proffered it with both hands.

"April," said Sir Edwin with contempt, and sucked down the last of his crumpet with a kind of inverted belch. "No more crumpets in a day or two, I suppose?" He took his tea from Patricia with a courteous nod. "April. Spring. I've always hated it. Brings nothing but trouble. And where's Isobel?" he demanded, the connection of ideas being ominously plain.

"Gone for a walk to the village, Daddy," said Patricia smoothly.

Sir Edwin decided to let this pass; but being determined to

be put upon one way or the other, for he derived much pleasure from grievance, he reverted to the intrusiveness of Morrison.

"Trouble," he said with relish, as though it were the name of a family estate. "We knew just the sort of man we wanted in Alastair Dixon's place for Bishop's Cross. And when they took up this chap Somerset Lloyd-James, it couldn't have been better. People knew his father, Shagger Lloyd-James" – for a moment he looked a bit dubious – "and they also knew that the boy was clever about money. Just what we wanted: someone to help keep the money straight. Because," he said, fixing his future son-in-law with a look that mingled irritation with respect, "even you left-wing fellows will admit that there isn't an unlimited supply. And what there is is getting jolly wonky, believe me."

Tom believed him.

"So everything was fixed up for Shagger's boy," continued the Minister in the smug tones of rational complaint, "and then what happens? Along comes the spring, and along comes trouble with it, in the shape of Mr Peter Morrison pushing himself in where he isn't wanted. Rocking the boat. Alastair Dixon says that's all he'll ever do; rock the boat. It's all he did last time he was in the House – him and that Young England Group. The fellow's just a confounded prig. Prig," he repeated delightedly, as though he himself had just invented the word.

"At least one can trust him, Minister," said Tom quietly, "which is more than can be said for Shagger's boy Somerset."

"Oh," said Sir Edwin, who, unlike many other important men, was always prepared to listen to what he didn't want to hear. "You know Lloyd-James well enough to say so?"

"For several years now I've done a lot of work for his paper. He is a brilliant editor and an amusing companion. He has a very shrewd grasp of practical economics, which is well supported by knowledge of relevant theory, both mathematical and political. He is a stylist. Despite a deplorable physique and bad utterance, he can charm. He is socially adept. He knows how to order a well-balanced and imaginative dinner, and he can cut a dash at the card table without getting himself into trouble. To know Somerset Lloyd-James is a first-rate education and at times an exquisite pleasure. But," said Tom, slapping both hands down on his thighs, "he is a killer. He is as mean as hell with money and there's nothing he won't do to get it. He is also, when it suits his book, a betrayer. He has the authentic Judas touch."

Patricia sat goggling at this insight into the world and its wickedness. Sir Edwin, who disapproved of Tom to the point of obsession but was sharp enough to know when he was on to a good thing, gave him the look of commendation which he reserved for upper servants, and remarked:

"Something of the kind used to be said about Shagger. A lot of people pooh-poohed it, but he was always regarded with caution."

"It has something to do," said Tom, "with the special morality of Roman Catholics. They have always been adept at adjusting moral issues to suit their own circumstances . . . at claiming for themselves, as adherents to the original faith, a sort of divine licence for obliquity. And in England, where their faith has been actively persecuted, they have an even stronger excuse."

Sir Edwin snorted. This was mere speculation – not what the fellow was paid for. More and more Sir Edwin found himself thinking of Tom as the hired secretary or adviser he devoutly wished Tom was – someone to be ejected with a month's notice if he got out of hand, not a permanent addition to the family. When first told of the engagement, Sir Edwin had been dumbfounded; but the habit of letting Patricia have her way had become so much a matter of course over the years that it was unthinkable that her intention should be thwarted or her wisdom questioned. For had it not been he himself who had always fostered and underwritten her pretensions? Too late to impugn them now. And so, conscious of his weakness and studying to compensate for it by craft, he had devised, in self-defence, a fiction whereby he accepted Tom as a disagreeable but talented assistant, whose personal shortcomings (the long curly hair, the sexual knowingness, the left-wing attitudes) were none of his affair provided only the young man did his job. Quite how he was going to adapt this system of deceiving himself when Tom and Patricia were actually married, he had not yet thought. Meanwhile, however, he contrived to tolerate Tom as a general tolerates a conceited but able aide-de-camp. Which did not mean, he now told himself crossly, that he had to listen to the fellow's theories about the psychology of Papists.

"I should prefer a more concrete and factual assessment," he said pompously. "Somerset Lloyd-James: in what respects has he *shown* he is not to be trusted? Never mind his religion."

"I mind it very much," said Tom: "without it he'd just be another amusing rogue. But his religion lends him a conviction of righteousness which makes him pitiless. Nobody's safe: not friend, lover, servant . . . dog."

"Please to be specific."

"Very well. Usury – at fantastic rates."

"It takes two to agree the rates."

"Granted. What about bribery?"

"Give me an instance."

"He once offered me three times the normal fee," said Tom blandly, "to fudge the facts for an article he wanted written."

"Editorial privilege," rasped Sir Edwin. "They're allowed to be selective."

"Attempted blackmail then?"

This time Sir Edwin turned thoughtful.

"For money?"

"There was money in it. But mainly for power."

"*That*," the Minister said, "is certainly something. You can vouch for it?"

"I was cat's paw . . . I didn't realise till too late."

"You seem to have been much . . . involved . . . with Somerset Lloyd-James."

"One can't help it if one lives in certain circles. He haunts them like a ghoul."

"But *now* . . .?" put in Patricia hopefully.

"*Now*," said Tom, "I am by way of being an expert on him. But I still have to look sharp. It's like dealing with Proteus: you don't know what shape he's going to take from one second to the next."

"Hmm," mused the Minister. "Not the sort of chap one puts up for one's club."

"He'd get in just the same if he set his mind on it."

"But for all this," said the Minister, "I don't care for the idea of Bishop's Cross adopting Morrison. He'll stir up that Young England Group again, for a start. And damn it all, it's not three years since he resigned because of that scandal."

"Nobody believes in the scandal."

"Some of the public will. The public memory is as long as it's inaccurate . . . for any kind of dirt, that is. It's just too *soon* for Morrison, and that's all about it. His name should never have been kept on the list at Central Office."

"From what I hear," said Tom, teasing faintly, "there was a number of very important people who took great care that it should be."

This reminder that Sir Edwin's disciplinary hold on the Conservative Party was not as absolute as he would have wished produced, at last, a sense of injury too strong to be merely pleasurable. The Minister put his cup down with a crack and strode to the door.

"Black tie for dinner," he said, as though proclaiming an interdict. "Eight for half past. The Canteloupes are coming with the dowager and a house guest. Chap called Detterling, who says he knows you and that Jew publisher of yours." For a moment Sir Edwin looked as if he had been about to institute a pogrom but had thought better of it at the last minute. Instead, "Please not to pass the port too freely," he enjoined with gloomy rancour: "Canteloupe's head does not improve."

"So when," asked Lady Canteloupe with a saccharine smile, "is the wedding to be?"

"Time enough to think about that," Sir Edwin said, "when we're through with the general election."

"The wedding's to be at mid-summer," said Patricia firmly.

Sir Edwin turned up his eyes and stuck his spoon into the middle of his peach melba, with the air of a soldier planting a sabre to mark a fallen comrade's newly filled grave.

"I'm going to be chief bride's maid," said Isobel. Even the ice-cream running down her chin seemed somehow to have sexual significance. "Patty and I have fixed on the dearest little short green dresses."

"Flowers?" said the Dowager Marchioness Canteloupe, mopping up the last of her melba juice with a stray piece of toast.

"Carnations."

"*Green* carnations?" said Lord Canteloupe, who affected to think that all young men with long curly hair and left-wing opinions must of necessity be sodomites.

"Yes," said Tom; "we've already arranged to have them dyed."

Lord Canteloupe laughed generously. He liked young men with spirit, whatever their social provenance, nor did he give a tinker's fart, as he himself might have put it, whether Tom was a sodomite or not.

"Hear that, mother?" he shouted – quite gratuitously, for the old lady's hearing was perfect. "They're having them specially dyed."

"*Very* expensive," said the dowager, looking maliciously at Sir Edwin.

"What nonsense," the Minister mumbled from the head of the table.

"Don't be such an old stick, Edwin," said the Marquis. "You can perfectly well afford it. Now, suppose you were like me, with the Lord Lieutenancy hanging over you. . . . *That's* going to be like having a wedding every week."

The Marquis Canteloupe would never be Lord Lieutenant, because he drank too much and his flushed bruiser's face frightened the ladies. In sober daylight, he knew this very well and did not resent it. He had the consolation of being an immensely rich man who was daily growing richer, this from the exhibition of his house and gardens, which he directed with a kind of stunted genius: for since he combined considerable native shrewdness with the tastes of a retarded adolescent, he knew just what would appeal to other adolescents, and arranged rallies and spectacles which drew them in tens of thousands from all over Wessex. But although the money and notoriety thus accruing more than compensated him for lack of official place, there came a stage every evening (after about three whiskies and two thirds of a bottle of wine) when he suddenly conceived that as the senior nobleman in the area he *ought* to be offered the Lord Lieutenancy, and from this it was a short step to claiming that he very soon would be. Thus far the illusion was harmless; unfortunately, however, brandy in any quantity would then lead him to reflect that the long postponement of the honour was a deliberate slight to his order; a grudge that issued in a spiteful peevishness, which he would express by accusing his host of conspiring to keep him short of drink. Since the accusation was often well founded, it was hard to rebut save by making him free of the decanter; and since such indulgence only inspired him to comment the more cuttingly on the antecedent stinginess, the problem was considered insoluble throughout the county.

The Turbots' answer to the dilemma was to invite the Canteloupes as seldom as possible, old friends though they were; but as Canteloupe had recently threatened, in a fit of boyish mischief, to take himself and his strawberry leaves over to the Labour benches of the Lords, Sir Edwin had felt obliged to undertake a series of entertainments to flatter and dissuade him. The best time to do this was over the port – while Canteloupe was still good-humouredly convinced that he would soon be Lord Lieutenant and before later doses of brandy had turned the conviction to rancour. When, therefore, the dowager had finally finished dunking at her melba, Sir Edwin gestured at Patricia, who rose and led off the ladies. The Minister now turned briskly to the reclamation of Canteloupe's political loyalty, leaving Tom to talk to the Canteloupes' house guest, Captain Detterling (M.P.), with whom he had been vaguely acquainted for some years and had recently come to know more closely as the new colleague of his publisher.

"I suppose I ought to congratulate you on this engagement," Detterling said, "but the very notion of people getting married irritates me beyond endurance. Nothing personal, you understand. It's just that the best of couples behave so smugly – as though they thought they'd done something original."

"I entirely agree," said Tom: "but as the years go on I feel the need for a little smugness in my life. I promise you I'll not pretend that I'm doing anything original."

"You won't be able to help it," said Detterling morosely. "It's a necessary condition of bringing yourself to get married at all. And another thing: all married couples – even working class ones – seem to think that the mere fact of marriage confers status . . . privilege. I put up with a lot of it in the Army. Quite junior men, subalterns, would ring up to say that they couldn't do this or that – whether it was playing squash or going on a night exercise – because it didn't suit their wives. Seemed to think that was the last word to be said."

"So what did you do?"

"Told 'em not to be so damned silly and be there on time, *or else*. . . . It made me quite unpopular."

"The theory is," said Tom, "that bachelors lead a pleasant and carefree existence, and ought to make allowances for those who are rearing the new generation."

"Nobody asked them to," said Detterling, his voice brittle with irritation: "in fact before long people will be begging them not to. The country's too full already; a man can hardly *move*. But still these bloody women sit about breeding like mice, and then expect to be told they've done something clever."

"It *is* rather onerous," said Tom: "they must be given some comfort."

"Why? It's not compulsory. People just don't think straight. Old friend of mine turned up at the club the other day with a face as long as a riding boot. Wife expecting third child, he told us: got to give up the club, give up his cricket tour in the summer, even give up his occasional round of golf. Why? I said. Money, he said, and went into a long spiel about education policies and the Lord knows what. But the thing was, he thought he was being dutiful, that everyone ought to say what a splendid fellow he was. In fact he was just one more bloody fool, and so I told him. You didn't have to get married in the first place, I told him, and even if you did you don't have to spawn like a frog. He was quite put out, I can tell you."

"Have you no crumb of consolation for me?" Tom said mildly.

"Yes," shouted Canteloupe, who had been trying to engage their attention from the far end of the table: "whenever you sleep with another woman it'll be adultery and not fornication. Sounds more stylish, don't you think? Now *pass the port*."

Detterling made a long arm and passed it. Sir Edwin gave a persecuted look, seized the decanter as soon as Canteloupe had filled from it, and impounded it in the crook of his arm with the officiousness of an excise man.

"Drink runs in the Canteloupe family," Detterling explained softly to Tom. "Canteloupe isn't too bad, but his brothers and sisters are in and out of the bin like cuckoos on a clock."

"You seem to know a lot about them."

"I'm a second cousin. Canteloupe asked me down to look at some memoirs his father wrote. Although, he's as rich as Midas he's always sniffing round for a little extra, so he reckons I can get Gregory Stern to publish them."

"And will you?"

Detterling turned his eyes up.

"I'll see they're read."

"Someone else," said Tom, "is shortly going to ask the same favour. I'm afraid I put him on to you. Major Fielding Gray."

This time Detterling did not turn his eyes up. He narrowed them into a look which conveyed a shrewd interest rather oddly mixed with remorse.

"I heard what happened," he muttered. "He should never have been in the Army. Not as a regular."

"Will his books be any good?"

"Could be," said Detterling non-committally, having quickly reverted to his normal manner. "He was a clever chap. Something had gone wrong – I never quite knew what."

"But you'll help him?"

"Of course. We served together. Pass the port," he called sharply to his host.

"Yes," boomed Canteloupe; "before we all die of thirst."

"The ladies. . . ." began the Minister.

"Can wait. Port," said Canteloupe. The decanter passed round. Canteloupe filled, drained, filled again, and then clasped both hands round the decanter, like a rich child who refuses to part with his toy to a poorer one. Sir Edwin, blinking with self-pity, resumed his blandishments.

"We'll have to get him out soon," murmured Detterling to Tom; "but one can't sit with an empty glass all night just because there's a drunk in the party. I'll tip Molly the wink to have the car called early." He looked meditatively at Tom. "And since there's something I want to tell you before I go," he said, "I'd best tell you now. You know Max de Freville? The man who runs the big chemmy game?"

"I've seen him occasionally."

"He's by way of being a chum of mine. The thing is that lately he's developed a very odd sort of hobby. A new game, you might say."

"I should have thought," said Tom, puzzled, "that he'd had enough of games."

"That's just it. He's bored and needs distraction, and this is new and different. It's a kind of power game. He collects information. He doesn't use it, he just collects it, so that he can feel he's got to the bottom of things and that if he *did* want to interfere. . . . You see what I mean?"

"Roughly."

"Well," said Detterling. "He's already got a lot of sources and he's busy getting more. He shows me a lot of the stuff, you see. And I thought you should know that he's got an informant in this house. I mean, if you're going to marry into the family. . . ."

"Not . . . not the Minister?" said Tom with a giggle.

"No. Isobel."

"*Isobel?*"

"It seems she got into one of his gaming parties with a boy friend one night. The boy friend guaranteed her, so although she was obviously under age Max let her play. She lost a thousand odd, couldn't pay of course, and didn't want Max to make her look silly by coming down on the boy friend for it. So they did a deal. Max would cancel the debt and Isobel would send in regular bulletins about the Minister's home life."

"I can't think that amounts to much."

"I don't know. Dinner parties like this. Canteloupe's a

name, to say nothing of Llewyllyn. And as Max says, the most boring information very often contains the essential clue to something really big . . . the missing number in the combination. . . ."

"Isobel's a perfect little madam," Tom said. "Any day now she'll get herself knocked up by an errand boy."

"Max thinks she's cleverer than people know. So I thought I'd give you the tip."

"But you say de Freville doesn't actually use what he's told."

"He could turn dangerous later. He's vain, bitter, obsessed. . . . So if I were you, I'd keep clear of Isobel."

Detterling rose as if he himself had been host.

"Come on, cousin Canteloupe," he said. "You can't sit there sozzling the whole evening."

"No," said cousin Canteloupe. "I'm sick of port anyhow. I need a little brandy." He pushed the port decanter peevishly away. "A lot of brandy," he emended.

In the drawing-room the four women were discussing hymns for the wedding. Isobel had just contributed "Perverse and foolish oft I strayed," when the men entered in some disorder which had been occasioned by Canteloupe's neglect to button his fly after going to the loo. When reminded, he had simply opened it wider and announced that these days there was never anything worth seeing. Sir Edwin, who was more put out by this than anyone else, had constituted himself a movable screen between Canteloupe and the public, and was now bobbing uneasily from side to side in order to sustain the role. Fortunately or otherwise, he did not have to do so long; for Canteloupe turned his back on the company as soon as he entered the room and made a rush for the sideboard, where he announced his intention of trying every single bottle. After signing to Lady C., who nodded wanly, Detterling went to the telephone to order the car up from the village; while the dowager sat back happily, long since inured, like a member of a Greek chorus, to any form of disaster – and indeed rather grateful to it for passing the time. Desultory conversation continued in front of the fire. Patricia took up some sewing and attacked it with moral fibre. There was an occasional slurp from the sideboard.

"Kent has a good chance in the County Championship this year," said Detterling as he re-entered.

Sir Edwin, who had been interrupted in the middle of his favourite story about Lord Curzon, looked like an affronted guinea hen. What he didn't realise was that Detterling's remark was a special code for warning Lady Canteloupe that the car was on the way without letting her husband know; for if he twigged that he was being taken home early he used to hide or lock himself in the lavatory, and had once even pretended to have a fit, in the hope that a particularly parsimonious host would come across with more brandy. This evening all went well. On receipt of a second code-message, "I wonder why Colin Cowdrey's bottom is so huge," ("*What?*" said Sir Edwin), Lady Canteloupe and the dowager moved into the hall to put on their coats. After another two minutes Lady C.'s head came round the door, to indicate that the car had arrived and the dowager was safely inside it. This was the testing moment: the essential thing was to get Canteloupe out of the house and into the car before he realised what was happening and could start a scene. Expedients ranging from cries of "Fire" to promises of naked ladies on the lawn had all been used and superannuated in their time; and it was getting difficult to think of anything effective. Oddly enough, however, on this occasion Lord Canteloupe, without a word being said to him, suddenly muttered, "Car's here, I suppose," and moved from the sideboard towards the door with no attempt at protest.

"I'm going quietly," he said, "so nobody need worry." He struck a match and carried it shakily to his half-smoked cigar; the flame never came within six inches of its target, but he seemed satisfied with his effort and sucked contentedly on the dead tube. "And I'll tell you why I'm going quietly," he continued between sucks: "my car's not the only one out there. If you look through the window by the sideboard, you'll see that you are about to be visited by three car-loads of police. The fun – such as it ever was – is over for tonight."

Canteloupe had exaggerated. There were only two cars, and only one of them connected with the police. His lordship was further mistaken in supposing that he could slip away quietly, as it was himself who was wanted.

"Quite a rumpus the other night" (as Isobel was later to write to Max de Freville). "Canteloupe dined here with Lady C. and the old woman, and by ten o'clock he was absolutely squiffed. Just as they were all going home about a million cars came up the drive brimming with policemen. Lord C. is scared stiff of the police, rather odd for someone in his position, but apparently they were beastly to him on Boat Race night years ago. Anyway, there he was scowling away on the front steps with his trousers open from top to bottom and just about to lunge into his Rolls, when out of one of the cars which *wasn't* a police car steps a squat, queeny little chap in one of those joke dinner jackets which look like all cuffs and collar.

" 'Ah, Lord Canteloupe,' says this nance; 'I thought we'd never find you. These country lanes . . . like a labyrinth, my dear . . . my dear Lord Canteloupe, that is.'

"So Canteloupe stands there with his underpants streaming in the breeze and says nothing, then out comes Daddy in a frightful bait, takes one look at the siss in the D.J., and says:

" 'Oh, it's you, Weir. What the devil's all this?'

"So then lovey-dovey, who turns out to be an M.P. called Carton Weir, explains that he couldn't find the way and had to get this brigade of bobbies to guide him. It seems that he's by way of being the Downing Street go-between and he's got an important message. So then Daddy preens himself up, thinking it's for him, but it isn't at all, it's for poor old pissy Canteloupe. So then the policemen salute like crazy and we all go inside again, having first dredged Lady C. and the other old cow out of the Rolls, and Lady C. tells C. to do up his trouser buttons, and C. as good as thumbs his nose at her, and Daddy looks ready to shit with temper because *he's* not the centre of attention, and C. looks so full of juice that it's clear he can't understand a single thing that's being said to him. He's funny when he's sozzled, he can talk more or less like he was sober but he can't take anything in. Anyway, the end of it is that Daddy and Canteloupe and the faggot go off to Daddy's study, and Patty and me and Patty's boy Tom are left to make polite noises at Lady C., the dowager, and some chum of C.'s called Captain Detterling who they brought along to din-din . . . rather a poppet this one, a bit long in the tooth but with that *distinguished* hair, he must have done his captain bit about ten generations ago. Both the captain and Tom know all about the poovy man in the tux, and the dowager, who's as sharp as the razor she shaves with, asks about a trillion questions, while Lady C. looks as sour as goosegogs because she's afraid her old man is in no shape to rise to the occasion. . . . Which it turns out about three hours later is quite some occasion, because Lord C. is being made a kind of mini-minister, a Parliamentary Secretary I think they call it. All drop dead."

"Parliamentary Secretary for the Development of British Recreational Resources," said Sir Edwin to Tom when the guests had at last departed. "It seems that this is an experimental appointment to give the Party a . . . new look, as they call it . . . for the election."

"You yourself were consulted?"

"Of course," said Sir Edwin. He went to the sideboard and mixed himself a very stiff whisky. "And I must tell you straight away that I was violently opposed to it. It appears that my wishes have been disregarded."

Sir Edwin was in many ways an honest man. Although he often found it expedient not to form an opinion, he was jealous and eager for those which he did hold, and he was, moreover, prepared to own to their consequences. In admitting that he had been snubbed he was paying Tom no special compliment: he had done and said what he felt was right, and anyone who enquired into the matter should be told so.

"It's not even," Sir Edwin continued, "as if he was a reliable member of the Party. He treats the Lords as 'a jolly good laugh' – his own expression. As you know, he's so lacking in responsibility that he was even threatening to change sides."

"For a jolly good laugh, presumably. Perhaps that's why they've made the appointment. To keep him loyal."

"That's not Party discipline as I was taught it."

"True. But these stately home impresarios are right in the public eye. They are considered to be modern, progressive, *with it*. Canteloupe's defection would have been *noticed*. . . . Though for the life of me I can't think why Carton Weir had to drive down here in the middle of the night."

"Likes a bit of drama. He was charged, he told me, to acquaint Canteloupe with the P.M.'s intention as soon as possible and persuade him to accept as a matter of vital urgency. Said he thought it might be easier if the man was mellow. As if there was any doubt of Canteloupe accepting."

"Did he know *what* he was accepting?"

"He affected to think that he was being made Lord Lieutenant . . . but he'll get it straight when he wakes up with Weir in the house. I gather Weir's to represent him in the Commons."

"That's shrewd. With Weir to shore him up he can't go far wrong."

"All the same," said Sir Edwin clenching both fists, "it won't do. It's too bad and it won't do. This isn't the eighteenth century, and you can't appoint clowns like Canteloupe to govern. If he wouldn't do as Lord Lieutenant of the County, he won't do as a Parliamentary Secretary."

"With respect," said Tom slowly, "I think the P.M. has been rather subtle. The fact is that Canteloupe has shown a conspicuous talent for entertaining the young. He knows the kind of rubbish they want and he gives it to them in just the right package. Given enough scope, he can lay the same sort of thing on for the young of the whole nation . . . for all those who are just old enough to vote, or soon will be. And this in a so-called age of leisure. It could help to give your crowd just the look they want – attractive, forward-looking, the party of progress and pleasure. An illusion of course, but it'll take everyone some time to twig that, and by then there'll be some other bright bubble to gawp at."

"None of which is government as I was taught it."

"Well, there you are," said Tom. "If you will support people like Somerset Lloyd-James and keep out honest men like Morrison, you must expect this kind of thing."

"Hrrmmph," said the Minister, and stumped off to bed.

4

PAN AND SILENUS

MARK LEWSON wrote to Max de Freville from Venice. "What a dear little chap Lykiadopoulos is. Like the Michelin man and as bald as a balloon, a life-size toy for rich children to play with. Not a cold fish either, as you'd expect a Baccarat banker to be, but warm and frothy. I suppose that's what fools the punters. 'We *can't* lose money,' I can hear them all say, 'playing against a sweet little man like that', and in they go laughing; and even after they have lost, it must seem more like giving it to a good cause, as though Lykiadopoulos were an orphan or something, so they feel all warm inside and hurry back to lose more. He really is a poppet.

"But of course you know all about that. So down to work. I arrived in Venice the day after I left you and booked in at the Cavaletto, not quite the luxiest thing going, but I'm afraid the Contessa and I got ourselves a bad name in most of the bigger ones. The next morning betimes I rang up Lykiadopoulos at the Danieli and begged leave to present your note of introduction. The telephone nearly cracked with excitement, because it seems the poor old thing is very much alone in Venice as the police are so severe that he has to be horribly careful. He didn't say so in so many words, of course; but I gathered that the idea of a nice, clean tourist chum with a British passport was very *bien vu*.

"So we met for a delicious lunch in Harry's and got on together like a kibbutz on fire. But then the trouble started. Lykiadopoulos (call me Lyki) wanted me to move in on the Danieli, and that was all right with me – had I not known that the minute I set foot in the place the manager would storm out with a load of the Contessa's duds drawn on the Banco di Spirito Santo, which would really be v. shaming in front of a new friend. So what to do? Well, clearly I'd got to get the entrée to the Danieli sooner or later, because if the letter was anywhere it was probably there, so I made a sort of semi-clean breast. There had, I simpered, been a little misunderstanding some years ago, when the currency regulations were still very fierce. . . . The dear, tactful, generous fellow took that at face value and volunteered to square the management. Quite what he did, I don't know; if they produced the Contessa's stumers, he never mentioned it then or later; but the upshot was that within three quarters of an hour I found myself installed in a suite at the Danieli, with everyone from the manager to the lift boy fawning on me like the Pope. My bag came over from the Cavaletto on a sort of magic carpet, the bill there was fixed with a flick of someone's finger, and I was to regard myself, it seemed, as the guest of "Signor Lyki" at the Danieli Royal Excelsior Hotel until (and here, despite the tooth-flashing, there was *precision*) the Signore moved out to the Lido to be nice and handy for running his bank.

"Well, a suite with a drawing-room amounts, in hotel convention, to a built-in chaperon, so you'll have guessed the rest. Hardly had I unpacked before there was the pitter-patter of Signor Lyki's little feet. *Son cosas de la vida*. And really life is quite pleasant. There are delicious meals and amusing trips to look at churches, both in Venice and on the islands, about which Lyki is remarkably informative. His speciality is the Ghetto – did you know the Venetians claim to have invented the system? – where we have just spent a very long morning. Lyki is so energetic about his sight-seeing, to say nothing of his other amusements, that unless I find the letter and get out I shall soon be a total wreck.

"And what about the letter? you'll ask. Nothing doing so far. For a start, he always comes to *my* room; and so far, if you can believe this, I haven't even been able to find out where or which his is. If I ask at the desk, they just ring through (*"Camera di Signor Lyki* – never a number) and tell him I want him, whereupon he either joins me straight away or fixes a meeting place over the buzzer – never, although I constantly suggest it, his own room. Very odd. The other tack I've tried is drawing him out about his gambling career, in the hope we'll get on to des Moulins and the letter. No luck. He's told me stories – v. good ones – about every trick in the game, but nothing about des Moulins and his *coup de dishonneur*.

"So I'll just have to keep trying. I've been in the Danieli for three days now, which gives me another six, I make it, before he moves out to the hotel on the Lido. He might take me with him but I doubt it. I gather that while the bank's running he leads a dedicated life, and anyhow I don't know that I could stand up to the wear and tear. Six days then: I'll do my best but I guarantee nothing. And incidentally, if you meant what you said about making it worth my while to keep you informed, a little on account would not come amiss. I have to make *some* pretence of paying for the odd luncheon. By telegraph to the American Express is quickest – or so the Contessa always said. And that's it for now. We're just off out to the Lido to have din-dins and go to the Casino – a preliminary reconnaissance, I gather, to see what nick the place is in. . . .'"

Max de Freville, just back from Menton, made a note on a desk-diary to send Lewson £50 by wire the following morning. Although the information was thin, Lewson had at least got inside the castle if not yet inside the keep. If he had spoken the truth about his efforts to date, he deserved a refresher now: if he had been lying, he would get his deserts later.

"Not bad," said the Marquis Canteloupe, surveying a hundred square yards of thickly carpeted office complete with cocktail cabinet and day bed, "not bad at all. So what's to do now, eh?"

"I dare say the civil servants will have something to say about that," said Carton Weir; "but as far as *we're* concerned, we want a bigger and brighter image of government-sponsored public recreation."

"More opera?" said Canteloupe dubiously. "That kind of thing?"

"No," said Weir: "*not* that kind of thing."

"And where do the civil servants come in?"

"Advice. Ways, means, money. Legal difficulties. There are a lot of laws against entertainment, you'll find."

"Let's get them repealed then."

"Oh dear me, no. Although the public demands to be entertained, it would be most upset if it thought the government approved of pleasure. The public must be entertained in spite of itself: in spite of the opposition which it will feel in duty bound to put up."

"But you just said it *demands* to be entertained."

"So it does. But in the teeth of its own puritanical traditions. So first of all it wants to be reassured. You've got to convince it that entertainment is somehow a social right, almost a duty, like having its kiddies educated. That will make it all respectable. But pleasure for the sake of pleasure . . . oh dear me, no."

"I'd thought," said Canteloupe, shyly, "of government brothels."

"*No*," said Weir.

"But all this talk of teenagers riddled with clap. *My* brothels would be medically vetted."

"NO."

"I see. . . . State Casinos?"

"In six or seven years, perhaps. Provided you charge a 50 per cent tax on winnings and only allow hard seats."

"Ah," said Canteloupe, "I'm beginning to get the idea.

Now what about this? Government-sponsored caravan sites for holidays. Make a filthy mess of some well known beauty spot – they'll love that – and then publish a lot of balls about The People enjoying Its Rights in the Countryside, that kind of blab. Jam the bloody caravans as close together as possible – you know how they love being crowded – make a song and a dance about being good neighbours, give a prize for the best behaved family, and perhaps throw in compulsory P.T."

"That's it," said Carton Weir: "that's just the ticket."

"Further to my last," wrote Mark Lewson from Venice, "we're a little warmer now though hardly hot.

"After I signed off the other evening, we duly set sail in Lyki's motor-boat to take a butchers at the Casino. The only plan I had, and a pretty poor one, was to wait till we got back to the Danieli and then follow Lyki to his room, so that at least I'd know where it was. If he caught me, I was going to pretend to be tight and say I'd lost my way; so the first thing I had to do was to prop myself against the Casino bar and consume, or appear to consume, an immense number of drinkies.

"The end of it was that I really did get tight. Lyki, who disapproves of drinking in casinos, had gone prowling off on a tour of inspection, and I was enjoying an interval in my dipso act, when in came Burke Lawrence, the advertising man. Now, believe it or not, Burke is one of the few people on earth who might be said to owe *me* money, because the Contessa, who was a nutty old cinephile, once put up a few hundred quid for some amateur film he was trying to make. Whenever we meet he always buys me champagne to stop me going on about what happened to the money, and this time was no exception. In fact he called for a magnum. Very pleased with himself was Burke. It seems that he's in Venice to help organise some festival to do with advertising films – I believe the Venetians

would throw a Festival of Plumbing if anyone suggested it –
and he regards this as professional recognition of a high order.
The only trouble, apparently, is that he's lumbered with an
out of date model called Penelope Holbrook, who was once
his mistress and now follows him around wherever he goes
making scenes and whining for work. Not that she needs it,
as her ex-husband pays her a handsome alimony, but she's
anxious to make a come-back. This evening, however, he
reckons he's safe, because one of the other geniuses to do with
the festival has made a pass at her and she's busy goosing him
up in high hope of an offer.

"So there we were, tucking happily into Burke Lawrence's
magnum of fizz and talking about the dear old days, when a
sort of frisson goes over the entire room and we see an
agitated crowd forming round the top roulette table at the
far end. And guess what's going on. Lyki, looking like a man
in a fever, is plastering the table with maximum bets all round
the number 20. 50,000 lire *en plain*, 100,000 for each of the
chevaux, and so on through the *carré* bets and the *transversals*
right out to the even chances – *noir*, *pair*, *passe* – on each of
which he places one and three quarter million. God alone
knows what's got into him. As soon as the chef sees what he's
up to, he suggests to Lyki that he should call the bet and
deposit the total sum needed with the croupier, thus leaving
room on the cloth for someone else to play; but Lyki's beyond
listening and just goes on wanging down plaques as though
they were dominoes until he's made the entire spiel. You
never saw such a sight. The table piled high with plastic of
every colour in the spectrum, Lyki's eyes glaring through the
smoke like fog lamps, the croupiers all sweating buckets, and
the spectators squawking and yakking like a parrot house.
Only the chef kept calm; he was a chap with a pan like Tiresias
who'd obviously seen the lot in his day and was beyond being
impressed by anything. Which was just as well, because otherwise they'd still be sitting there; he had to flick his fingers

three times before he could get the croupier responsible to pick up the ball and throw for the coup, and even then the poor fellow bungled it and had to stop the wheel and start all over again.

"But eventually we were off. Wheel turning, ball whirring round the groove at the top of the bowl, dead silence now, Lyki's whole body trembling like a witch-doctor throwing a seizure, ball begins to drop, bounces on one of the diamonds, rides for a second on the rim of the wheel, and then *clunk*.

" '*Uno*,' calls the croupier; '*le premier*.'

"So that was that, it seemed. But as you of all people will know, one lies next to twenty on the wheel; and when the wretch looked again, his face turned a rich green and started sort of oozing. Whereupon the chef took over.

" '*Venti*,' he called after a stern inspection of the wheel, '*vingt, zwanzig*, twenty. *Noir, pair, passe*.'

"After this they led Lyki away to the manager's office to make him out a cheque. He re-emerged, rather flushed, about twenty minutes later, came over to Burke and me, ordered more champagne, and started lapping it up like a figure of farce. And he didn't forget his chums. Pretty soon we're all floating in the stuff, and what with the brandy I've already put down in order to pass my drunk act off on Lyki, and what with the gamblers pressing round to gawk at him and touch him for luck, I'm beginning to feel mildly hysterical.

" 'The first time,' Lyki was saying, 'the first time I have ever drunk wine in the Rooms. And you know why? It is not the money, though that is pleasant. It is that I have now fulfilled one great ambition: to make the *Grand Coup de la Table*, to back the winning number in every possible way, all seventeen bets, and to do it at the maximum. Roulette is a miserable game, a game for old women and children, but this I have always wished to do, as some men wish to climb a mountain or sail alone across great oceans.'

" 'An expensive hobby,' Burke suggested.

" 'Yes. But this evening I was certain. It was as though a little devil was standing on the number and beckoning me. . . . I was always lucky.'

"At this stage our pleasant evening was sharply interrupted. A tall scowling woman, with a low forehead and mean, prying nostrils, marched up to Burke and demanded to know what the hell he thought he was doing. This was the passée model, Penelope Holbrook; it seemed her escort for the evening had ditched her soon after dinner and had not been at all helpful about her career. Bad temper and disappointment had turned her very ugly, and the wonder was, from where I sat, that she'd ever made it as a model at all. Why Burke has anything to do with such a frightful bitch I can't imagine; he was clearly irritated by her arrival, as he'd taken a fancy to Lyki and *vice v.*, but he treated her with considerable courtesy all the same, got her a chair, introduced her all round, and never once batted an eyelid though she was pumping pure poison at him without stopping to draw breath.

" 'My whole career at stake,' she was saying, 'and you have to sneak off here without telling me.'

" 'But my dear,' said Burke meekly, 'you said you wouldn't need me.'

" 'You should have let me know where you were. So that I could get you if I wanted you.'

" 'I did try to tell you. But you were so absorbed in the prospect of your dinner with Perry – '

" ' – Perry,' she snorted. 'Another dried up queen. No wonder it's so hard for a girl to get proper recognition.'

"She was one of those women who've got homosexuals on the brain. You know the sort of thing: anyone who doesn't fawn round *them* all day long is automatically a criminal pervert and ought to be put in chains.

" 'Get me a coke,' was her next contribution.

"Lyki offered her champagne, but no, she'd got some idea Coca-Cola was the smart thing, she'd read that story about the

top model who'd insisted on drinking it at Maxim's and afterwards married a Viscount, so *she* was going to have Coca-Cola
too. Brother, what a woman. You could just hear her tiny
little brain clicking over as she wondered what was the surest
way of making herself the centre of attention and spoiling
everyone's evening at the same time. Eventually she thought
up a real winner.

" 'Since we're here,' she said, 'we may as well gamble. Give
me some money.'

"So Burke passed over 10,000 lire.

" 'I said money.'

"Burke gave her 10,000 more, whereupon she sniffed at
Lyki and me as though we were samples of inferior cocaine
and stalked off to one of the chemmy tables, with Burke trot-
ting after her like a page boy.

" 'We should see this,' Lyki said. 'It will be interesting.
That woman lives in her fantasies, and her present fantasy is
that she is an ex-king's mistress losing a spectacular sum in
full view of all at Monte Carlo.'

"How right he was. As soon as she got to the table she
called 'banco' to 60,000, lost, handed over the 20,000 Burke
had given her and 40,000 more which he reluctantly produced,
and then called 'suivi'.

" 'No, dear,' Burke whispered, 'I haven't got it.'

" 'You'll just have to find it, won't you?'

"God knows what sort of hold she'd got on him. It was
certainly a great deal stronger than that of a former mistress.
Whatever the answer, Burke went quite haggard; his face
drooped in despair and anguish just because he hadn't got
120,000 lire on him for this ghastly woman to toss away at
chemmy. Not that she was taking the slightest notice of what
he said. She'd already picked up her cards and asked for
another – which she didn't get because the bank held a natural.
So far from being put out, she was obviously delighted, and
stood there triumphantly flicking her fingers at Burke for the

money, for all the world (as Lyki had foretold) like a royal courtesan.

"But Burke just hadn't got it. Flick, flick, flick went her fingers, while he looked miserably at her and shrugged, terrified at what was coming. After a bit even she got the message; at first she looked at him like Medusa, then she stuck her nose in the air, started to walk away from the table – and was stopped by two polite men in dinner jackets. Burke stood there trembling and moaning; and finally it was Lyki who moved in to mend matters.

" 'You have no money?' he said.

" 'No.'

" 'At your hotel?'

"She was ready to spit with rage. If there's one thing a woman like that can't stand, it's being made to pay her own losses.

" 'Ask him,' she said, pointing at Burke.

" 'No,' said Burke, shuddering. 'I've enough, just enough, to pay the hotel when I leave. You had 60,000,' he said piteously: 'I did tell you there wasn't any more.'

" 'You see?' said Lyki. 'Either you must pay yourself or you will be charged by the police. In this country it is a criminal offence.'

" 'All right,' she said, snarling like a vampire in one of those films: 'I'll send the money in the morning.'

" 'One of these gentlemen,' corrected Lyki, 'will probably choose to accompany you now.'

"So that was the end of her. Off she went with one of the casino officials, while poor Burke scurried and fussed about behind them. God help *him*, I thought; and I should add that I'll be very interested to find out, if ever I can, just what's between that pair.

"Well, you'll have been wondering what all this has to do with the letter. Simple. What with the excitement of his coup and all the champagne and the pleasure of putting down

Madame Holbrook, Lyki was disposed to be garrulous; and since the Holbrook incident had set his mind working that way he started up about similar cases of default. Now, the significant thing was that though he told me about several of these, involving sums of anywhere between ten pounds and ten thousand, he never once mentioned des Moulins. Unhelpful, you say? Certainly; but at least I now knew that he regarded the matter so warily that even in his unwonted cups he wasn't going to tell the story. Conclusion: he was nervous. Further conclusion (tentative): other people had found out about the letter and were after it. Perhaps he even suspected me. Final conclusion: – no good pussy-footing round playing at Raffles in the Royal Danieli. If he was being so cagey, the letter was probably locked up somewhere very safe; perhaps his bank. There was only one thing to do: come right out with what I knew, watch his reaction, and play it by ear from there.

" 'You know, sweetheart,' I said, 'you've left something out. I know you were taken for a big ride by a frog called des Moulins – and I know how he paid you off.'

"I'm not sure quite what I'd expected. Shock, suspicion, anger. Fear, perhaps, or just curiosity. But he showed none of these. He just looked terribly, terribly sad.

" 'Poor des Moulins,' he said. 'He was a truly religious man. That's what ruined him.'

" 'Religious?'

" 'He was for ever trying to ascertain the will of God. You don't read Dante? No, none of the young do now. "In His Will is our Peace." Since des Moulins thinks it was God's will that he should be totally destroyed, he has accepted his degradation almost with rapture.'

" 'And it was God's will that you should be given the letter?'

" 'You are interested in the letter?'

"He seemed resigned and faintly amused.

" 'Everyone is who knows of it.'

" 'Yes,' he said; 'that letter. It could do much harm . . . not least to innocent people. There is a boy, a youth, the one who carried it . . . he would be crushed. It is a burden. I wish I could so dispose of it that it no longer had power to hurt.'

" 'Why not destroy it?'

" 'It was a gift, my dear. It is evidence of a most important historical truth. One must not destroy such things. There is little enough truth left in history.'

" 'Then have it locked up.'

" 'Then I die suddenly and it is discovered.'

" 'Sooner or later it must be.'

" 'Later is my hope. When everyone concerned is dead.'

"Meanwhile, it appeared, I was not the first to show interest. When the minister from whom des Moulins stole the letter had discovered the theft, he had known who must be guilty and made enquiries. These had started talk in certain circles, des Moulins had been approached in Beirut, his hovel and himself turned upside down without result. Then, since something was known by the seekers of des Moulins' former involvement with Lykiadopoulos, he in turn had been approached.

" 'They will never find it,' he said.

" 'They might turn nasty.'

" 'They already have. And they may turn nastier yet.'

" 'Then you must destroy it. Historical evidence or not.'

" 'They would not believe me when I told them. To such men it is unthinkable that a document which could bring money or power could be wilfully destroyed.'

" 'Then you must get rid of it. Give it away. Sell it.'

" 'These men – the ones who have been pestering me – offered me a high price. But I do not need money, Mark, and I must protect that boy. What I really wish is to forget the whole thing. That is why I do not tell the story of des Moulins. Anyway, it does not belong among a gambler's anecdotes.'

"So there we were going round and round in circles. I've

reported all this at some length to let you know, in case you didn't realise already, what a very odd bird your chum is. Rather fascinating. These scruples of his, about not destroying historical evidence on the one hand and yet not incriminating that French boy on the other, indicate a moral conscience one would not expect to find in a professional gambler (beg pardon, my dear, but you know what I mean). And again, in many ways he's so subtle but in others so crass. It's just as you said. He's taken no trouble to find out whether these people who are after him want to publish the letter or to suppress it, or what sort of agreements they might be prepared to come to if he let them have it. He's as short-sighted as he's devious. Or is he? What he really wants is for scholars to find the letter in 100 years' time; and I suppose his hiding place has been chosen with that in view. Which is *something* to go on. At least I now know that the letter still exists and what processes of thought have dictated the methods of concealment. 'They'll never find it.' That surely indicates, for a start, that it's not in this mysterious hotel room of his; so for the time being at least I've decided not to risk annoying him by trying to track it down. Nor could it be on his person, as they say. Positive conclusions are harder to come by, and you'll agree that the odds are unpromising. But I'll keep at it like the Trojan I am and I'll keep you posted. *Arrivederci*. Mark.

"P.S. This has been a long and painstaking account, you will agree. Pray let this be borne in mind when pay day comes round once more. Which can hardly be too soon. M."

Max de Frèville, though amused by Mark's second despatch, was by no means as pleased with it as he had been with the first. While he had always realised that for Mark to put his hands on the Greek's letter would be difficult, he had yet assumed, such was his confidence in the instinct which had led him to assign the task, that the thing would somehow be done. Now it seemed likely that the thing could not be done.

A substantial disappointment; for although he did not want
the letter for his own use, he had looked forward with keen
enjoyment to following Mark's machinations for its profitable
disposal. Powerful and pompous men, once confronted with
such a document, could have been made to cut some humili-
ating capers; and to Max in his role of political voyeur the
spectacle would have been choice. This pleasure, as it now
seemed, he must make up his mind to forego. But there were
consolations: there was other folly doing in the world for
him to relish. Spring had brought with it the usual rich crop
of sexual antics and disasters in important circles; a prominent
trust lawyer, whose name was a byword of integrity, was about
to be apprehended (so he was informed from a reliable source)
for embezzlement in the sum of half a million pounds; and
there was a heartening promise of low comedy in Lord
Canteloupe's sudden promotion.

One of the first people to call on the new Parliamentary
Secretary was Somerset Lloyd-James. The interview, which
ostensibly had to do with the economic problems which faced
Canteloupe, had been set up by Carton Weir, who opined that
the Marquis might now constitute a politico-social ally of
some prestige. Aware of the threat posed to his leadership of
the Young England Group by Peter Morrison's possible
return to Parliament, Weir, who would in any case have supported Lloyd-James in return for favours past, was now
doubly assiduous in his cause.

"There's nothing direct the old fool can do for you," as he
remarked to Somerset the day before the meeting; "but it will
do you no harm at all to be well in with him. *To be known* to
be well in with him."

And so Somerset had called on the Lord Canteloupe – in
correct morning dress, a courtesy which he rightly surmised
would both flatter the patrician ego and appeal to the patrician
sense of style.

"*Strix?*" said Canteloupe dubiously. "Never had much time for reading. I'm afraid. Not what you'd call cultured. That," he added with characteristic insight, "is why they've asked me to do this job."

"*Strix*," said Somerset smoothly, "has nothing to do with culture. We're interested in money."

"Ah," said Canteloupe with undisguised warmth.

"The thing is," Somerset pursued, "do you see your way to running this show at a financial profit for the exchequer?"

"Any damn fool can run at a profit. Find out what they want and make 'em pay a proper price for it."

"Exactly," said Somerset; "but how does one find out what they want? Impresarios, P.R.O.s, film magnates, men who are accounted experts in interpreting the public taste, are constantly getting it wrong and losing millions."

"Because they don't keep in touch. If a thing works once it'll probably work twice; the mistake they make is to think that it'll work for ever."

"But won't it?" said Somerset. "Basically, what they want stays the same. Sex, flattery, and a spot of mystery to keep them curious."

"Right," said Canteloupe. "But you've got to shift the emphasis from time to time. It's a matter of suiting presentation to the public mood. You take that period just after the war. People were frustrated because they'd won a great victory, or so they were told, and they hadn't got a damn thing to show for it – not even enough to eat. They felt cheated. So what to do with them? Simple. Invite them to revenge themselves on those who are cheating them (i.e. the authorities) by cheating back. That's why the spiv was the most popular character in the late forties – the fellow who got whatever he wanted despite all the regulations saying he musn't have it, and got it, what's more, for nothing. That gave me the clue: let them think, I told myself, that whatever I'm offering them or showing them in my house is somehow illicit, that they're getting what they're not allowed."

"Rather difficult in the stately home business?"

"Not at all. Emphasise the luxury, the social injustice, the immorality of it all – and then invite them to join in. Encourage them to feel like lords and ladies living in the lap and grinding the faces of the poor. There wasn't much they could actually *do*, of course, except feel each other in my park, but I made them *think* they were being awfully wicked by getting everything up to look naughty. Horny paintings, the third marquis's silver jerry for pissing in under the table while the port went round, the odd man trap in the cellars, the authentic bed where they caught Lady Kitty rogering her black page. That sort of thing."

"And how shall you apply this formula to public recreation?"

"I shan't. That was just after the war, and the mood's changed since then. Many times. We've had romantic moods and aggressive moods and so called creative moods and teenage moods and hands off the Empire moods – we've had the lot. Just now the mood is one of aspiration and high ethical principle. Everyone's got everything he wants and more – except a purpose. So civic virtue, respectability, married love, moral rearmament – that's the line now."

And Lord Canteloupe went on to enlarge on his scheme for caravan parks and to explain how their ugliness and regimentation would appeal to the contemporary taste for moral endeavour. Somerset, impressed by Canteloupe's theory and wondering why the man was commonly written off as a moron, reflected that if his premise about a prevailing passion for virtue were correct, the Conservative Party might be well advised to change its pre-electoral policy of plugging material benefits and introduce a more spiritual tone.

"But don't you worry," said Canteloupe, as though reading his mind: "if anyone was to take this morality line so far as actually to suggest people could do without a few things, could lower their own standard of living to help feed a few of their black brothers, they'd lynch him. They want it both ways: they want to live wealthy and feel worthy."

"Moral seriousness is a prerogative of full bellies?"

"Something like that," said Canteloupe, who mistrusted other men's epigrams. "They'll come and play at austerity and moral seriousness in my caravan parks, like Marie Antoinette played at being a dairy maid. But when the chips are really down, when they've got to vote about their future, it'll be cars, cookers and fancy cans, and up yours I'm laughing."

"You wouldn't mind if I wrote an article for *Strix* about these caravan parks? Illustrating your theory of the economics of entertainment?"

"Is it a theory?" said Canteloupe, pleased. "I thought it was plain common sense."

"It'll look like a theory by the time I've finished with it," Somerset promised.

"Good of you to take the trouble."

"Not at all. It's my business to go into these things – not only as editor of *Strix* but as a prospective Parliamentary candidate."

Somerset lowered his eyes demurely and allowed this to sink in.

"I see," said Canteloupe. And then, "From what I can make out we need a few more chaps like you. Chaps who know a good thing when it's under their nose. Who look into matters first and make their theories afterwards. It's usually the other way round."

The interview ended a few minutes later, when Somerset undertook to complete the first draft of his article within five days and invited Canteloupe to dinner on the sixth so that he might read it and give his comments.

Both parties were highly satisfied with their meeting. Somerset considered that he had found a useful supporter who, while his political influence was as yet small, was destined for higher circles of government as time went on. Clearly, in this instance someone (the Prime Minister?) had at last decided to revert to the sound pragmatic principle of giving jobs to men who understood what was needed and how to provide it. In a generation which was increasingly concerned with fighting off boredom during its ample leisure, opportunities for Canteloupe to practise his proven expertise, and so magnify the power of his office, could only multiply. True, the probable outcome was such as to make a civilised man shake in his shoes, but that was not the point. The point was that Canteloupe, despite his rank and background, was of the age and understood it. This transformed his rank and background from liabilities into assets and opened up for him all save the very highest places in the kingdom, and possibly even those. His diagnosis, that what was currently required was something ugly and uncomfortable, was a minor stroke of genius, Somerset considered. Here was a new and bright star in the mid-century firmament, and Somerset proposed to hitch his wagon to it . . . at a discreet distance, of course.

For his part, Canteloupe was much impressed with Somerset. Here was a fellow who knew how to dress and behave, who was (as Carton Weir had made plain) soundly connected, who understood and appreciated what Canteloupe was trying to do, and who was prepared to give it a boost in his mag. Canteloupe knew nothing about *Strix* (though he was to learn a great deal in the months which followed) but he knew a gentleman when he saw one and he recognised intelligence. In short, Somerset Lloyd-James would do. That he was manifestly not only a gentleman but also a howling shit did not deter Canteloupe one iota: for one thing, as he reflected, he was a shit himself, and for another he preferred working with them. For the great thing about shits was that they got on with it (provided the price was right) and didn't ask damn silly questions.

Max de Freville, setting out for a meeting with his accountant, was handed a telegram:

SUCCESS SUCCESS CATCHING FIRST POSSIBLE PLANE EXPLANATIONS LATER MARK.

5

SOMETHING OF VALUE

RUPERT PERCIVAL and Alastair Dixon sat on Percival's terrace and gazed towards the Quantocks. The cards on the table between them were ready for Piquet, but Dixon, restless and fretful despite an excellent luncheon, had twice refused to begin.

"It's no good sulking," Percival said, "just because you can't have it all your own way. You're old enough to know that."

"I'll have it my way yet. But I don't at all care for it when men like Edwin Turbot prove unreliable."

"He's got his own troubles. They appointed Canteloupe against his considered advice. One in the wind-pipe for his *amour propre*."

"That's no reason," said Dixon, "why he should vacillate over other matters. Some time ago, as you'll remember, he asked me to enquire what was doing down here. When I told him what you told me, he was quite plain: he supported Lloyd-James for the candidature – "

" – Which, by the way, has nothing to do with him – "

" – And he didn't want Morrison at any price. And now what? He's not exactly howling with enthusiasm for Morrison, but he's indicated very firmly that he would prefer him to Lloyd-James. Why the change?"

"You're nearer these things than I am," said Percival smugly, "but as I understand the story, his future son-in-law has been giving him a few straight tips."

"But he doesn't like young Llewyllyn, so why does he listen? It's common knowledge he was against the engagement."

"But he's letting it go on. Wedding in June, they tell me. And whether he likes Llewyllyn or not, he knows a clever man when he sees one."

"Llewyllyn's just a common scribbler."

"Or a distinguished contemporary writer. It depends how you look at it. But why," said Percival, picking up a pack and shuffling it for the twentieth time, "are you so put out? What does it matter to you which of 'em gets in?"

"I want my seat to go to the man I want it to go to," said Dixon mulishly. "Lloyd-James is a gentleman. He's in the correct tradition for this part of the world."

"Apparently others are beginning to doubt that. Anyway, Morrison's a gentleman too."

"Damned trouble-maker. Barrack-room lawyer."

"Well," said Percival, "as I've told you before, we in Bishop's Cross don't take orders from Edwin Turbot. So you needn't be afraid that his change of mind will affect Lloyd-James's chances. Such as they are."

"And as I've told *you* before," said Dixon with rising petulance, "Edwin Turbot has more ways of putting the screw on you and your selection committee than you might think. You just wait and see. . . . Which reminds me: when does the committee make its final choice?"

"End of July," said Percival, "before everyone disappears. Which leaves plenty of time, I grant you, for Edwin Turbot to try his hand for what it's worth. Or anyone else who fancies his cards."

He nodded courteously towards the blue, familiar Quantocks, then turned his eyes on his old friend and began to deal.

"So there I was," said Mark Lewson to Max de Freville, "getting nowhere at all really, when Lyki picked up a morning paper and read about a bomb outrage in Paris. Algerian job."

"And so?"

"And so there was a list of people whom the bomb had done

for. And right at the top was the son of the Minister from whom des Moulins stole the letter. You know, the boy who carried it back from Israel and whom Lyki was so anxious to protect."

"So now one of his strongest reasons for hanging on to it was gone."

"Right."

So Stratis Lykiadopoulos had taken Mark Lewson up to his mysterious room, from which he had debarred him hitherto because it contained a miniature shrine, complete with cross and eikons, and was not to be profaned by the activities associated with Mark. Now, however, the shrine had been dismantled for carriage over to the Lido and in any case the business on hand did not amount to desecration. It was the business of making a seemly farewell.

"He told me, in the nicest possible way, that since he was moving to the Lido in a day or so to start his bank, it was time to hand me my cards. He was wondering what to give me as a parting present, he said, and he'd decided that as I seemed so interested in it he'd give me des Moulins' letter. It was a gift which would suit my character and the character of our friendship. Now that the Minister's son was dead he could dispose of it with a good conscience; and in many ways he'd be relieved to get rid of it. He added a word of warning: if people continued to pester him about it, he'd tell them who had it, and in the event of his being believed I could look out for trouble. In sum, he was telling me politely, 'You're a crook, and you've been paid off, and to hell with you'."

"No more talk of the letter being a historical document?"

"No. But you know what I think? I think he reckons I'm in such a hurry to cash in that the whole thing will explode into headlines. Which would now suit his book very well: the boy's dead, everyone else deserves anything that's coming to him, the letter itself would be preserved and appreciated at its proper value, and all the cloak and dagger boys would leave him in peace. He's using me as a kind of bomb disposal outfit. Cunning old Lyki. . . . But *cunning*. You just guess where he'd hidden that bloody letter."

Max shrugged.

"In one of the eikons? Or the cross?"

"Not bad, but not up to his standard. It worked like this. . . ."

For the last time, Lykiadopoulos and Mark had set out for the Gaming Rooms on the Lido. There Lykiadopoulos had gone to the Caisse and signed a cheque for five plaques, each of them worth 5,000,000 lire.

"He explained to me that there were only these five worth that amount kept in the place. They weren't used often – only for big games in the high season – and naturally enough they were always cashed in immediately after use. People might leave the Casino with the odd chip for five or ten thousand, but no one was going to lug one of these great bastards off with him. . . ."

So there were the five plaques, always in the safest of keeping, always available, save possibly for an hour or so during an unusually high game, on demand and payment. On this occasion Lykiadopoulos had retired with Mark to his private speed boat, where he used a small screwdriver to unfasten tiny screws at the four corners of each of the plaques. When this was done, the plaques split open into two sections, so moulded that when fastened together they left a hollow space between them of ten inches long by four inches wide by one-sixteenth of an inch high – just room enough to contain one of the five folded sheets which comprised the purloined letter.

"So he removed the five sheets and passed them over, then screwed the plaques together again, took them to the Caisse and got his cheque back, and that was it. Rather neat, don't you think?"

"Typical Greek elaboration, and not even foolproof. They might have decided on a new issue of counters and scrapped the old lot without his knowing."

"But they hadn't, had they?"

"You've got the letter with you?"

Mark tapped his breast pocket.

"Documentary dynamite. Any use to you?"

"No. I told you. I want *you* to handle it. I'm only interested in what happens next. . . . But I'd like to check it through."

"Touching costs extra, darling," Mark lisped.

Max nodded assent and Mark passed him the letter. When he had read it through, Max said:

"Much as I thought. It's all there."

"Isn't it though? So now you're satisfied, dearie, it's time for a little arithmetic."

"Very simple arithmetic. You were sent fifty when you first reached Venice. For reports since then, plus the privilege of reading this letter, I'll pay you another seventy-five."

"Very *detailed* reports. I was rather hoping for a hundred. Remember all those little extra bits . . . like that scene with Burke Lawrence and the model girl."

"What's that to me?"

But nevertheless there was hunger in his eyes.

"Nothing just yet," said Mark carefully, noting the hungry look and drawing his own conclusions. "But unless I'm mistaken there's something very odd going on there."

"Burke Lawrence," mused Max. "Conceited little man in advertising, with pretensions to know about cinema. Right?"

"Right. And Penelope Holbrook, the girl he was with, she was married to Jude Holbrook, who let her divorce him about the time he disappeared, something over two years ago. Jude wanted to marry our nice chum in Menton, Angela Tuck, but she walked out on him at the last minute."

"So she's told me," said Max stiffly. "I gather there was good reason."

"The very best. Jude was always a nasty little man, and just about then he was busy blackmailing half London to help with some shifty business deal he wanted to put through. When all this blew up, it was too much for old Angie. She'd just inherited some money, so she told Jude his fortune and pulled out."

"You seem very well informed. What happened to Jude Holbrook?"

"No one really knows. On top of everything else his little son died suddenly of meningitis, so his business partner, Donald Salinger, gave out that Jude had had a nervous breakdown and gone on a long holiday. After a bit 'Salinger & Holbrook', their printing firm, quietly became plain 'Salinger', and no one's heard of Jude from that day to this. It's thought that Donald bought him out, in which case he won't be short of money."

"And this slut he was married to. You say she gets alimony?"

"Paid through lawyers, Burke said. She's heard no more from Jude than anyone else."

"And what about her modelling?"

"She was quite near the top," Mark said, "about five years ago. But too many late nights out and about put an end to that. So now, as I told you, she just tags around with Burke, nagging him to find her work she doesn't need and for which she's no longer suited."

"You also said she used to be his mistress."

"That was way back, before she got her divorce. Not any longer, as far as I could tell. But she's got some hold on him which amounts to considerably more. That's what interests me. Those two have something in common far more . . . *serieux* . . . than bogus festivals in Venice."

"All right," said Max. "You find out what it is and you won't be the loser. I'd be glad to hear something of Jude Holbrook, too. From what Angela says, he was a thrusting little chap, and I can't think we've seen the last of him."

He went over to a desk, unlocked a drawer, and took out a sheaf of five pound notes.

"Now," he said, "back to more immediate concerns. There's a hundred pounds here. Let's say seventy-five for services rendered, and the extra pony to see you on your way to dispose of that letter."

"But what am I to do with it?"

"Find out who's willing to pay what for it and why, and let me know. That was the plan from the start."

"I know. But when it comes to it . . . I mean, I can't just waltz up to No. 10 and say, 'Prime Minister, dear, I've got something here which might amuse you'."

"You'll find a way," said Max, "because you stand to make money. And don't just flog it for the first offer. Interest as many people as possible and let them compete in the bidding."

"I'm beginning to feel like Lyki. I don't want to wind up on a slab."

"Then you should choose more conventional ways of getting your bread. One hint I will give you. If there's one man in England who'll be interested in suppressing that letter, both for his own sake and the government's, it'll be that egregious major-domo of the conservative party, Sir Edwin Turbot. It so happens that I'm in correspondence with his younger daughter, Isobel. You'll find her co-operative . . . in more ways than one, very likely. You could make a start there."

"What about the press?"

"That would be wasteful. With the press everything – even this – is here today and dead tomorrow. The highest bids will come from people whose interest is *abiding*. People like Sir Edwin, who want the letter to suppress it. Or those who want it to apply pressure by threat. Find someone like that, and you could make yourself comfortable, very comfortable indeed, Mark, for the rest of your natural life."

"What little was left of it, dear," said Mark, "but thank you for the tip."

When Mark left Max de Freville, he had already made three decisions.

First, he would certainly go to see Isobel Turbot, because Max made her sound amusing, something might come of it, and the whole Turbot set-up, so English and rural, seemed reassuringly tame. The contents of the letter revealed that Sir Edwin had that to answer for which, whatever his motives, would cause many to call him archfiend; but one thing you could be sure of – he wouldn't stick a knife in your ribs while you were his guest, or even while you weren't.

Secondly, however, before he went to see Isobel Turbot or anyone else, he would seek advice from his old friend, Jonathan Gamp. For while Mark was a scoundrel of some experience, this experience was all hand to mouth, superficial. He was, truth to tell, little more than a second-rate con-man, and an amateur one at that. To get perspective in depth in the present affair he must consult someone of more powerful and objective insights into grand chicanery, and who better than Jonathan, who was both connoisseur and scholar in this field?

Thirdly, most firm decision of all, he was not going to stick his neck out for the amusement of Max de Freville. It would be silly to let his property go for a song, and it would certainly be sensible, as Max had suggested, to stir up a little competitive interest; but the first offer that was "anything like" he was going to grab with both hands, and then clear off for a well earned rest on the loot.

When Max de Freville was left alone, he too had already come to three decisions, or perhaps "judgments" would be an apter word:

First, that Mark, despite his undoubted luck in winning the letter, was a moderate performer now batting right out of his league.

Secondly, however, that this was a good thing, as it might lend the subsequent intrigues that kind of ineptness and even absurdity which gave scandal its true relish. That highly placed people should be detected in evil was much to Max; that they should be laid, open to ridicule at the same time was much more.

And thirdly, almost as an afterthought, he blessed the moment when he had thought of bringing Mark together with Isobel Turbot. In that combination lay endless possibilities both dangerous and comic.

What Max failed to take account of was that Mark had an acute sense of self-preservation (an attribute which is often very strong in second-rate performers and does much to explain their mediocrity) and that this, when it came to making a settlement, would more than outweigh his vanity and greed. What Max also failed to take account of, and what had been obvious to Mark, was that the former was not far removed from insanity ("barking", as Mark later expressed it to Jonathan Gamp). For what had at first been an amusing interest, to counteract his boredom and disgust at making easy money from fools, had now become an obsesssion. Max had reached the stage at which he must know more and ever more, when information, about small people now as well as great, was the staple of his existence, when he yearned to be privy to the secrets of the entire human race. Max, in short, was playing God. Had he been able, he would have constructed his own little universe, that he might sit and brood on every movement of his creatures. As it was, omniscience of this world was his end, and his resources, even his resources, were feeling the strain. His accountant, the day before, had had some cautionary things to say to him. His reserves were depleted, some of the oldest of the clients at his chemmy tables were taking shameless advantage of the long credit he allowed them, the payments to his many informants now amounted to several thousand a month. 'What do you pay them for, Mr. de Freville?' 'Assistance.' 'All I can say, sir, is that you must do with less.' But how could he? For Max de Freville was hooked; he had allowed a whimsical pastime to grow into an imperious necessity which was devouring both his substance and his soul.

In Menton, Angela Tuck mixed herself a stiff brandy and soda, looked at the American sailor slumped on the bed, and wondered how to get him back to Nice before he was missed from his ship.

In Venice, Burke Lawrence said to Penelope Holbrook:

"I think we've done all we can here for the time being. May as well blow tomorrow."

"*Blow?*"

"Army slang for shove off."

"I never knew you were in the Army."

"Everyone my age was. How quickly people forget."

"The money," said Penelope. "Has Salvadori paid you the money?"

"I've arranged for it to be credited in London. In case you get another of your gambling yens before we leave."

"That wasn't a gambling yen. It was temper."

"It worked out just as expensive."

"And what about the festival?" she said. "That's what you're meant to be here for."

"That's in good shape. They can manage without me."

"And the next ... the next assignment?"

"Salvadori will let me know. Stockholm, he thinks. In a month or six weeks."

"As long as that?"

"Sales technique, love," Burke Lawrence said: "in this trade it pays to keep the customer waiting."

Two days later, in her flat off Curzon Street, Maisie opened the parcel which Burke Lawrence had just delivered. Carefully she counted the little tins, then locked them up in a drawer. She didn't understand it very well, but it was wonderful the difference a sniff or two made to some of her customers. Apparently it made what usually took ten seconds go on – or seem to go on – for more than a minute. Very odd. Perhaps Fielding ... when he came that afternoon? No, she decided: he was a thoroughly nice boy and she didn't want him getting nasty habits. Besides, it was very expensive, and Fielding ought to be saving as much as he could just now. Strange boy; keen enough, yet always so gentle and polite; such a pity about his face.

She looked at her watch and decided there was just time for a toasted tea-cake and a cup of Earl Grey.

In his room at the Cavalry Club, Fielding Gray finished the first book review (of the memoirs of a retired West End locksmith) which he had been asked to do by Somerset Lloyd-James. The book had no literary merit whatever, but he supposed the economics of the lock trade must be of interest to Somerset's readers. In any case, it was no business of his to quarrel with such work as he was given, and he had done his best in his short piece to ensure that Somerset would be satisfied and give him more. In other ways as well his new career had got off to quite a promising start; for Gregory Stern, who had read his two novels surprisingly fast, had asked him to come in next week and discuss them.

For all that, he thought, he could not go on living in the Cavalry Club much longer. Quite apart from the expense, the setting, however agreeable, was wrong for a man of letters and encouraged him in certain modes of thought and behaviour which he felt he must now eschew; for an instinct told him that they were incompatible with humility, and that humility, a disposition to expect only the worst, was essential in an aspirant artist of any kind. This led to the question of whether or not the humility would be genuine in his case, and how far, if it were merely assumed (to deceive the gods, so to speak) it could still be efficacious; but this question he deferred for later thought. The immediate point was that he must find suitable and economic digs for a bachelor called to his new station in life. Perhaps Somerset, who had always had a turn for economy, would be able to help.

And now, he thought with a quick lift of the blood, it was time to visit Maisie. (He had considered economy here too, but without sincerity.) With hands that shook slightly he folded his review; he could post it on the way. But no; he must make *sure* it got there. He would deliver it to *Strix* himself. Since he was already pressed for time if he was to be punctual at Maisie's, he took a taxi from the Cavalry Club to the far end of Gower Street and then round and down to Berkeley Square. Not really a very economic performance, he supposed; but after all, this was his debut as a professional literateur, an occasion unsuited to parsimony.

"The Board of *Strix* assembled at half past two of the clock on the twenty-second day of April, 1959. Present were the Right Honourable the Lord Philby, Proprietor; Henry Arthur Dilkes, B.Sc., Secretary to the Institute of Political and Economic Studies; Robert Reculver Constable, M.A., Professor of Economics in the University of Salop and Provost Elect of Lancaster College, Cambridge; Carton Weir, M.A., Member of Parliament for Chirt and Wedderburn Regis; and Somerset Lloyd-James, M.A., Editor.

"Lord Philby having taken the Chair, he proposed a motion of congratulation to Professor Constable on his recent election as Provost of Lancaster College. The motion was seconded by Mr. Dilkes and warmly received by all present.

"Mr. Lloyd-James: May one ask, Professor, when you take up residence at Lancaster?

"Professor Constable: In September, in time for the new academic year.

"Mr. L-J: Your new appointment. . . . It may perhaps affect your attendance at this Board?

"Prof. C: Why should it?

"Mr. L-J: I was wondering, among other things, whether the Council of Lancaster would approve of your association with a journal well known to be conservative in tone.

"Prof. C: Since it has been my constant concern to make it less so, I have no reason for embarrassment before the Council of Lancaster.

"Mr. Dilkes: Anyway, they're not as red as all that. I'm told that several of the younger dons are starting a new fashion in Toryism. They'll be delighted you're on this Board.

"Prof. C: Their approval is of no moment to me.

"Mr. Weir: I wouldn't be too sure of that. Take Jacquiz Helmut, the historian. You wouldn't want *him* for an enemy. As rich as a money-lender – come to think of it, his father *was* a money-lender – friend of royalty, blue-eyed boy of the Billingsgate Press –

"Prof. C: Inside Lancaster College, Mr. Helmut is Assistant Tutor and a member of the College Council. As such he has one vote, no less and no more.

"Mr. W: Don't you believe it. Half of them vote as he tells them because they hope he'll get them asked to Buck House.

"Lord Philby: All very interesting, gentlemen. But, with respect to the new Provost of Lancaster, we're here to discuss the affairs of *Strix*.

"Prof. C: I entirely concur.

"Mr. L-J: So we were in a way. I was hoping Professor Constable would take the hint, but as it is I must now remind him that his place at this Board is *ex officio*, deriving from his position as Professor of Economics at Salop. Since his appointment to Lancaster will necessitate his resignation from the Professorship, it follows that he must also resign from the Board.

SILENCE.

"Mr. D: Surely not. I too might be described as an *ex officio* member of the Board, in as much as I was asked to join it because of my position at the Institute. But as I understand it, it was not part of our founder's intention to displace sitting members. When, in the fullness of years, Professor Constable sees fit to withdraw his services from *Strix*, then of course his place here will revert to whoever is then Professor of Economics at Salop. But just because he himself is now honourably relinquishing that office –

"Mr. W: – There is surely no need of speculation. Our founder, the first Lord Philby, will have made his intentions quite plain in the Articles of this journal.

"Prof. C: I must say, I have always considered the matter in much the same light as Mr. Dilkes.

"Mr. L-J: In the past, Professor, on several occasions you have insisted that we follow the Articles to the letter. I take it you are still of the same mind?

"Prof. C: Er . . . yes, of course.

"Mr. L-J: Then let me quote you the relevant clause . . . 'Two seats at the Board shall be reserved, respectively, for the Secretary of the Institute of Political and Economic Studies, and for the incumbent of the Chair of Economics at the University of Salop.'

"Mr. D: Nothing about resigning.

"Prof. C: But the meaning is clear. The clause refers to the 'incumbent' and can only mean the actual and present holder of the chair. Your point is taken, Mr. Lloyd-James, and I shall act accordingly.

"Ld. P: We shall be sorry to lose your services.

"Prof. C: Such as they are, sir, you will have the benefit of them for some months to come. My resignation from the Chair at Salop will not be effective until August first of this year. It follows that until that time I shall continue to do my duty at this Board. . . ."

"Neat work," said Carton Weir to Somerset after the meeting. "It'll be a relief when Professor Constable removes his dreary face from the table."

"It was only a question of following the Articles . . . which may not suit our book so well when it comes to filling the empty place."

"Automatic, surely. The next Professor of Economics at Salop."

"Suppose we wanted someone else?"

"Have you anyone in mind?"

"I had thought . . . perhaps Canteloupe."

"You were impressed by your meeting?"

"With reservations, yes. I hope you're seeing to it that he doesn't drink too much."

"Hardly my job. He spends a lot of his time in White's, of which I'm not a member," said Carton Weir resentfully.

"Do your best to keep him out of mischief. I'm giving him a bit of a build-up in this journal. These camping sites of his."

"Good on you."

"I might even do a second piece later on . . . if he comes up with anything else."

"Don't go overdoing him, Somerset."

"I told you. I have my reservations. But the image is dead right. Morality with profit."

"If he can hold on to it. . . . Change of subject, Somerset. There's something you ought to know. As far as I can make out, Edwin Turbot's going to back Morrison for Bishop's Cross. We all thought he'd be behind you, but now. . . ."

So Tom's been busy already, Somerset thought. Well, it was only to be expected. Aloud he said,

"What can Turbot do? Will they listen to him at Bishop's Cross?"

"He's a persuasive man."

"I dare say something will turn up. They tell me the Selection Committee at Bishop's Cross won't decide till late July. That leaves three months . . . for me to bustle in."

"And for others to bustle in."

"Morrison won't bustle."

"There are those that'll bustle for him."

"And for me," said Somerset, scraping a blackhead out of his ear with a jagged finger-nail.

6

BUYERS AND SELLERS

"I THOUGHT YOU'D like to know," Captain Detterling said. Peter Morrison finished his coffee and said nothing. Helen Morrison put her head round the study door.

"The boys are waiting for you," she said. "It *is* Nickie's last day before school. . . ."

"Tell them we'll be right out. You're strong enough," said Morrison to his guest, "to bowl a few overs at the nets?"

"It'll do me good. So Nickie's off to school already?"

"Eight and a half. I thought it'd be jollier for him to start in the summer."

"Yes, the summer was always the best. . . . That reminds me, Peter, though I can't quite think why. Fielding Gray's back."

"Back?"

"Out of the Army. You knew about the accident in Cyprus? What happened to his face?"

"I'd heard something. Poor Fielding. Nothing ever went right."

"I hope it will now. He's been writing books, and I've got Gregory Stern to take an interest."

"Good," said Peter non-committally, and rose to his feet. "What you were saying just now," he said, "before Helen came in. . . . That's all?"

"All I can tell you so far. Edwin Turbot is now on your side. It's thought that Tom Llewyllyn has been talking to him – as the future son of the house."

The two men walked through a door and on to the lawn,

at the far end of which Nicholas Morrison stood ready in pads while Jeremy tended gloves like a squire at a tournament.

"Tom," said Morrison, "is like a poltergeist. A well meaning one, but apt to create confusion."

"I think you will find that he's more discriminating these days. He's certainly done a good job on Sir Edwin. But even so, Peter – "

" – Come along, Daddy," called Jeremy: "Nickie's waiting."

" – Even so," persisted Detterling, "it's time you took the field yourself."

"What could I do at this stage?"

"Show yourself at Bishop's Cross. Get to know the Selection Committee. And start keeping a very sharp eye on Somerset Lloyd-James."

"Come *along*, Daddy."

"I can't compete with Somerset at his game. You know that."

"We want you back, Peter."

"Very nice of you, but you must let me get back in my own way."

"*Daddy*."

"Your way," Detterling said, "is much too easy-going . . . much too fair for these days."

"I don't know," said Morrison, and caught the ball which Jeremy had thrown him. "It is possible to bowl fairly according to the rules and yet to be deceitful and aggressive. Come along. We'll try some elementary tricks on Nickie."

"I quite agree with you, dear," said Jonathan Gamp to Mark Lewson. "You're way out of your class. Way out of mine too, for the matter of that."

They were talking in the dainty drawing-room of Jonathan's house in Hereford Square.

"What do you suggest?" said Mark.

"We'll have to think, darling. The great thing is to keep

the game going. Poor Max may be going off his rocker but he's still good for lots of lovely lolly. So you must keep finding *amusing* things to tell him, mustn't you?"

"It's a strain. I'd like to cash in and be done."

"Of course you would, darling, but it's not that easy. People like you are always dreaming of lump sums, when in fact their best hope is to go on drawing small ones. Lazy and greedy, that's your trouble; always butchering the poor goose because it won't lay more than one golden eggie at a time."

"Well, what *do* you suggest?"

"As for that letter, we'll talk about it in a minute. A little frivolity first, dear. You did say you'd got Max interested in that ghastly Burke Lawrence and his trollop?"

"If she is his trollop."

"Well then, dear."

Jonathan unlocked a drawer, produced a small tin and took out a cylindrical capsule with rounded ends and about an inch in length. This he snapped in two; then he held the broken ends just under Mark's nose.

"Not very appetising."

"No?" Jonathan threw the remains of the capsule on to the fire. "But expensive. And in certain circumstances – believe me – effective. An oriental recipe for prolonging natural pleasures. Ever seen one of those Japanese pictures of a woman holding a saucer under a man's nose? Well, that" – he gestured at the fire – "is what the man's inhaling. And *that* is what Burke Lawrence is peddling round the place."

"Where does he get it?"

"He's not saying, dear. And those little jobs aren't the only things he's got for sale. He's got goodies much more dangerous and more expensive – though I don't touch them myself."

"I see . . . and Penelope?"

"It's only a guess, sweetie, but I'd say she was helping with transport. She still calls herself a model, right?"

"Right."

"Well, models can haul trunk loads of kit round the place without making anyone suspicious."

"Someone'd jolly soon get suspicious if he opened one and found it full of little tins."

"*Darling*. . . . Pills and packets can be sown into dresses. Stuffed into hollow heels of shoes. An ordinary make-up case – all those pots and things – can conceal enough junk to keep half London high for a month. Though mind you, it's only a guess."

"It would certainly explain why he was so polite to her in Venice."

"And it'll make a nice little tale for Uncle Max."

"Indeed," said Mark, "though it's pity we don't know where the stuff comes from . . . who's behind it all."

"I think, dear, that that is one of the things it is better *not* to know. Anyway, you mustn't be so demanding."

"Sorry. . . . Now, what about this letter?"

"I think Max is right, dear. Approach Edwin Turbot through Isobel, let him see a copy, and then promise to suppress the jolly news for so much a month. On the other hand, you could do worse than try that old crook, Somerset Lloyd-James. It's right up his street."

"He'd print it in *Strix*?"

"Not him. Like Max said, sweetie, it's far more valuable for threatening, and Somerset will love that."

"Which of them would pay best?"

"Hard to tell, darling," Jonathan said; "Sir Edwin will have more in the bankie, but Somerset's very resourceful. So why not try a little chat with both parties, and see who's most forthcoming? Your main trouble will be to get them to believe that the original letter's authentic without actually letting them get hold of it. If you're called upon to give a demonstration, you can't reasonably refuse, but don't let it out of your hot little hand for a moment."

"I'll make no bones about it," Gregory Stern said to Fielding Gray. "I'm interested in those two novels of yours, but they won't quite do as they stand."

Gregory Stern was a tall, elegant man with a long lugubrious face. He had fussy hands which moved constantly over the buttons on his dark check suit, testing and re-testing for weaknesses and thereby effecting them. His voice, in contrast to his physiognomy, was light and girlish; his eyes candid and intelligent; his teeth much metalled and wired.

"And another thing," Stern went on. "Although I hope to publish these novels – provided we agree the alterations – I shall be doing so less for their own sake than for their promise. You see, they're lacking something . . . something which you've deliberately withheld. Detterling here agrees with me on that."

He nodded towards Detterling, who was examining a bookcase which contained all Stern publications to date.

"It is felt," said Detterling, "that your work could do with more . . . of yourself."

"These two novels you've read," said Fielding: "there is no place in them for more of myself."

"I don't question that," Stern told him. "As far as they're concerned, it's just that they're both a little too short and too compressed. Some of the technicalities need expansion."

"I'll gladly provide it."

"Then you can have a contract this morning. But," said Stern, his voice fluting slightly, "that contract will bind you to let us publish the next three books you write; and in these we shall look for more . . . well more. . . ."

"Of myself. In what respect?"

"More emotion rooted in experience . . . which has affected your – well – psyche. These two" – his fingers slid nervously over the typescripts on his desk – "are merely theoretical. Like riders in geometry, which end in a pat solution but offer no . . . human . . . comment."

Fielding pointed to his single eye.

"This?" he said.

"If you like."

A telephone rang, Stern started angrily, tested the buttons on either cuff while he recovered himself, and lifted the receiver.

"Send him up," he said after listening briefly. "Tom Llewyllyn," he announced to the room at large. And then quietly to Fielding, "You don't mind him being in on this?"

"I'll be glad to meet him again."

"Good. . . . The thing is this, Mr. . . . er . . . Major Gray. I like to publish good books which make money. I don't expect all that much money and sometimes I'm prepared to make none at all, but in your case I think we've got the makings of a minor prestige novelist with a broader appeal than most such. Which means both cachet and cash." He giggled rather wildly. "Forgive my little joke; I have an old-fashioned taste for puns. Well then . . . I think you write good English in the traditional manner and I think, though you have yet to show it, that you have a highly individual approach to – er – the human predicament. The combination promises well . . . if I am right. But where is the evidence for this individual approach? Not in these." He fingered the typescripts. "And yet it *is* in these – in the strong feeling I get from them of deliberate omission. Now, have you written anything from which you have not omitted . . . what has been omitted . . . here?"

He drummed on the typescripts, then sat back and clawed at his Old Etonian tie. Tom Llewyllyn entered without knocking, gestured to Stern to ignore him, and went straight on to join Detterling by the bookcase.

"I've written a journal," Fielding said at last.

"Ah?"

"It's unprintable as it stands, but it contains . . . the kind of reactions . . . which seem to interest you."

"It could be turned into fiction?" said Detterling, without turning from the bookcase.

"Yes. . . . A lot of people might recognise themselves. Including you."

"I promise not to sue. Others might be less amenable."

"We could sort all that out," said Stern, fluttering his hands. "It's what we pay John Groves for. Is there a theme to this journal? Something to provide a basic plot?"

"You might call it a love story. A vision of . . . of the true and the beautiful. I need hardly tell you that it has an unhappy ending."

"Through whose fault?" asked Tom Llewyllyn.

"Mine. With a bit of exterior malice thrown in. Jealousy, deliberate misunderstanding."

"Right," said Stern, who seldom asked for details once he was satisfied as to competence. "I'll take your two novels for an advance of £200 each, on the understanding that you'll loosen them up in the way I've suggested. Our editor has details."

He pressed a buzzer on his desk.

"You'll be given a cheque now," he said, "and you can fix an appointment with our editor for tomorrow. We'll do our best to publish the first of them – the Court-Martial one – in October. *But*" – his fingers flew over his coat buttons and then up to test his lower teeth – "what I'm really interested in is what you can do with that journal. I'm commissioning you to make a novel of it in the sum of £100 down, a further £100 on delivery, and yet a further £100 on the day of publication – all this, of course, being an advance against royalties on the usual scale."

"This is generous," said Fielding Gray, who was resisting a strong impulse to cry.

"Let us say that I am prepared to . . . er . . . back my beliefs with hard money. So many publishers are not. With the result that in the end they lose both money and author."

"Was that altogether wise?" said Tom Llewyllyn after Fielding had gone.

"Yes," said Stern. He tapped the typescripts on the desk. "There's quality here. And if he can find a little something else as well . . . which I hope is in that journal . . . a love story, he said . . ."

"I think I know what it's about," said Detterling. "Among other things, the boyhood of our friend, Somerset Lloyd-James."

"Don't tell me Gray was in love with Somerset," said Tom.

"Perhaps it was the other way about."

"And where do you come in?"

"Peripherally, I should imagine. When things went wrong with Fielding, I had a lot to do with finding him a place in the Army."

"What did go wrong?" asked Stern.

"Better wait for his version," Captain Detterling said. "After all, you've just offered him 300 quid for it."

As for Fielding Gray, for him it had been a morning of triumph. In his pocket was Stern's cheque, which not only represented a substantial sum of money but acknowledged him as a proper and practising novelist. On top of this, when he returned to the Cavalry Club, he found a note from Somerset Lloyd-James, who was very pleased with his first little piece and was now prepared to offer him a basic fee of £300 a year to write reviews and articles for *Strix*; subject, the note said, to giving *Strix* "first refusal" of all his journalistic work, but this did not seem an unreasonable condition. For a moment Fielding thought uneasily of Somerset's probable displeasure when his third novel should appear (for Detterling's surmise about its matter was largely correct); but it had all happened, he told himself, over ten years ago, he would try to be tactful in his treatment, and in any case the novel's completion, leave alone its appearance, was many moons away. So he turned with satisfaction to consider his third piece of good luck: in answer to an enquiry in Stern's office, Tom Llewyllyn had advised him that the cheap and suitable digs he had been wanting were to be had in a place called Buttock's Hotel. Indeed, Tom had said, he would arrange for Fielding to inherit his own quarters there, for these he must shortly vacate against his bridal day, which was not long. . . . Sweet Thames run softly, Fielding mused, until I end my song. A vision of the true and the beautiful, he had told Gregory Stern: if others would only see it too, through his eyes, then everything would have been worth while.

In the event, Somerset sent a copy of his article to Canteloupe two days before they were to dine so that he might be fully prepared for its discussion.

"I notice," said Canteloupe over the lobster soufflé, "that you call them 'camping sites'. Nothing about caravans."

"Caravans imply something cosy and casual – even anarchic: gipsies and so on. 'Camping' is more stern, bringing to mind campaigns, expeditions . . . herosim on Everest."

"I see . . . I was thinking; perhaps it won't do to be *too* stern at first. After all, I've got to attract people to these places."

"The sort of people you hope to attract won't read my article in *Strix*. We're interested in building you up as a politician who combines practical good sense with high moral ideals. You'll prove your practical good sense by making a profit – and we shan't enquire too closely how you do it: you can run your sites like Butlin's for all we care. But in order to put across your moral ideals we've got to . . . *let it be understood* . . . that campers are leading a life of self-denial, dedicated physical effort and so forth. You understand? Like Edinburgh's Outward Bound rubbish, only a family version."

"In your view then," said Canteloupe, "I'll end up providing the working class with the usual candy floss and slot machines, while the readers of *Strix*, who won't bother to come and see, think that everyone's sweating up mountains and practising first aid."

"That's about it," said Somerset, as the duck press was wheeled up. "Of course, there must be a certain attention to appearances in case someone should investigate. You might hire a few Army throwouts to hang around; call them 'camp leaders', 'fitness guides', that sort of thing. And give the sites impressive names: 'Hilary', 'Wingate', 'Montgomery'. You might even get Edinburgh to open one. Which reminds me: what actual progress have you made? When will the first site be ready?"

"Late June," said Canteloupe. "But don't you think it might be safer not to hurry? I mean, people can get all this moral uplift and so on just by reading about these camps: need we risk actually having one?"

"There's a lot," said Somerset, "in what you say. But I think you should have *one* in existence, if only to get the publicity of the opening ceremony. You could always close it quietly down afterwards. This one that'll be ready in June . . . where is it?"

"Somerset. No, not you – the Quantocks."

"Splendid. We'll give it some sensible west country name . . . 'Drake', perhaps – "

" – Wasn't he a Devon man? – "

" – No need to be pedantic. A bracing west country name, a royal opening on television, and presto, in moves the first lot of campers – "

" – Wearing lederhosen – "

" – Singing Jerusalem – "

" – Men and women hand in hand, but peeling off emphatically to separate quarters – "

" – Except for the family parties with bright-eyed children to prove it – "

" – A service of dedication – "

" – Taken by Donald Soper – "

" – Accompanied by a skiffle group – "

" – And I've got just the name. Westward Ho!"

"But how," said Canteloupe as the crêpes flamed skyward beside him, "can I be sure of getting suitable campers for the occasion?"

"Out of work repertory actors. You can hire them by the gross. Tell me," Somerset said, "now we've got all this buttoned up, have you got any more projects in mind? I'd like to do another piece for *Strix* in about a month."

"Well," said Canteloupe, "Carton Weir suggested that we ought to do something for the popular arts. More recognition for band leaders, and so on – why should the Shakespeare boys hog all the honours? All right as far as it goes, though no money in it, but it gave me a better idea. Government recognition of popular pastimes. Bingo, for example. It's all the rage just now, and why shouldn't H.M.G. cash in? Publicly owned Bingo Palaces, that kind of a thing?"

"But the moral line? Not very elevating."

"Ah. Leave aside our profit, a big proportion of the prizes would be awarded in special bonds, which in theory at least would be financing medical research into incurable conditions. 'Win Bingo Bonds to Beat Disease.' Make it a moral duty, you see. And you know how sentimental the English are about health; so the bonds could carry bugger-all in the way of interest, and even so no one would ever dare cash them in. Imagine going to the Post Office and selling a bond with 'Paralytic Old Folk' or 'Spastic Kiddies' written all over it. You'd feel like a murderer."

"Go on," said Somerset; "this is fascinating. . . ."

Mark Lewson, though undeniably second-rate in his chosen, profession, was subject to flashes of inspiration. He was, and always had been, hampered by incompetence, fecklessness, captious changes of plan and negligence in their execution;

but he was seldom short of good ideas. In the case of des Moulins' letter, it occurred to him that if he could get more than one party to bid for it he might also get more than one party to pay for it; and with this firmly in mind he paid a call on Somerset Lloyd-James, taking with him a photostat copy of the original document.

To Somerset the letter was just what he had been waiting for, the answer to his most fervent prayers, in Westminster Cathedral, the Brompton Oratory, Farm Street, and on his knees by his own little bed, for the last month. Here was matter to compromise several leading members of the Cabinet and in particular the party's Dean of Discipline, Sir Edwin Turbot. With this letter in his possession he could demand anything he wanted short of a dukedom, and Sir Edwin, pastmaster of ways and means, would be compelled to devise a formula to see that he got it. There could be no question now of Sir Edwin refusing his support over the candidature for Bishop's Cross; and that was only the beginning.

But clearly there were dangers and difficulties: for a start, was the original document genuine? The photostat was impressive; the contents of the letter were consistent with everything he knew or suspected about the Suez affair; but even so, it was not beyond Mark Lewson to have got the whole thing up himself. What was it Jonathan Gamp had once said? "My dear, he's *famous* for cheques." Just so; if cheques, why not letters?

"You know Max de Freville?" Mark said.

"I've played at his parties."

"He put me on to this. Why not ring up and check with him?"

"He can't *know* it's genuine any more than I can."

But Somerset, clammy with excitement, was anxious to believe, and on re-examining the text he found something which convinced him, if not that the original was beyond suspicion, at least that here was a gamble worth making. For the letter purported to be written by a cosmopolitan Israeli of German birth; it was in English; and in two respects the English, otherwise excellent, betrayed a weakness common among those to whom German is their native tongue. In the first place, there was a pedantic tendency to write 'shall' where 'will' would have sounded more natural: 'I shall not claim to understand quite why, but it seems that the Cabinet Minister, Sir Edwin Turbot. . . .' Secondly, and far more convincing, was a confusion of subjunctives: 'If the Prime Minister would go' for 'if he were to go' (or 'went'); and 'If your Government would wish (wished) to provide such co-operation, it could swiftly make this plain.' It was of course possible that these errors had been deliberately planted by Lewson, but Somerset doubted this: had the thing been a forgery, the fake errors would have been cruder.

All right, thought Somerset, so I accept the document as genuine. But the original will be very expensive. Can I do without it, can I work with a copy? The answer to this, in the long run, was 'no'. To bring pressure to bear effectively he must be in a position, not only to print the letter, but to adduce the original when he was challenged. A threat to print when he was supported only by a photostat would scare nobody. *Ergo*, he must first make sure that the original still existed and then he himself must possess it.

"The thing is," said Mark, who had a fair notion what Somerset was thinking, "that a lot of people will be feeling the same. I wonder whether you can afford it?"

"Afford what?"

"Let's say . . . twenty thousand."

Somerset retched.

"After all, it's the scoop of the century, so I should have thought *Strix* could pay that much. Or were you perhaps thinking of going into business on your own account?"

"I'll give you five thouthand down," Somerset lisped.

"*Darling*," said Mark, pretending to be Jonathan Gamp.

"Theven."

"Now look, thweetheart," said Mark, "let's get one thing straight. Are you bidding for *Strix* or for Somerset Lloyd-James?"

"For the latter," said Somerset, gagging.

"So I thought. But you can't pay enough, can you? On the other hand, you have got what is sadly lacking in little me – application and expertise. So listen carefully, darling, and I'll tell you what we're going to do."

It had all come to Mark as he entered Somerset's office. Here was a Headquarters; here was authority and organisation; here was a man able and ready to pay attention to the tedious details, which he himself could never abide. The answer was obvious: in return for a substantial but not impossible payment, he would admit Somerset into partnership, thus obtaining a nice sum of ready and a competent executive who would assist him in further extortions. Blithely he now declared his terms. For seven thousand pounds he would entrust the original letter into Somerset's keeping. Somerset could use this as he saw fit; but it must not be resold or published without Mark's agreement. Further, Somerset must be prepared to produce the letter whenever required to do so for Mark's purposes, and must be prepared, moreover, to advise Mark on the furtherance of these.

"So long as it doesn't go out of my sight," said Somerset. The idea of being in a syndicate with Mark Lewson gave him little pleasure, but he was in no position just now to argue. Later on perhaps. . . .

"And don't go getting ideas about double-crossing me," said Mark; "because I've got Max de Freville behind me and he might turn nasty."

On this Somerset made no comment.

"If I'm to help you," he said, "I must know what you have in mind."

What Mark had in mind, he explained, was a visit to Sir

Edwin Turbot, whom he proposed, in accordance with Max's advice, to make his first victim; one point being that Max's connection with Isobel would smooth the way.

"We'll go together," Somerset said.

"How friendly. If you'll undertake to manage the old boy, we'll split down the middle."

Mark Lewson was an open-handed man by nature, particularly to those who relieved him of bother. As for Somerset, he did not trouble to explain that his own price would not be reckoned in pounds sterling.

"This," said Tom Llewyllyn to Tessie Buttock, "is Mr. Fielding Gray. Or should I say 'Major'?"

" 'Mister' will serve from now on."

Tessie, warned by Tom about Fielding's appearance, nevertheless examined him with the frankest attention, and finally shook her head, as though to say, "That's what comes of playing with dirty children."

"Well dear," she said: "naughty Tom tells me you want to move into his room when he leaves next week?"

"If I may."

"You may, dear. Any friend of Tom's. Did he tell you the rules?"

"No."

"Only two, dear. Weekly payment in advance, and no dragging back."

"Dragging back?"

"No rubbish off the street. They nick things and spread crabs all over the house."

"I see."

"Not that I'm a prude. If you've got a *nice* girl, you know, a lady, bring her in and welcome. But try to pop her out again before the maids get here in the morning."

"I'll remember."

"Now dear," said Tessie turning to Tom, "that little back

room I thought you might like as a *pied à terre*. You're sure you don't want it?"

" 'Fraid not, Tessie."

"Because I've had another offer. Funny little chap came in here yesterday, common voice but dressed like a gentleman, wants a room for a few weeks, he said. Kept picking at his fingers, which I didn't care for, and Albert Edward didn't like him – did 'oo, woozums? – but I thought, if Tom doesn't want it, and if he pays as sharp as he looks – "

"Kept picking at his fingers?" said Tom with interest. "What was his name?"

"Holford, Holworthy, something like that."

"Holbrook?"

"That's it, dear. He's coming again today. Know him, do you?"

"Yes."

"All right?"

"No," said Tom, "very much not all right. But as far as you're concerned, he'll pay weekly in advance and I don't think there'll be any dragging back."

Later on, when Tom and Fielding were walking together in Hyde Park, Tom said:

"I think I'll move out even sooner than I told Tessie. I don't want to see more of her new guest than I can help."

"Holbrook? What's the matter with him?"

"He reminds me of what I'd sooner forget."

"Most people have that effect on me," Fielding said.

"I know what you mean. But Holbrook's a special case. My very own personal plague rat."

"Where will you go?"

A spring breeze skimmed the Serpentine and the trees rustled with the familiar invitations.

"Off into the blue. A walking tour. I always planned it, to nerve myself before getting married." Tom hesitated. "You

. . . wouldn't like to come with me? There's a lot we might talk about."

"There's nothing I'd like better," said Fielding, obscurely moved by this suggestion. "But I must get down to work. Stern's been very good, and if I'm to – "

" – You're quite right," said Tom, flicking his fingers. "That's where I nearly came unstuck when I started – kept delaying. You get down to work and stay down. But you'll take a day off for my wedding?"

"With the greatest pleasure."

"Patricia's family are rather grand, you see. I'll need a few friendly faces on my side of the church."

Fielding shuddered slightly and Tom looked him straight in the eye.

"I meant exactly what I said, Fielding. To me, your face is now that of a friend. And so, however disfigured, it is a friendly face . . . a face to call up love."

Max de Freville was spending a week in Menton with Angela Tuck. On his fourth day there he received a letter from Mark:

". . . So as soon as Somerset's cheque went through, I got out the jolly old letter and off we pranced to Wiltshire to talk turkey with Edwin Turbot. I was in favour of having a word with Isobel first, but Somerset said no, we'd announce ourselves as the editor of *Strix*, and that would get us straight in. He'd already rung up from London, it seemed.

"In the hall was a galumphing lass with a lot of jerseys and a po face.

" 'You must be Miss Patricia Turbot,' Somerset said. 'I'd like to congratulate you on your engagement to Tom Llewyllyn.'

"She thawed out a bit at that, though she still seemed suspicious. I don't know Tom well, but it's funny he should choose a kind of female gladiator after all these years of dainty

ladies from the chorus at the Tin Tack Club. Wants a change,
I suppose, and he'll certainly get it: like going to bed with that
statue of Nurse Cavell. Anyway, this Patricia just stood there
simpering and blocking up the doorway, till Somerset
reminded her we'd got an appointment with her old man. At
this she let us in and strode along in front at heavy infantry
pace on the way to what she called 'the study'. But before we
got there, she suddenly stopped, did a parade ground turn,
and said to Somerset,

" 'Do you know where Tom is?'

" 'He's on a walking tour," said Somerset. 'Didn't he tell
you?'

" 'Yes. But I'd like to know where.'

" 'He didn't know where he was going. He told me he was
just going to start and see where his feet took him.'

" 'How childish,' she said. 'And what about his work for
your paper?'

" 'No more now till after the honeymoon.'

"At this she went a deep, sweaty scarlet, not only bashful,
if you ask me, but ripe and randy, so perhaps Tom has picked
well after all. But it seems that she doesn't approve of Tom
wandering away over the countryside like his namesake Jones,
and though she gave permission she's now thought better of
it (wildly jealous of possible picaresque adventures) and wants
to get her great big capable paws on him again. If Tom had
seen the look of greed in her face, he'd start sending back the
wedding presents tomorrow.

"Well, Somerset couldn't help her, so she clanked off to
her own quarters, and we went in to see Sir Edwin, who was
busy stuffing himself with digestive biscuits and spraying the
crumbs all over *The Times*.

" '*Strix*,' he said, 'of course. I suppose you've come to ask
my views on the forthcoming election?'

" 'No, we haven't,' says Somerset, as sharp and nasty as a
rusty bayonet, 'we've come to do business with you. We have

proof positive that you and other ministers conspired with Israeli agents to force a crisis over Suez. We're here to tell you how you can make amends.'

"One in the teeth for Sir Edwin. But he took it like a real trooper. You've got to hand it to the old gang – they've a monopoly in sheer brass neck.

" 'Llewyllyn told me about you,' Sir Edwin said. 'What he didn't tell me was that you were foolish as well as unscrupulous. What sort of storyteller's rubbish is this?'

"For answer, Somerset held the letter under his nose. Sir E. was just about to take it, when Somerset withdrew it and gave him a photostat.

" 'You read this,' Somerset said, 'and then you tell me what sort of storyteller's rubbish it is.'

"You could almost see the poor old chap shrinking as he read it. But when he'd done, he stood up with his back to the wall (Steady the Buffs), reinflated himself, and took a steady return aim.

" 'It's a fake,' he said.

" 'There are those that can prove otherwise.'

" 'What it says is untrue.'

" 'That will be for others to judge. They might think it fitted in rather well with what they already know.'

" 'You publish a word of this, and I'll sue you through every court in Christendom.'

" 'Even if you won, you'd still be finished after what was said.'

" 'And to think,' Sir Edwin said, 'that originally I was going to back you for Bishop's Cross. I'm glad I changed my mind.'

" 'Won't you have to change it back again?'

" 'Very probably. But at least I've the satisfaction of knowing that I reached the right decision . . . even if circumstances now prevent me acting on it.'

"For of course he was too old an operator not to know

when he was beaten. But once again, you've got to hand it to him: there was a kind of offhand dignity about his surrender which implied that although he was having a bad run just now, he was still in the game and ready to wait for his own turn. It was very well done. Somerset had hoped to have him grovelling, instead of which he was a model of self-possession and turned out, when they came on to the terms of treaty, to be much the cooler and more accurate of the two.

" 'Very well.' he said: 'so you're asking for my support at Bishop's Cross?'

" 'I'm asking to be assured of selection as conservative candidate there.'

" 'I can't assure you of any such thing.'

" 'They'll listen to you.'

" 'No doubt. But I can't make them do more.'

" 'Then somewhere else?'

" 'Look,' Sir Edwin said; 'the truth is, and a lot of people are beginning to know it, that you're not fit to represent Bishop's Cross or anywhere else. So I can't promise. You must see that.'

" 'And you must see that I've got enough here to blow you to fragments.'

" 'After which I wouldn't be able to help you at all.'

"This elementary piece of logic went home. While Somerset chewed away on it, Sir E. started on me.

" 'And what do *you* want?'

" 'Money.'

" 'Thank God for that. I can cope with your sort. But him' – pointed at sulky Somerset – 'he'll want a ministry before I can turn round.'

" 'I can't see,' huffed Somerset, 'that there's anything ridiculous in that.'

" 'Except that for some years now these things have been rather difficult to arrange. How's your father?' he shot at

Somerset, then turned away without waiting for an answer, went to a desk, and came back with a cheque book.

" 'His father's called Shagger,' he told me as he started to write. 'You know why? He had a reputation for bedding half the shop girls in Cambridge. Put about by himself, of course. If you ask me, he just stayed in his room and had dirty thoughts. Like his son, I wouldn't wonder. Here's £500 to be going on with. You can have another £1,000 in September, and the same after Christmas. All right?'

" 'All right,' I said. 'But after that?'

" 'We'll have a little talk about a regular arrangement. That's if smarty-boots here hasn't opened his spotty mouth.'

" 'Look here,' said Somerset, who was looking positively sorry for himself, 'there's no need for all this personal talk. All I'm asking is your assistance and good report.'

" 'You shall have both. The question is, who's going to believe me?'

" 'There's only one person need believe you. Rupert Percival. He can answer for the Selection Committee at Bishop's Cross.'

" 'Granted. But what makes you think he'll like the cut of your jib?'

" 'That's up to you,' Somerset said.

" 'Well, I don't really know the chap,' said Sir Edwin, as easily as if we'd been talking about the local cricket club, 'but I'll ask myself over there and see what's to do. And now, in order to keep up the domestic fiction that you are welcome visitors, you'd better come and meet my daughters over lunch'."

"Tell me," said Angela to Max de Freville in Menton, "is anything the matter?"

"What should be?"

"You've been odd. And all that time you spend brooding over those letters."

"That's my business," snapped Max: "don't interfere."

"Darling, I don't want to. I was only asking. . . ."

"There's not enough to tell, not yet. One day I'll know it all, and then I'll tell you. One day I'll have the key, and then – "

He broke off when he saw how strangely she was looking at him.

"Just don't interfere," he muttered. "You wouldn't really understand."

"Gloomy old faces," Isobel had written to Max, "at luncheon today. Daddy had two guests, a scabby old journalist thing called Lloyd-James, and a younger man, raddled but devastating, who told me on the side that he's a chum of yours. The silly thing was that everyone was meant to be all palsy, but I could tell that underneath Daddy was ready to widdle with fuss, while the Lloyd-James creature, though he behaved smoothly enough, was quite rancid with frustration about something. He was like a little boy who finds that his new toy isn't nearly as big and as blissy as he thought it would be from the picture, but still has to go on being grateful in order not to annoy mummy. On top of all this, Patty was in a rare old bait because she still hasn't heard from Tom on his walking tour and she suspects him of having it off with every other woman he meets. All nerves of course. Tom's now as staid as an old cow in a field, whatever he may have been like once; but nothing's going to stop her worrying till she's got him locked up in a glass case on the mantelpiece. I wouldn't wonder if she comes out in shingles – and *that'll* be nice on the honeymoon.

"Anyway, what with one thing and another, the only people there who were enjoying life were me and this celestial Mark Lewson. We played a bit of footy under the table, and then a bit of kneesy, and after lunch I managed to get him to myself, because Daddy went off for his nap and Patty was conducting an inquisition on the Lloyd-James monster about Tom, though Mark said she'd already had one go that morning. It was now Mark told me he knew you, so then I realised there was more in all this than an interview for L-J's dreary paper and I asked Mark what was frying.

" 'Your old daddikins, dear,' he said.

"Then he told me all about the Suez do-da and Daddy being so naughty, and how L-J wanted a seat in Parliament, and how galling this was for Daddy because of L-J being such a piece of sparrow-crap, and so on and so forth. And I said, was it wise of him to be telling me, and he said he didn't suppose I'd want to land my old pater in the manure, and that anyway he'd done quite well out of it all by now and didn't really care if the news did get out.

" 'It'd annoy Somerset,' he said, 'and Somerset's a prick. And as for making more money, I've thought of another scheme to take care of my old age. Much less risky and much more fun.'

"And then he kissed me in a way that hasn't happened before, and even though his mouth tasted foul he thrilled me into little bits, so that he could have had the whole caboodle there and then (which no one else really has, I'm not such a tart as I look) only Patty and Lloyd-J. came in, both of them looking like empty slabs in a morgue, and Lloyd-J. said it was going time.

"So that was that. But I'm seeing lovely Mark in London again next week."

For Fielding Gray in Buttock's Hotel the days passed quickly. First of all he altered his two novels along the lines suggested by Gregory Stern and the firm's editor. Then he took out his journal, sorrowed briefly over the memories which it revived, and began to calculate how it could be cast as a work of fiction.

From time to time, in hall or corridor, he passed a small,

tense man, of about thirty-five years old, who moved as though he were always on his way to take an urgent part in great events. This, as he had heard from Tessie Buttock, was the new resident, Jude Holbrook. He found it difficult to understand why Tom Llewyllyn's aversion was so pronounced; for Holbrook, while shifty and tight-lipped, had in his manner a lack of co-ordination, a spasmodic nervous jerk, which, taken with his size, gave him the appearance of a marionette: a villain, possibly, but a villain on a stage of puppets.

For Tom Llewyllyn too the days went swiftly by.

One afternoon, walking through the Quantocks, he breasted a rise and found himself on a small wooded plateau lying along a spur which jutted from the range to the north of it. To the south the county unrolled itself like a great patterned eiderdown: green pastures sprawled at leisure, woods nestled, and orchards lay tidy and demure.

The plateau itself, with its groves of lady birch, would have been enchanting – were it not that gangs of men and machines were clearing away the woodland at a rate of ten yards a minute, and that a large space already cleared was occupied by closely packed caravan-trailers of identical design with a perimeter of prefabricated stalls and huts. There were two large notices: one carried the name of a contractor; the other proclaimed,

WESTWARD HO !
First of the Government-sponsored
Canteloupe Country Culture Camps
FITNESS FAMILY
FAITH.

As he walked downhill towards the south, Tom wondered whether he should telephone Patricia that evening. He decided not. In his good time he would move east again to Wiltshire, where he would be with her, as promised, some seven days before the wedding in order to settle any last minute arrangements. Meanwhile, she must do without further reassurance; she had already had plenty, and she must learn to put up with his long withdrawals which, for one reason or another, would be bound to continue during their married life, probably to the great benefit of them both. So let the days pass in silence and soon enough they would bring him to his bride.

Two meetings with Isobel in London confirmed Mark in the idea which had come to him in Wiltshire. A regular arrangement, Sir Edwin had said. Very well; let him hand over his younger daughter and a suitable dowry, and Mark would abandon any further claim upon him. In this way he would have achieved security and social status (for both of which he had always had a secret longing), to say nothing of an amusing, vivacious, appetising wife. He wanted a bit of peace and permanence; he was fed up, worn out with the constant struggle for petty cash and 'the endless antics in strange beds. All ways round, Isobel would do very nicely: she was his Sophy Western, waiting with arms wide open at the end of the turbulent road.

But there were two formidable obstacles. First, Sir Edwin, who was already somewhat put out by the imminence of one dubious marriage, might be reluctant to hand over his remaining daughter to a penniless adventurer. And secondly, although his objections might be overcome by reference to the letter, he would surely want this to be given up to him, as confirmation that he had now paid the final price. Since the letter was in Somerset's possession, and since Somerset had no intention of giving it up to anybody, Mark was in no position to close the deal . . . even on the assumption that Sir Edwin would consent to make one.

But as the days went by and the grass grew fat and rank in

the Royal Parks, he conceived a plan. A bold, roistering plan, full worthy of his gay Sophy Western.

Sir Edwin Turbot consulted warily with Alastair Dixon in London. After all, he said, he had decided that Somerset Lloyd-James was the better choice for Bishop's Cross: would Dixon, as outgoing member and mutual friend, do his best to convince Rupert Percival? Dixon would, but wanted to know what part Sir Edwin himself proposed to bear in the matter. The trouble was, Sir Edwin said, that while he would much prefer to make a discreet and personal approach, he was but little acquainted with Percival. Dixon, who knew that the old country lawyer would resent and resist any pressure exerted through hierarchy but might perhaps yield to personal suasion, approved Sir Edwin's choice of method and suggested that Percival should be asked to the wedding, where their acquaintance might be renewed as a preliminary to further negotiation. Dixon himself would be staying with Percival the night before the wedding, so Percival's invitation would appear quite natural: it would be seen as a graceful if not mandatory way of recognising that his house was harbouring one of the more prominent wedding guests. Sir Edwin opined it a pity, since time was passing, that their movements should be quite so stately; but Alastair Dixon pointed out that any sign of fuss or urgency would put Percival against them for good.

"We've been asked to Tom Llewyllyn's wedding in Wiltshire," said Peter Morrison to Helen.

"It seems a long way. . . . And I've hardly ever met Tom. Except for that awful time when he was so drunk at Chevenix Court."

"He's changed a good deal. I think we'll go, if you can bear it. There'll be several people there who'll be in the know about Bishop's Cross. And if Turbot really is going to back me, as Detterling says, it'll do no harm to be polite to him."

"Will Somerset Lloyd-James be there?"

"I expect so – Tom's editor, you see." Peter chuckled. "I wouldn't mind seeing his deceitful old face again. I might even ask him what he's up to. You never know, he might tell me; he's got a peculiar sense of humour – like all Papists."

"You're much too kind about him."

"He's got a bit of a kink, that's all. I expect someone dropped him on his head when he was one."

He looked along his lawn, and then beyond it to his fields, which were already well forward.

"Not bad for early June," he said; "and the old men say we're in for a hot summer." He gripped his wife's arm just above the elbow. "I think – don't you? – that we can afford to be kind about Somerset Lloyd-James."

And so the days lengthened and drew on towards midsummer; days bringing Fielding Gray to slow fulfilment and Canteloupe's first caravan camp to punctual completion; bringing Burke Lawrence and Penelope Holbrook to their engagement in Stockholm and Jude Holbrook ever closer to the information which he sought; bringing Somerset Lloyd-James and Peter Morrison nearer to the time when one of them must be chosen; bringing Mark to Isobel but little comfort to Max de Fréville; and bringing Tom Llewyllyn back from his wanderings to his affianced wife.

Neither Patricia nor anyone else learnt much of where he had been. Something indeed he told of the men and machines which were making hideous the little spur of the Quantocks; but nothing at all of the middle-aged woman whom he had visited in her cottage by the Severn, a woman whom Tom called 'mother' but who would not be in the church to see him wed. For it had always suited Tom to come from nowhere; and of those that would gather to drink at his marriage feast, he and his bride alone would bear his name.

7

MIDSUMMER WEDDING

"GROOM, DEAR," said Jonathan Gamp, winking saucily at the usher, and trolled himself up the aisle to find a place next Somerset Lloyd-James. From the bride's side a block of county faces regarded him incuriously; they had been warned what to expect. In the front row, Canteloupe fidgeted thirstily while his lady and the dowager eyed him with contempt. Carton Weir, who had not been invited but had come, on Somerset's suggestion, in the capacity of Canteloupe's *aide*, passed his master a copy of the order of service in the hope of keeping him amused. Just like a bloody great Christmas card, Canteloupe thought, only no pictures, worse luck. What was this on the front?

> With that I saw two Swans of goodly hue
> Come softly swimming down along the Lee;
> Two fairer birds I yet did never see:
> The Snow which doth the top of Pindus strew
> Did never whiter show. . . .

Great God, Canteloupe thought, so that old fraud Edwin Turbot's taken to writing poetry.

"Overdoing it rather," said Jonathan to Somerset. "Two geese if ever there were. But I must say, Tom looks rather sweet."

Tom, hair disciplined, shoes gleaming, his hired morning coat only a size or so too large, looked unprecedentedly respectable as he waited for his bride. The audience on the groom's side averred to one another that this must be the

work of Gregory Stern, who stood beside him conducting a
furious last minute test of his waistcoat buttons.

"He looks all right to me," said Rupert Percival to Alastair
Dixon: "why was Turbot so put out about it?"

"No one knows who he is. He just turned up at the 'Varsity
one Michaelmas with a scholarship and went on from there."

"I should have thought it was perfectly clear who he is. A
writer with three rather distinguished books to his credit and
a prominent by-line as a political journalist."

"No one knows who he was, then."

"Does that matter these days?"

"His . . . er . . . morals" Dixon deposed with vague deprecation.

"Is that anything new?"

"It's all right if you *know* about people. But if you don't
you have to be careful."

> So purely white they were (read Helen Morrison)
> That even the gentle stream, the which them bare,
> Seem'd foul to them . . .

A man with a badly disfigured face and only one good eye
sat down next to her. Poor thing, Helen thought, as her
husband leaned across her.

"Fielding," he said softly.

The disfigured face tormented itself into what was presumably a smile.

"Peter. Peter Morrison."

"You've never met my wife? Darling, you've heard me
talk of Fielding Gray."

The one eye looked at her suspiciously. The head inclined
in formal salute.

"Mrs. Morrison."

"I've heard. . . . That is, Peter has. . . . Please call me Helen."

"When I know you better."

Blinking slightly, Helen read on while the two men whispered across her.

> . . . Seem'd foul to them, and bade his billows spare
> To wet their silken feathers, lest they might
> Soil their fair plumes with water not so fair
> And mar their beauties bright. . . .

Stone the crows, thought little Alfie Schroeder of the Billingsgate Press, waddling in the wake of a phalanx of Parliamentarians, Tom's really hit the jackpot with this crowd.

"Press?" said an usher, looking at Alfie's shining Sunday suit.

"No," said Alfie with spirit. "For the bridegroom."

For Tom Llewyllyn had not forgotten his old companion.

"Pardon me," said Alfie, as he trod first on Captain Detterling's beautifully polished Mess Wellingtons and then on Mrs. Donald Salinger's pointed patents.

"My bloody bunions," Mrs. Salinger said.

"Funny friends Tom has," said Salinger to Detterling.

"The lot on the other side look just as odd to me. Look at old mother Canteloupe."

And indeed, while Carton Weir squirmed, Lord Canteloupe scowled, and Lady Canteloupe looked faintly unhappy, the dowager was munching with gusto an egg sandwich which she had brought along in her handbag. What her party didn't know was that she also had several slices of garlic sausage stored up against the sermon.

"Already five·minutes late," said Percival to Dixon.

"I hope nothing goes wrong for him now," Alfie Schroeder prayed.

"There's something so *naïve* about country churches," remarked Jonathan Gamp.

"I had to get special dispensation from His Eminence," Somerset Lloyd-James replied.

"Seven minutes late," the county faces murmured without anxiety.

"Stern's looking a bit fussed," said Captain Detterling.

"They say his father's still orthodox," mused Mrs. Salinger.

"No, his grandfather," corrected her husband.

"They always said Turbot didn't like it," mumbled the Parliamentarians. "Do you suppose. . . .?"

"Please, madam," Carton Weir entreated the dowager; "they should be here at any moment."

"It's no good," said Canteloupe. "Much better ignore her."

The Dowager Marchioness dropped a bit of egg on the seat and bent happily to pick it up again.

"I'll tell you what little I know after the service," Fielding was whispering to Peter across Helen Morrison: "but it's not much. As far as I'm concerned, Somerset's only my editor these days."

And mar their beauties bright, (read Helen Morrison
on the third time through)
    That shone as Heaven's light,
    Against their Bridal day, which was not long:
    Sweet Thames, run softly, till I end my song.

And now at last, with a peal of triumph from the organ, came Patricia Turbot on her father's arm, confounding the malicious, making glad the heart of every female, stepping strong as a sentry on his beat. A kilted page, fussed over by the radiant Isobel, bore the train, and six more bridesmaids, in swanky short green dresses, pressed on behind, urging the virgin sacrifice to Hymen's altar. Tom's face lit up like a winter's sun breaking through mist and he held out both his hands to greet her.

"Mistress Isobel looks very pleased with herself," mused Somerset.

Gregory Stern bowed a tall and noble bow. Sir Edwin drew back.

"Here in the sight of God, and in the face of this congregation. . . ."

Helen Morrison grasped Peter's hand.

". . . First it was ordained for the procreation of children. . . . A remedy against sin. . . ."

"There's something definitely queer about Isobel's demeanour."

A strapping wench, thought Alfie; I hope he can manage her.

". . . Such persons as have not the gift of continency. . . ."

"I'm sure I heard it was his *father* who's Orthodox."

"Nonsense, Vanessa. His father served in the Brigade."

"Let him now speak, or else hereafter for ever hold his peace."

Peter Morrison disengaged his hand from Helen's; she always got so sticky at weddings. I don't suppose Fielding can help about Somerset, he thought, so I'll have a word with the old crook myself. Odd about Fielding. He's a wreck, yet there's a . . . a serenity there which I don't remember – even if he was a bit sharp just now with Helen. Guiltily, reluctantly, he repossessed himself of his wife's sweaty palm. The big ones always have a lot of juices, he thought; that great hoyden of Tom's will be just as bad.

"Wilt thou have this woman to thy wedded wife, to live together after God's ordinance in the holy estate of Matrimony?"

"I will," Tom said in tones which rang round the church.

Edwin Turbot looks rather down, thought Somerset: perhaps he's not finding my little affair too easy. Later on I'll have a word with him. What to do about Peter? Just be polite – he's not one to bear a grudge.

"To have and to hold from this day forward, for better for worse, for richer for poorer. . . ."

I wonder about this Morrison woman, Fielding thought;

capable, I dare say. I wish I hadn't come; I wish I'd stayed in London and got on with my book. *My book.*

". . . in sickness and in health, to love and to cherish. . . ."

God, make them be happy, Alfie Schroeder thought.

God, make me be happy, Isobel Turbot thought.

Something . . . queer . . . about Isobel today.

God, I could use a drink, Lord Canteloupe thought.

God, this revolting hag and her sandwiches, Carton Weir thought; and tomorrow we've got to inspect that bloody caravan park.

Oh God, I don't know, Captain Detterling thought; it was never for me, all this cherishing and so on. Though there's a nice bit in Homer which the old man used to read us at school. About a man and his wife, a great joy to their friends and a grief to their enemies. But the old man was a bachelor himself.

". . . till death do us part, according to God's holy ordinance; and thereto I plight thee my troth."

And now what had at first been a mild snivelling, then a repressed sobbing, then a barely controlled bodily heaving, became an open and impassioned bawling, full-throated and lusty, the tribute of a tried but generous heart. It was Tessie Buttock weeping, part in happiness and part in sorrow, for her lost favourite, naughty Tom.

For as long as possible, Sir Edwin Turbot had postponed considering what attitude he should adopt to Tom once he was fairly married to Patricia. Until just before the wedding he had coped with his aversion by regarding Tom as a talented nuisance, as an irritating employee who must be tolerated for his undoubted ability. Plainly this view of the matter would serve no longer. The wretched fellow was now his son-in-law and must be admitted to full family privilege: the question was, how should this be done without imposing too much of a strain on Sir Edwin's *amour propre*.

But now, as Sir Edwin surveyed the long queue which was waiting to pay compliments to the newly married couple, and as he reflected that neither here nor anywhere else in the house was a single relative of Tom's to be found, the answer came to him. Tom, so to speak, was the scholarship boy with no background; while he, Sir Edwin, was the traditional but far-seeing headmaster, making concessions to a new age. Tom would be accepted forthwith as absolutely "one of us", indeed as one likely to do "us" great credit in the long run, but also as one who had not had quite our advantages: a fact which we would never mention but would always keep at the back of our minds, to excuse ourselves (and Tom) in case he should make some fatal blunder – which would otherwise have disgraced us wholly but could now be promptly attributed to an upbringing deficient because unknown. Patronage, that was the word, Sir Edwin thought: he was the eternal patrician braving and taming the eternal parvenu, he was the enlightened head of house welcoming the young F. E. Smith to Oxford, or even the King of France summoning Cellini to his court. Sir Edwin glowed with pleasure at his new *imago*. A pity, of course, that Patty hadn't let him enquire more closely into the young chap's past, but it was all settled now, with a good get-out clause in case of nasty accidents, so *noblesse oblige* and he'd better go round encouraging people to make free with these beastly refreshments, which looked as if they'd been specially dyed for the occasion.

"My dear old boy," he said, punching Tom in the back as he passed behind him and Patricia. Make the chap feel at home, eh – how was that for a start?

But Tom, who was facing an even more brutal attack from the front, hardly noticed.

"Oh, Tom," Tessie was saying; "and is this your lovely bride? Oh Gawd, I feel quite faint."

She kissed Patricia greedily but not without all restraint; Tom she might have swallowed whole, had not Fielding Gray prodded her from behind to indicate that it was time to desist.

"There's rather a long queue," he said.

So Tessie unclamped herself and waddled off, and Fielding took her place.

"Major Gray, darling," said Tom before he could stop himself. Somehow the formality seemed appropriate today.

"Your servant, madam," Fielding said, with about eighty per cent irony. He bent to kiss her hand and was gone. Next came Peter and Helen Morrison. While the two women eyed each other warily, Tom whispered to Peter,

"Have a word with old Edwin. I've done what I could."

"So I heard, and thank you."

"But," said Tom, "he's been very shifty these past few days. I don't know anything for certain, but there's beginning to be a familiar smell in the air. Half sulphur and half stale sweat, if you see what I mean."

"A smell one associates with an office in Gower Street?"

Tom nodded and then inclined himself towards Helen, remembering their last meeting three years before.

"I'm sober today," he said. "Kiss and be friends?"

"Kiss and be friends."

"What – ?" began Patricia sharply as the Morrisons moved off.

" – A squalid lapse," said Tom airily, and deliberately left her guessing. "Ah, here comes Somerset," he said.

Further down the queue, back in the ante-room, Jonathan Gamp complained,

"I don't believe there's an ash-tray in the entire house." He held up quarter of an inch of cigarette between two finger nails. "It must be a special torture which that prim Patricia's thought up."

"Throw it into the fire-place," said Captain Detterling, and turned away crossly because he hated social ineptness: in Detterling's view, if there were no ash-trays provided in a room one refrained from smoking there.

So Jonathan threw his butt towards the fire-place and didn't bother to see where it landed, which was a good two yards short and on a thick carpet. This was noticed by Carton Weir, who thought it would be amusing to say nothing and see what happened. Carton Weir liked to complicate situations because he was quick-witted and could appear to advantage.

They filed on into the next room.

"*Darling*," said Jonathan to Tom several times, while the county faces pretended not to notice.

Meanwhile Somerset, having said something polite to Alastair Dixon and having received a cool but courteous nod from Rupert Percival, passed through the crowd to Sir Edwin, who was wondering where Isobel had got to and, still delighted with his new role as aristocratic patron, was drinking quite a lot of champagne, despite its palpable acidity.

"Ah," he said to Somerset, "I suppose you'd better have some champagne."

Somerset sipped and winced.

"I don't wish to appear importunate," he said, "but how are things going?"

"Things?" said Sir Edwin, knowing what he meant.

"Bishop's Cross."

"Mills of God, dear boy. I've got Percival here to fix up a proper discussion."

Somerset looked dissatisfied.

"More urgency – ," he began.

The Minister waved him down like a policeman.

"It's like stalking deer," he said. He took a large gulp of champagne and decided to expand the simile. "You've got to get downwind of them. And even then, the slightest noise and they're off. If Percival suspects . . . You'll excuse me." His glass was empty and he wanted more. "Other guests . . ."

"Please don't forget what's at stake," said Somerset, smiling urbanely to reassure a covey of M.P.s who were scratching their way towards his host.

"My dear fellow, I'm a professional."

Cut off from the bar, Sir Edwin marched up to the covey of M.P.s with the determination of a beater and sent them fluttering in all directions. Politeness could wait; he wanted more champagne. "Oh Patricia," he thought, "all these years I've guarded and loved you like a mother, how could you?" But this would never do. All that, he reminded himself, had been settled once and for all: he wasn't losing a daughter, he was gaining a scholarship boy. A protégé. Rumpff. Playful stuff, this champagne. He reached the bar and poured himself a tumbler of it. "Oh Patricia – " *No.*

"Sir Edwin?"

Young Morrison. What did *he* want?

"This is my wife, Helen. You never met . . ."

"How de do?"

Strong, reliable sort. But you never could tell. He would have sworn before God and man that his own Diana . . . And then, as soon as Isobel had been born . . . Rumpff.

"So sorry," he said to the surprised Helen. "Trying sort of occasion, you know. No, we never met. And it must be nearly three years," he said to Peter, "since I've seen you."

"I hope that will be different after this autumn. You may have heard – "

" – I've heard." Sir Edwin reflected. Finally he said,

"Always tricky, this sort of thing. Wish you the best of luck, of course."

Not the voice, thought Peter, of a firm supporter. Tom was right: there was a smell of sulphur here.

"Won't be a moment, darling – excuse me, sir," he said on impulse, and screwed his way through the crowd to where he could see Somerset, who was standing alone at one corner of a large table which held the wedding presents.

"What did you send . . . you old crook?"

"That," said Somerset, pointing to a florid edition of Saint

Augustine's *Confessions*. "Rather appropriate if one considers Tom's younger days."

"Proselytising, Somerset?"

"It is a duty enjoined upon us. How are you, Peter?"

"Pleased to see you, in a dreadful sort of way. And curious."

"Curious, my dear?"

"Bishop's Cross, Somerset. What's going on?"

"Naturally I'm very anxious to be chosen. It's high time I got started."

"I'm anxious too. I want to get back. But you haven't answered my question. What's going on?"

"You know very well," Somerset told him, "that you can't expect a direct answer to a crude question like that. What makes you think that anything's going on?"

"The way certain people are behaving. And the glazed look in your eye. It always used to come when you were up to something."

"Oh dear," sighed Somerset, "I hoped I'd got over that."

"I find it rather endearing. A reminder of our childhood."

"When all the best prizes went to you," said Somerset with sudden and naked resentment. "Well, Bishop's Cross is one prize that isn't coming to you. That much I will tell you. And if you want to save time and trouble for yourself and everybody else, you'll withdraw your name. Because just this once the clean-limbed hero of the school is going to be put down by the school swot, and it might look better if he resigned gracefully first."

"I wonder," Helen Morrison was saying to Sir Edwin, "what my husband is saying to Mr. Lloyd-James. They look rather flushed."

"I could tell you why," said the Minister as he refilled his tumbler, "but I'd much sooner not. I'll tell you something else instead. You remind me of my wife."

Helen looked distressed.

"She left me, you know, when my younger daughter was

a baby. I wonder," he said, looking vaguely round the room, "where Isobel is?" For a moment his eyes misted, then focused again on Helen. "As I was saying, she left me very suddenly and no one ever found out why. There wasn't even another man, not a proper one, just someone who – Well. So I had to look after the girls, and I've done my best, but sometimes, today of all times, I wonder whether – Oh dear. I don't know why I'm telling you all this. I expect because you look like – "

" – Please," Helen said. "Patricia is a very fine young woman," she instructed him stoutly, "and Tom Llewyllyn is – " She tried to say a "fine young man" but for all the world she couldn't manage it. " – Very clever and distinguished," she concluded.

"Rumpff," went Sir Edwin. "Sorry, dear lady. A trying occasion. Have some more champagne."

He gestured with vigour but made no attempt to get it for her, then, seeing Peter on his way back to them, excused himself hurriedly and made across the room towards Dixon and Percival, for it was time, his instinct told him, to start throwing a bit of charm about in that quarter.

"Something's up with Somerset," whispered Peter as he rejoined Helen; "but I'm blessed if I know what."

"Something's up," whispered Alfie Schroeder to Tom on the other side of the room.

Alfie had waited at the end of the queue so that he might have a better chance to make his point. Patricia had now strayed a few yards away to talk to some of the bridesmaids, and Alfie was urgent.

"There's something up," he said.

"On the job, Alfie?"

"I came here as a friend, laddie, you know that, so I'm telling you. Get that girl of yours and get out – before something happens to stop you leaving. I wouldn't want to see your honeymoon spoilt. It was about the one good thing that ever happened to me – but never mind that. You get going at once. That's my advice, and it's the best wedding gift you've had so far."

"But Alfie. There are going to be speeches and a cake and God knows what." He glanced at Patricia; but she was safely occupied, it seemed. Even so he moved Alfie further away. "What on earth's the matter?" he said.

"Never you mind. It's just that there's going to be a nasty shock round here before the day's out, and I'd like to see you well away from it."

"But Alfie. . . . How can you know?"

"Let's just say I looked in the woodshed. Or the stables, to be more precise."

"Whatever you saw, we can't just push off."

"You would have done three years ago."

"Things change. There must be speeches, Alfie. It must all be done properly. For Patricia's sake."

"I suppose so," said Alfie miserably. "Try to get a move on, that's all."

But the proceedings, Tom reflected, would take their own time. There were too many rules and too many people; nothing he could do. In any case, Alfie had roused curiosity in him rather than apprehension. If something was going to break, Tom wanted to be in on it. As a writer, he could not afford to miss a good scene; and he was – always would be – a writer before he was a husband. No, he thought; let things take their course: the wedding trip was to last six weeks, and he could well afford a day or two's delay if there was anything to show for it. Absent-mindedly he took a glass of champagne from a tray, then realised this was the first drink he had had time for and drained it in one.

"*Christ*," he nearly shouted, as the malignant fluid rasped down through his chest.

"*Christ*," Vanessa Salinger was complaining to her husband Donald. "They must have made it themselves."

"Champagne's always like that at weddings," Donald said; "it's the occasion that counts, remember."

"Stop being so smug."

Donald pouted.

"We ought to have a word with Lord and Lady Cante-loupe," he said.

"Why?"

"Good manners require it."

"For Christ's sake, Donald. We don't even know them."

"That's just the point. We ought to. The firm's printing the stuff for the advertising campaign about Canteloupe's Country Culture Camps."

Deferentially Donald stalked Lord Canteloupe, who was standing, glumly and with an empty glass, between Lady Canteloupe and Carton Weir. (The dowager was busy gather-ing a representative selection from the buffet to take home in her handbag.) Since the Salingers knew Weir slightly, having met him over de Freville's chemmy table from time to time, Donald signed to him for assistance; but Weir, preoccupied with the sight of Sir Edwin courting Rupert Percival, did not respond.

"Lord Canteloupe, I'm – er – Donald Salinger," Donald eventually said.

"Who?" said Canteloupe savagely.

Carton Weir, his attention recalled by this exchange, whispered in the Secretary's ear.

"Of course," boomed Canteloupe. "Delighted to meet you. Doing a great job with the printing. Be a good chap," he said to Weir regally, "and get me some more of this poisonous stuff."

Refusal being tactless in present company, Weir took the empty glass and moved off towards the bar.

"And this," Donald Salinger began, "is my – "

But Vanessa, anxious for a little light relief, had followed Weir.

"Shall I tell you something amusing?" she said.

"I could do with it. Trailing round with that lot isn't very joy-making."

"Well then. Sir Edwin Turbot's pissed."

She nodded towards where the Minister was talking, red with effort, to Percival and Dixon.

"What of it? So would Canteloupe be if I gave him half a chance."

He poured an ungenerous glass of champagne and started back with it.

"Sir Edwin's pissed," Vanessa said, "because he doesn't like this marriage."

"We always knew that. He doesn't care for Tom Llewyllyn."

Deftly, Carton Weir forged a passage between a jowly M.P. and a shapeless county lady, Scylla and Charybdis.

"You haven't seen the point," Vanessa said. "It's not that he doesn't care for Tom. He's *jealous*."

"Old Oedipus again? Quite normal."

Vanessa put up her hand to detain him while they were still out of earshot of Donald and the Canteloupes.

"When a girl hasn't got a mother," she said, "she sometimes has a very special thing with the father. And *vice versa*. Far more than the usual father-daughter thing. I had a girl friend once . . . it was much the same story as this, important family, almost as much money. Just before the couple went off from the wedding breakfast in their car, her father went berserk. He raged round the car cursing at the top of his voice, and started cutting all the old shoes and things off the back bumper with a pair of garden shears. Then he ran into the house again snapping the shears at the guests – dangerously, not just pretend – and wouldn't leave his bedroom for a week."

"Why are you telling me this?"

"Helpful hints, sweetie, for a young politician on the make. Afterwards, my friend's father was a changed man. Within a year of the wedding he was caught with his hand in the till. Embezzling clients' money. Only a few hundred quid – which he didn't begin to need. You see what I mean?"

"Edwin Turbot's made of sterner stuff."

"I wouldn't be too sure, sweetie. Change of life, you see."

"*Please*, darling."

"Men can have it as well as women – particularly if they've been doing a woman's job, standing in for mummy like Sir Edwin here. Now, most women have their change at just about the same time as their children are growing up and leaving them, so if Sir Edwin's going to have one, it'll happen now. Elder daughter getting married – just the time when her mother would have been going funny and having all those operations. As surrogate mother, he must do it instead."

"*Angel*," said Carton, who was getting rather restless and was not at all sure how seriously Vanessa's theory should be taken.

"And if you throw in a dose of jealousy to help unsettle him – "

" – Are you suggesting he'll go potty like your friend's papa?"

"Not potty. Odd. It can take a number of forms – like this boozing today. One thing which happens at the change of life is they start taking to the bottle."

Carton Weir dilated his eyeballs at her, then led on firmly to the Canteloupe group, which had now been rejoined by the dowager. Canteloupe, who was panting slightly, snatched at the glass of champagne. Donald flashed vicious annoyance at Vanessa and went on being ponderously bonhomous to the marchioness. The dowager offered wedding canapés all round out of her handbag and then, taking an immediate fancy to Vanessa and having an instinct for likely informants, propelled her on to one side to ask questions about Tom Llewyllyn's private life. Carton Weir, keeping a careful eye on Canteloupe, considered Vanessa's theory about Sir Edwin.

It was, of course, preposterous; but there was no doubt that the Minister had been soaking up champagne – out of a tumbler at that. Smaller things than this had been known to herald important changes in important men. . . .

"So that's fixed," Sir Edwin was saying to Rupert Percival.

"What is?" said Percival, who was being wary.

"That I'll drive over and talk to you on Monday. Before I go up to London."

Suddenly Sir Edwin felt exhausted. If only they'd all go away; Patricia, Tom, Dixon, Percival, the lot. Go away and leave him in peace. Never mind Lloyd-James and his threats, never mind squaring this smug provincial solicitor, never mind this abominable wedding and the concomitant follies: sleep, that was the thing, sleep. . . . Come, come, this wouldn't do. In a minute or two he must make a speech, he must pull himself together, life must go on to the last, what he needed was more champagne.

"Alastair," he said to Dixon in a brittle voice, "please get me something to drink."

Dixon, accustomed by years of political life to fagging and bootlicking, took the empty tumbler and moved away. Percival, who had long since sensed an ulterior motive behind the Minister's attentions and regarded Dixon's despatch as the preliminary to a private assault, bristled and made ready.

"Yes?" he said sharply.

"Yes what?" sighed Sir Edwin.

"Your proposal – to visit me on Monday – is a little sudden. I'm not very clear as to its purpose."

"Exchange of ideas. It's always a good thing for those of us at the centre of the party to hear what you're thinking down in the constituencies."

"It's a long time since anyone of your . . . eminence . . . has shown such an interest."

"Too long perhaps," muttered the Minister. Where was Dixon with that drink?

"We aren't fools," Percival said. "We know that this kind of interest . . . this condescension . . . is only the preface to some demand. Why can't you leave us in peace?"

"I sympathise with your attitude, believe me."

"Then why not leave us in peace?"

"Because something has come up . . . to disturb the peace."

"Ah. So there is something you want."

Dixon returned with the Minister's champagne. In a wine glass, Sir Edwin regretfully noticed: what had he done with that commodious tumbler? And then, Percival's not giving much away, he thought: how will he react? After all he's no catch-penny moralist, he's one of us, one of the old guard, he should be able to take it. But with these country chappies one could never tell; they might turn out to be the most colossal prudes, or they might develop some kind of feudal mania and start asking for earldoms. Not, he gathered, that Percival was the type who asked for things . . . and so much the worse. But he was really too tired to consider the details now. He would give the fellow some idea and leave the rest till Monday. Sir Edwin drank off his champagne and for a moment felt slightly better.

"We need your help," he said in a level voice: "don't we, Alastair?"

Dixon, as yet unconscious of the real issues at stake, assented with a practised air of conviction.

"In what respect?" said Percival.

"Over your choice of a successor to Alastair here."

"Indeed," said Percival, his eyes rippling with hostility: "not a topic for a wedding breakfast."

"No," said Sir Edwin suavely: "for Monday."

Trained to achieve the last word (and thus to leave every contest, if not victorious, at least for the time undefeated), he turned before Percival could answer and moved off to arrange for the speeches to start. As he went he passed Peter Morrison, who was talking, he noticed, to that odd chap with one eye.

Still euphoric from the last glass of champagne, he smiled genially, forgetting that Morrison was now an obstacle which must, at any cost, be shifted.

"Well, well," said Peter to Fielding. "Earlier on he hardly knew me. What's all this you were trying to tell me in the church? About Somerset?"

"That he'll be a tricky opponent."

"Not news, Fielding."

"I dare say not. But there's one thing more." Fielding lowered his head slightly. His good eye was both amused and shifty. "Mind you," he said, "Somerset's been kind to me since I've been back. But it seems to me from what I've heard . . . from what Llewyllyn and others have been saying . . . that it would be better if you were given the seat at Bishop's Cross."

"Better?"

"Yes. The House of Commons may no longer enjoy much esteem, but there are limits, and they don't include Somerset. So for old times' sake I've something to tell you."

Peter said nothing but turned his enormous face full on to Fielding.

"Something," Fielding went on, "about yourself rather than Somerset. Something which your supporters are too close to you to see. Or perhaps too respectful to mention."

"Well?"

"Just this. Your trouble is that you're such a frightful bloody prig. Oh, I know what you're going to say," he continued steadily as Peter opened his mouth to speak; "you're going to say that I've hardly seen you in fourteen years, so what can I know about it? Well, I've always followed your career, more recently I've listened to friends of yours in London, and just now I've spent the afternoon watching you and your wife. So I'll say it again, Peter. You're a pompous, self-satisfied prig. All this prate about duty and honour and loyalty, and not a row of beans to show for it. Nothing: except for this resignation three years ago – just when things were beginning to look difficult. You're so infatuated with your own vision of yourself that you think it's beneath you to make an effort, to do something concrete. You won't lift a finger – in case you spoil your pose. Say what you like about Somerset, at least he joins in. He's not afraid to get his hands blistered."

"Or dirty. I thought you were on my side," said Peter, sweaty and flushed.

"I am. That's why I'm telling you that it's no good just sitting on your arse and expecting to be wafted back into Parliament on clouds of virtue like a baroque picture of God."

"Decency imposes certain rules."

"So does necessity. First you've got to get back. Then you can start talking about decency – and I grant you that a little's badly needed. But for God's sake stop being so self-righteous and get yourself moving. Otherwise Somerset's going to walk all over you."

"So he's just been telling me."

"There you go again. The retort courteous. It's no good any more. People don't want your unruffled gentleman act, all patronising and paternal, they want interference, action, indignation – even pettiness, so that they know you're one of them."

"At Bishop's Cross they're still rather old-fashioned."

"Not so old-fashioned that they want to send a stuffed dummy to Westminster."

"I think," said Peter, irritated but kind, "that you had better stick to what you know about. I liked your last piece in *Strix.*"

"Don't change the subject. It's always the same with you people who inherit money when you're young, nobody contradicts you and you soon start thinking you're Christ Al – "

" – Isn't there some talk of a book?" persisted Peter, knowing just where and how close under the surface vanity would lie.

"Two books as it happens. But we're not talk – "

" – Who's publishing them?"

"Gregory Stern. And I'm writing another one for him," said Fielding, his face becoming fatuous with conceit, Peter's shortcomings now graciously dismissed. Capitulation, Peter thought: what is it about writers that makes them so naïve, as if they thought that writing books was the only worthwhile occupation and that the whole world talked of nothing else? Self-absorption, he presumed; their careers, to be fair, were so difficult and precarious that without their egotism to protect them they wouldn't survive a week.

"Stern's over there with Detterling," Peter said. "I thought he looked very well as best man. Let's go and have a word."

On their way over they were joined by Tessie Buttock, who felt that she now had certain proprietary rights in Fielding. Stern, who looked a little tense, nevertheless bowed to Tessie with princely elegance when she was introduced.

"So you're the guardian angel of my authors?" he said. "I've often heard about you from Tom."

But since mention of Tom seemed likely to reduce Tessie to tears again, the subject was changed.

"I've got to make a speech," Stern said. "I've been trying to think of an original joke."

"There are none," said Detterling: "not for this occasion." The topic foundered.

"I see," said Detterling after a pause, "that Donald Salinger is keen to ingratiate himself with Canteloupe."

"Business, dear," said Jonathan Gamp, who had suddenly appeared in their midst. "Donald's printing the posters about Canteloupe's caravans, and he's hoping there'll be more where that came from. He's been steadily losing business for the last three years . . . ever since he got rid of Jude Holbrook."

"Jude Holbrook?" said Fielding with a glance at Tessie.

Jonathan, who had never met Fielding, started a polite explanation.

"Jude was Donald's partner, you see. Until he put up a whopping great black. But the thing is, he really did understand business, so after he disappeared – and disappeared is the *mot juste* – poor old Donald started running downhill. Slowly, mind you. Donald's no fool, it's just that he hasn't got the thrust Jude had, won't ever take a risk."

"Would it amuse you," said Fielding, "to hear that Jude Holbrook's back in London?"

"It would not," said Detterling, "but it would interest me. I wonder what he's up to."

"He pays regular," Tessie put in; "and no dragging back."

"Need he be up to anything?" Fielding asked.

"Oh yes, dear," mewed Jonathan, wriggling his hips with pleasure. "Jude hasn't come to London for the bracing air, you may depend upon that. Tell us *more*."

"Nothing to tell. He's taken a room with Tessie here and keeps himself to himself."

"Never stops for a chat," Tessie said. "Hardly says good morning some days."

"I *wonder*," Jonathan said.

Helen came to stand by Peter.

"I've been talking to Patricia Llewyllyn," she told him, "and some of the bridesmaids. Patricia's worried stiff about something. I hadn't met her before, so I couldn't press – "

There was a loud rapping and a call for silence. Stern went white; though he always acquitted himself beautifully on these occasions, he suffered torments of nerves beforehand. Alfie Schroeder belched loudly. "SSSHHH," everybody went. Sir Edwin, standing on a chair, began to speak. His voice was without tone of any kind, without authority, without warmth, like the thin, level drone (Fielding thought) with which the ghostly heroes greeted Odysseus from the banks of hell.

"I have an announcement to make," Sir Edwin said. "The house is on fire. Those that wish may leave through the door on to the terrace."

He pointed to the exit in question, got down from the chair, and started talking, as if nothing at all had happened, to a lady in a vast yellow hat.

"There's a nice thing," Tessie said, "to happen on Tom's wedding day."

But neither she nor anyone else made any effort to move. Apart from the conversation being rather muted, while people tried to remember what they had been discussing and take it up again, everything went on as before. It seemed generally agreed that Sir Edwin's interruption could be ignored.

"Bonkers," Vanessa Salinger was saying to the dowager: "the house is no more on fire than I am. I knew he was going funny."

"There *is* rather a smell of burning," said the younger Lady Canteloupe.

"Only cigarette smoke," said Donald, who had a horror of fires and was looking slightly peculiar.

"Gamp's cigarette," said Weir, remembering.

He hurried away past the bar, peered into the inner room through which the queue had stretched, and returned grinning.

"The carpet's caught," he said, "and there's a large sofa smouldering."

"That doesn't mean the house is on fire," Vanessa sniffed: "sheer exaggeration."

"Ought it to be put out?"

"Turbot must have seen it, otherwise he wouldn't have made that speech. So I expect he's made arrangements. Told the servants or something."

"Then why did he ask us to leave?"

"He didn't. He only suggested."

"I think," said Vanessa, who had been watching Tom and his new bride talking together in one corner with anxious faces, "that there's more in all this than meets the eye."

Lord Canteloupe was taking advantage of this diversion among his attendants.

"Can you get me a drink?" he said to a passing waiter.

"Sorry, my lord."

"What do you mean, sorry."

"Been told to drop everything and look for Miss Isobel. Sharpish."

"Miss Isobel can take care of herself."

"But the house is on fire, my lord."

"It's nothing of the kind. Please get me a drink."

"I'm only a servant here, my lord. Which means I believe what Sir Edwin says and do what he tells me."

And indeed, as the waiter moved away (none too eagerly, Canteloupe noticed), smoke started wafting into the reception room and with it a faint uneasiness among the weaker-minded guests.

"Do you suppose he really meant it?" said Tessie.

"It can't be anything much," Jonathan Gamp assured her. "I expect someone's dropped a cigarette."

"I think," said Gregory Stern, "that everyone feels it would be bad form to show panic. So no one can be the first to move, and they'll all roast to death rather than commit a social solecism. Very English."

Alfie Schroeder, who was perfectly prepared to commit a social solecism, hovered near the glass door on to the terrace, where he was joined by Tessie.

"Quite right, love," Alfie said. "Much the safest place."

"But what *is* going on?" bleated Tessie.

"If you want my opinion," Detterling was saying to Stern, "the motivation is slightly different. Refusal, by members of a ruling caste, to acknowledge that *they* could be inconvenienced. Therefore they must behave as if the fire did not exist. There was an officer in my regiment who was once mortally offended because a soda-siphon ran out while he was using it. He regarded it as a kind of insolence on the part of the siphon. That's what this fire is – a piece of insolence on the part of nature, to be pointedly ignored until it gets ashamed of itself and goes away."

Meanwhile the smoke grew thicker. Vanessa Salinger, who wasn't quite well enough bred to know that the fire mustn't be acknowledged, coughed and attracted pitying glances. The dowager selected from her handbag a canapé of a curious mauve and sat down to enjoy it.

"I think your theory is over-sophisticated," Fielding Gray was saying to Detterling. "I think this is more like a nasty smell in a car. You just drive on and hope for the best."

"Same thing," Detterling commented. "*My* car wouldn't *dare* break down. A member of the lower class, on the other hand, would get out to see what the matter was."

"Only," contributed Peter Morrison, "because he would know about engines and we don't."

They were joined by Somerset Lloyd-James.

"It reminds me of the time John Dorsetshire tried to kill himself," he remarked. "In full view of everyone at Newmarket, but they all thought it would be impolite to take any notice. They left him on the ground, I'm told, until after the result of the photo-finish was announced."

"That's because they were too interested in the photo-finish . . . unlike poor Dorsetshire. He knew where *his* horse had come in."

"They do say it was slowed down by one of the bookies."

At this stage Sir Edwin got up on the chair again. This time he was more animated.

"Ladies and gentlemen," he said, "I fully appreciate the delicacy of feeling which prompted you to ignore my first warning. But now, since the fire-brigade will be here at any moment, and since they will require space in which to manoeuvre . . ."

As Sir Edwin's courteous speech droned on, Alfie and Tessie, standing by the glass door, witnessed the following sequence of events. Along the road, which was visible beyond

some 300 yards of down-sloping meadow and which led to
the entrance of Sir Edwin's drive, came a large black limousine,
which Alfie correctly assumed to be the hired car that was to
take the newlyweds the fifteen miles to Salisbury station.
Behind the limousine, clanging its bell but unable to pass
because of the narrowness of the road, came a fire-engine of a
design which Alfie had not seen since the blitz. When the
limousine was still about a quarter of a mile from Sir Edwin's
gate, there was a loud roar from the area of the stables on the
other side of the house, and a few seconds later an open
sports car of blue and white, rather like a giant co-respondent's
shoe, could be seen by Alfie and Tessie shooting down the
drive. At the wheel was a young man whom neither of them
knew; next to him was a girl dressed in the striking shade of
green affected for the occasion by the bridesmaids.

"That's the chief one," Tessie said, "the one who was taking
care of the little boy in the kilt."

"I know," said Alfie with grim satisfaction.

As the sports car hurtled down the drive towards the gate,
it was hidden from the limousine on the road by thickets of
rhododendron, while its noise (Alfie presumed) was drowned
by the clanging of the fire-engine. The chauffeur of the
limousine was therefore quite unprepared for the emergence
of the sports car, which, without any pause and doing about
fifty miles an hour, shot out in a wide left-handed turn on to
the limousine's side of the road and then made straight for it.
True, the driver of the sports car was steering it back on to
the proper side of the road, and succeeded in gaining this
without hitting the limousine; but by that time the limousine
had braked very sharply and the fire-engine had run into it
from behind. The sports car – God knows how it squeezed
through on the narrow road, Alfie thought – did not stop
but roared away in the direction from which the limousine
and fire-engine had been approaching; a dazed chauffeur
lurched out of the limousine and tottered to the rear; some

men climbed off the fire-engine and began to inspect a twisted figure which seemed somehow to be impaled against the back of its open driving seat; and that, Alfie thought, is one poor bugger's one-way ticket home.

"And so," Sir Edwin was saying, "if you will kindly proceed on to the terrace . . ."

I told Tom, Alfie thought, to get away before anything happened; and now this. Not that it was quite what I expected, but it will serve even more surely to delay him.

"Oughtn't we to tell someone?" Tessie said.

Alfie nodded. First things first, he thought. Get this absurd fire put out, and then tell them about the girl and the rest of it. He pushed his way through the crowd to where the Minister was still politely perorating from the chair. Since Alfie was short, his head hardly reached Sir Edwin's knees; so he tugged at one tail of his morning coat, and was brushed off like a fly.

"It will not, of course, be possible to have the usual speeches before we go outside," Sir Edwin was saying, "and there will be logistic difficulties about refreshment. But if you will take your glasses with you and congregate at the southeast corner of the lawn, we will contrive to drink a toast. Thank you."

Sir Edwin got down from the chair and was rather surprised to see Alfie get up in his place.

"Ladies and gentlemen," Alfie said. "The fire-engine has had an accident. It can't get here."

No one disputed this, and there was a buzz of tired interest.

"Why didn't you say so straight away?" said Sir Edwin. "I'll go and telephone for another."

But as Alfie had anticipated, there were those who favoured action more direct. The Minister's first speech had simply been a scientific proposition, but his more recent mention of the fire-engine had constituted social recognition (so to speak) of the fire, and it was now permissible to have dealings with it. While Tom escorted Patricia, who was still talking at him intently, to safety with Tessie by the glass door, Captain Detterling picked up two buckets of melted ice and marched through to the conflagration. Peter and Fielding did likewise. Somerset took the opportunity of going over to the Canteloupe group to tease Donald Salinger, who had been nervous about fires ever since his hair was set alight during a drunken party at Oxford. Detterling came back out of the inner room.

"It's taken quite a hold," he said: "find all the buckets you can."

Fielding came after him.

"The water's been cut off. I've been through to the kitchen. . . ."

"It often happens," said Sir Edwin conversationally, "about this time of the afternoon. They're laying new pipes."

"The stables?"

"It will be the same there."

"Only one thing for it, Edwin," said the dowager. "Use the champagne."

"The *champagne*?"

"*Not* a time for economy."

Canteloupe came to life.

"Champagne," he roared.

He ran behind the bar, had two bottles open within seconds, took a swig from each, then rushed through to the fire and started hosing it with a twin frothy stream.

"More," he called from within.

"Champagne," the cry went up.

With gay abandon bottles were opened and passed down an improvised chain gang to where Canteloupe, supported by Weir and the dowager, poured the amber fluid through clouds of steam on to the immense sofa and large areas of carpet.

"About all it's fit for," Canteloupe was saying, though treating himself to copious gulps.

"More . . . more," howled the dowager.

"Over there in the corner," Weir said: "there's something odd behind the writing desk. . . . I can't quite see. . . ."

"Nonsense. Finish the sofa first."

In the reception room Alfie took Tom on one side.

"The chief bridesmaid," he said: "it *was* your sister-in-law?"

"Yes. Patricia's very worried because she's been behaving oddly . . . disappeared somewhere after the service."

"She's disappeared in the rough direction of Bristol," Alfie said, "doing about ninety miles an hour in a sports car which is driven by a young man who'll have manslaughter to answer for."

Alfie explained.

"Isobel has peculiar friends," was all Tom could find to say.

"Have you seen my little boy," a harassed woman was asking them, "the page in the kilt? Isobel Turbot was taking care of him, but she seems – "

" – I should look in the garden," said Tom gently.

The woman hurried off.

"Upstairs?" said Alfie.

"Perhaps. 'Now, darling,' " Tom said in a clumsy parody of Isobel, " 'Auntie Isobel's got to go. So you walk through there to find all the nice people. . . .' "

"But he couldn't have been – "

Tom set off down the champagne chain and into the smoke.

"Have you seen the page?" he shouted at Weir.

"The page," the cry went back along the chain, "the page."

"There's something behind the desk."

"*Oh my God.*"

The smoke was thicker now. Tom blundered over to the desk.

"The champagne's run out." "Has anyone seen the page?" "There's some men at the door with a stretcher and – er –

something on it." "A chauffeur, out of his wits with temper."
". . . The page. . . ."

Tom hauled out a small, dirty, blubbering figure in a kilt.

"What were you doing there, laddie? Why didn't you call
for help?"

"The man told me to hide. Half an hour, he said, and if I
didn't he'd find me one day and cut my head off."

On the lawn, after comfort had been administered by
paternal Alfie and then by Mummy, the rest of the story came
jerking out.

"This man. . . . Auntie Isobel's friend. . . . He said, here's
five bob for you, duckie, and you go and hide, and don't tell
anyone we've gone for a good half hour, that's what he said,
or I'll find you one day and I'll – "

" – Yes, yes. What was he like?"

"He had a funny bottle he kept drinking from. And he
smelt nasty when he talked."

But Auntie Isobel had liked him well enough, it seemed,
and had been expecting him, because they'd gone specially to
the stables to find him, and Auntie Isobel had put her arms
round him straight away and gone umshlllppp all over his
face. And then the man had had a drink from his funny bottle
and had said something about leaving a letter or something,
but Auntie Isobel said "No". So then the man had gone
umshlllppp all over Auntie Isobel's face, and after that Auntie
Isobel had gone all funny and hadn't said anything. So the
man had given him the letter and also the five-shillings, and
told him to hide, and he'd hidden, and then the smoke. . . .

Tom took the letter from the page and started to read it.
A second fire-engine came clanging up the drive. An angry
man in a chauffeur's hat stamped across the lawn.

"Who was it?" he shouted, shaking his fist at Alfie. "It
was someone from here. Who was it?"

"Ask him," said Alfie pointing at Tom.

"Isobel and I are in love and are going to be married,"

Tom was reading. "We hope for your consent, and that everything will be pleasant about money and so on. When you agree to this, just put a line in the Personal Column of *The Times*, 'All is forgiven. T.', and we'll come back. Meanwhile we'll be living together as man and wife, so the sooner you agree the better. And of course there are other reasons for us all to be friendly, as you well know. So please don't turn nasty and try to follow us, or get some doddering judge to issue an injunction. Let's all be sensible and make the best of what we've got, which is quite a lot when all's said."

> Yours sincerely,
> Mark Lewson. Isobel sends love.

The chauffeur came at Tom from one side, Sir Edwin from the other. Firemen came round the house with hoses. Some men appeared on the terrace and put down a stretcher which bore a suggestive object wrapped in a dirty blanket. The page boy observed this and was led away howling. Sir Edwin took the letter from Tom – "Mine, if I'm not mistaken" – and started to read. The chauffeur shook his fist.

"Who was it? That's what I want to know."

"Apparently," said Tom, "it was a man called Le – "

" – We don't know," said Sir Edwin, looking coolly up from the letter. "A stranger. Not one of the guests."

"But 'e was going to tell me." A nod at Tom.

"He's had a bad shock. His wedding's been ruined and he doesn't know what he's saying."

" 'E looks all right to me," the chauffeur said, and drew up to Sir Edwin with unmistakable menace.

"I am Sir Edwin Turbot, a minister of the Queen. If you lay hands on me, you'll go to prison for the longest sentence Her Majesty's Courts can award. You would be better employed summoning the police."

Sir Edwin turned and beckoned Tom to follow him. The chauffeur approached Alfie.

"Something odd going on, mate."

Alfie said nothing but looked anxiously after Tom.

"Why – ?" Tom began.

"It must be kept quiet," Sir Edwin said.

"It can't be."

"Not about Isobel, I agree. But no one must know who's with her."

"Why not?"

Sir Edwin snuffled and shook his head without speaking.

"Why not?" persisted Tom. "He's a wanted man. Over there on the terrace there's a – "

" – Did anyone recognise the driver as Lewson?"

"No, but now we know it was him – "

"No, we don't," Sir Edwin said. "You just help clear up the mess and get everyone out of the place. And when the police come, send them straight to me."

Very soon, the fire was brought under control, the guests were dismissed ("My favourite wedding ever," said Jonathan Gamp), the police were received, witnesses questioned, and statements taken.

"Saw them driving off but didn't know him from Adam," said Alfie, who along with Tessie and the page had stayed behind to help the enquiries.

"A funny bottle," the kilted page repeated, "and a nasty smell."

"So *that's* plain enough," the Inspector said. "You run off to mummy." And to Tessie, "You saw him, madam?"

"First time in my life. No idea who he was."

"So he can't have been at the wedding. What about this letter the little lad talked about? Might tell us who the fellow was."

"The page dropped the letter in the fire – when he was rescued," Sir Edwin deposed.

Both Tom and Alfie opened their mouths. Then they shut

them; Tom because Sir Edwin was now his father-in-law and must be given a chance to explain himself in private, Alfie because he trusted Tom and was prepared, for the time at least, to follow his lead.

"Well, it shouldn't take us long to find them," said the Inspector. "Mind you, it would be a help if we had the number. But a blue and white open sports car – conspicuous, I'd say."

That was what Sir Edwin was afraid of; but evening yielded to night, night to morning, morning to afternoon again, and there was still no word. Meanwhile it was agreed that the start of the wedding tour should be postponed – "It seem's there's one honeymoon in the family already," as Sir Edwin grimly remarked – and that Patricia and Tom should stay with Sir Edwin until the situation had been made plainer. On her wedding night, so long, so lovingly, so greedily awaited, Patricia turned away: "not now," she implored him: "not yet."

8

A BEAST IN VIEW

"RIGHT," SAID Lord Canteloupe to Carton Weir: "now for a little word with the staff."

They were in the Quantocks inspecting the completed caravan site, which was due for its ceremonial opening in three days' time. They had inspected the dance-hall-cum-gymnasium, the swimming pool ("Fed by Clear Mountain Waters"), the dinette, the nursery-crêche, the project and discussion centre, and the Maison Bingo. This latter had rather a contrived air, since it had been popped up at the last moment as a result of Canteloupe's recent decision that Bingo should be included in what he called his Country Culture; but all in all the camp's outer periphery, of which the Maison Bingo and the other amenities formed the greater part, was a credit to the Scheme, especially if one considered how quickly it had all been run up. The shock had come when they started inspecting the caravans and sanitary appointments in the central body of the camp, a shock in no way palliated by the attitudes of Camp Commandant Hookeby (an ex-lieutenant-colonel, once mildly celebrated as the laziest officer in the Royal Corps of Signals), who was showing them round.

The first thing that had been wrong was that half the caravans had no wheels and were supported by piles of oil cans and similar detritus.

"It's not as if they're ever going to move," said the Camp Commandant.

"Looks bloody awful," said Canteloupe. "Anyway, where are the wheels?"

"The peasants stole them," said Hookeby, gesturing out over Somersetshire, "before I arrived to take over."

"Then get new ones and post a piquet."

Hookeby nodded wisely, then sealed one nostril with his forefinger and winked at Carton behind Canteloupe's back.

"My wife," Hookeby said, "maintains that you can't trust the natives."

Canteloupe snorted and climbed into a caravan. Then came the next disillusionment. At the second step inside his foot had gone straight through the floor.

"They don't season the wood these days," the Commandant explained. "Too impatient to get their money back on it. It's the same with cricket bats, I'm told."

Again he winked at Carton, who despite his official dignity started sniggering like a school-girl. He had not expected such a bonus of entertainment.

The next caravan which Canteloupe inspected had survived the ordeal but turned out to be concealing a large pile of decaying sandwiches in a clothes cupboard.

"Contractors' men," said Hookeby cheerfully: "filthy brutes."

"Get it cleaned up."

"The man's off ill."

"Then clean it up yourself."

By this time Weir had recovered his gravity. If something went wrong at the opening, Canteloupe would be in trouble and so would he. And so now, as they moved towards the showers and the rears, which were at the very centre of the site ("The heart of camp life," smirked Hookeby), he began to think about ways of dissociating himself from the department at short notice.

The first shower, when tested, had spat rusty water like a snake, shuddered, and gone dead. The second, on the other hand, performed with such crazed intensity that the spray had shot off the pipe and hit Carton hard on the knee; further-more, it refused to be turned off.

" 'And here's the interesting bit,' " Hookeby quoted: " 'There was no way of stopping it. . . .' "

Canteloupe snorted at him and led the way to the toilets. As they entered someone slouched resentfully past them on his way out. This someone had a huge, yellow, drooping moustache, carried a pile of Sunday newspapers, was smoking a pipe and chewing something at the same time, was also buttoning his trousers, and made no attempt at greeting.

"Who in the name of God was that?"

"Sergeant-Major Cruxtable," said Hookeby: "physical fit-ness and so on. I think we caught him at what he calls his 'time'."

This had been the last straw. Canteloupe looked at the retreating Cruxtable, he looked at Hookeby, he looked down the long rows of partitions, turned away with a slight heave, and at last he looked, as if here at least he had hoped for sanity and support, at Carton Weir.

"Right," he said grimly and sadly: "now for a little word with the staff."

This was all too easily arranged. Since the refuse man was absent with what he termed "haemorrhoids" and the boiler man with varicose veins, since the cook and her two assistant sluts were not due until the next day and the Camp Matron was out to lunch with a colleague at the nearby mental home, there were left with Cruxtable, Mrs. Hookeby (a chinless, mem-sahibish woman whose role was not very clearly defined), and Hookeby himself. These being duly assembled in the project and discussion room, Canteloupe said:

"This place is a pig-sty. I have no alternative but to stay here myself until we open, in order to bring things into a condition befitting the honour which Her Royal Highness will pay us."

There was something rather magnificent about him as he

said this, something which even Hookeby and Cruxtable seemed to sense. As for Carton, he was reminded that Canteloupe had organised the most famous and profitable "Stately Home" of them all, and now he saw one reason why. If no one else would do the job properly, Canteloupe would see to it himself. Repenting of the disloyal thoughts which he had entertained earlier in the afternoon, noticing that he had unconsciously come to attention during his chief's short speech, Carton inclined his head to hear his instructions.

"You'll be no good here," said Canteloupe dismissively, "so go back to London and handle things there. Call in at my place on your way and send the car back here with a camp bed and a dozen of burgundy. I suppose," he snapped at Hookeby, "you can feed me?"

"Sir," Hookeby said.

"Off with you then," said Canteloupe to Weir; to Hookeby, "Get me that contractor on the telephone – Sunday or no Sunday"; to Cruxtable, "Find a suit of overalls and report back in five minutes"; and to Mrs. Hookeby, "You too, madam – with a bucket and a mop."

Sir Edwin Turbot had originally opined that Mark Lewson would be easier to deal with, since all he wanted was money, than Somerset Lloyd-James. The situation had now changed. In the first place, it now appeared that Lewson was demanding his daughter as well as his gold, and Sir Edwin was disinclined to concede her. But in the second place, if the police found Isobel for him, they would also find Lewson, which would not do at all; for there was a strong chance that Lewson, desperate and illogical, would seek to distract attention from his crime by revealing his secret.

Another problem was what to tell his son-in-law. Tom had so far kept quiet, out of deference to himself, about the identity of the hit and run driver; but if this silence was to be maintained, Tom must have an explanation. Yet what could he be told? Certainly not the truth, or anything near it. There was really only one thing to do: he would have to appeal to Tom's loyalty as a member of the family, and on that basis ask for his trust. And his help, which would be badly needed. And if Tom showed signs of restlessness, then Patricia must be told off to deal with him. After all, she was his wife, his newly wedded wife, and Tom (to judge by his grave and loving demeanour in the church) would surely heed her.

With all this in mind, the Minister summoned both Tom and Patricia to his study.

"You've seen the morning's papers?" he began. "Rather hostile, I thought."

"Perhaps," said Tom, "you should have issued a fuller statement. They feel thwarted. The police have had the devil's own job keeping them out of here over the week-end."

Sir Edwin looked thoughtfully at the paper which lay nearest to hand:

MINISTER'S DAUGHTER BOLTS WITH MR. X
Hit and Run Elopement.

"They seem to have enough to be going on with," he said: "what else could I tell them?"

"Yes," said Patricia, protective. "What else could Daddy have told them?"

"The press is the self-appointed guardian of public morality. In such cases, it likes to assure its readers that steps are being taken to uphold that morality . . . that chastity and family honour are being defended."

"But what could Daddy have done?"

"He could have obtained an injunction against Isobel's abductor."

"But if we don't know who he is?"

Tom and Sir Edwin exchanged glances.

"We do know who he is," said Sir Edwin with a small sigh. "He's called Lewson." He did not remind her of Lewson's visit with Somerset Lloyd-James as he did not wish Tom to know of this. Nor, as it happened, did Patricia, who was conscious that she had cut a very foolish figure on that occasion.

"Then why haven't you told the police?" she said.

"Because I don't want him to be caught," said Sir Edwin flatly.

"Why not?"

"I must say, sir," said Tom: "we are entitled to know."

"It's a matter of tactics," said Sir Edwin, firm and glib. "Here I am, a senior Minister of the Crown. My younger daughter has run off with a man at present unknown who is wanted for drunken driving . . . worse, for manslaughter. If they are caught together, investigation and trial will take months and Isobel's name will become indissolubly associated with a vicious lout and a scandalous case in the criminal courts. My position would be intolerable and I should have to resign."

He snapped open a packet of chocolate biscuits. In his way he was enjoying himself.

"But if," he continued, "we can contrive quietly to bring her back without anyone's assistance . . . and if the young man disappears still unknown . . . then the whole affair will die down, Isobel will be seen as injured innocence, or at worst as folly repentant, the fatted calf can be killed with discreet advertisement, and no more need be said."

"And the dead man?" Patricia said.

"That wasn't Isobel's fault or ours. Nothing we can do will bring him back. Best concentrate on our own essential problem – which is to avoid any further fuss."

He's lying, Tom thought. All this is plausible enough in its way, but it's not the whole truth. With the means at his command, he could get Isobel accepted as "injured innocence" without protecting Mark Lewson. There's something else. But before he could voice this suspicion in suitably ambiguous terms, Sir Edwin had passed from exposition to appeal.

"So I'm asking you, Tom," he was saying, "to find them. Find them, see Lewson on his way, out of the country if that's still possible, and bring Isobel back here. Of course it's a damned shame about your honeymoon – "

" – What makes you think I can find him?"

"Because you've got to. For my sake . . . and Patricia's."

"How?"

"Put yourself in his place. Ask yourself what you'd have done in his position."

"If you'll play fair by me – " Tom began.

"Of course Daddy will play fair by you," said Patricia, not understanding the hidden query.

"I meant, if your father will . . ."

He hesitated.

"Will what?"

"Undertake to deal . . . truthfully – "

" – What do you mean?" Patricia blazed. "Daddy's told us what the position is and what must be done. If you're the man I married two days ago, you'll not sit there hedging and hair-splitting, you'll get off your backside and see to it."

Tom looked at her, red and spluttering as she was, ashamed for her sister and anxious for her father, cruelly disappointed and shocked by this grotesque interruption to her happiness; and suddenly he felt pity enter into him, so sharply and brutally that it might have been a needle at the base of his spine. He had been, as it were, violated by compassion.

"Very well," he said. "I'll start at once. Come with me, love, and help me pack a case."

"One thing," the Minister called after him.

"Sir?"

"Your journalist friend, Schroeder. What does he know?"

"He knows we've suppressed that letter which was left with the page boy. So he'll be suspicious."

"What will he do about it?"

"Nothing," said Tom, "until I've spoken with him."

"What will you say?"

"I shall ring him up and ask him to join me in Salisbury or Bath."

"Join you?"

"To help me."

"But discretion," said Sir Edwin, taken aback: "the fewer people who are involved . . ."

"Alfie's already involved," said Tom. "If I put it to him, he'll probably be prepared to see it your way . . . if only for my sake. Provided, of course, he thinks you're on the level."

He took Patricia's hand and led her out. Well, Sir Edwin thought, I suppose I had it as much of my own way as I could reasonably expect. He took a handful of chocolate biscuits from the packet. Patty was rather a brick, he thought, cupping a biscuit securely into his hand and slapping it into his mouth; when the family's in trouble she forgets her silly moral fads and becomes a real Turbot. Should be a great help if things get tiresome later . . . if Llewyllyn and that journalist of his . . .

But never mind all that now, he thought; I've done what I can. With the practised insouciance of his calling, he dismissed Isobel and Lewson altogether from his mind and turned to the next item on the agenda. In just two hours' time he would be seeing Rupert Percival: how best to win his backing for Lloyd-James?

Max de Freville received a letter from Isobel.

". . . Mark and I are writing this together, among other things to thank you for your part in bringing us together. We know it sounds silly, but if things come right, about money and so on, we're going to be the happiest people that ever lived. Mark is so – super. I can't say anything more about him because he is looking over my shoulder as I write and it makes me feel a fool. Proud, but a fool.

"You'll have read about what happened at the wedding and drawn your own conclusions. Mark had been drinking – nerves, he said, and of course one doesn't elope every day. But it was frightful – though we'd no idea, until we saw the papers, that that poor fireman had been killed. Rotten luck, really, for everyone: that road is usually empty for days at a time. Mark feels horrible about it; but we both agree that there's no point in giving himself up at this stage. It wouldn't help anyone and it might spoil everything for us. Jolly lucky that according to the papers no one who saw us driving off knew who he was. And more luck: it seems no one had time to take the number of that car, so they can't trace us that way. But it's the sort of car which shows up rather, so Mark sold it for cash – no questions asked or answered – to a little man he knew of near Warminster, and took an old Morris shooting brake in part exchange. Mark says the little man will repaint it and anyhow keep it out of the way until the fuss dies down. What it is to know one's way around. But of course it might have been more sensible, for an elopement, to use a less prominent car in the first place. That's one of the things I love about Mark: he's awfully naive in so many ways, innocent almost.

"But whichever way you look at it, we shall have to lie low for some time. We can't go abroad, though Mark seems to have lots of money with him, because Daddy keeps my passport locked in the safe and I couldn't get at it. But Mark's thinking up a plan for hiding, he's superly clever at that. You must blend naturally with the surroundings, he says. Never hide under a table, sit down at it and start eating, and then no one will take a second look.

"And later on? Well, what we're hoping is that Daddy will play along with us, that because of this peculiar letter

he'll let us get married and give us some more money —
Mark's won't last for ever, he says, even if he has done quite
well just lately. I don't really see that Daddy can refuse, Mark
knowing what he does and being able to prove it, and it's a
good sign that he hasn't told the police who 'the hit and run
driver' is, though he must know because of the note we left
him. He daren't risk trouble, Mark says. So it really looks as
if there may be a happy ending. If only the police don't find
us. But of course it's *me* they're looking for, as they don't
know who else, so we're going to be cunning about that —
travelling separately and staying at different places, hardly
meeting at all until Mark's hit on the ideal place to hide. So
if they do find me, they still haven't found Mark, and what
can they do then?

"We're writing this in a wood outside a dear little village
near a place called Blandford. I'm going to take a bus later
on, and Mark will follow in the Morris — we're not quite sure
where, but that can be settled later. Because it is wonderful,
being in this wood with Mark, on this beautiful summer day
— hasn't it been a marvellous summer? — only the two of us
in all the world who know where we are, and only mattering
to each other. And that brings us to the last thing we've got
to tell you. Dear old Max, you've been so kind to us in your
way. I've had such fun writing to you all this time, and Mark's
enjoyed it too, not only the money you've paid. But now,
whatever happens, we've agreed it's got to finish. You see,
Mark and I are now *private*. Can you understand? Whatever
we may do, we shall be doing it so closely together that to
tell you would be, I don't know . . . Mark says exhibiting
ourselves, like a circus act, and from now on it's not going
to be like that any more. It was all right when we were
separate, it would even be all right if we didn't love each
other, but as it is . . . We do hope you understand.

        "Love from Isobel and Mark."

"Will he understand?" Isobel had said to Mark when she finished writing.

"I don't know. He's been very odd lately. I think perhaps . . . by the time he gets this . . . it won't matter to him."

"But we had to tell him," she said.

"Yes, we owed him that. If only all our debts could be so easily paid."

They both lay back. The mid-morning sun, penetrating a gap in the leaves, cast a small patch of light over Mark's eyes. He threw his arm across them, moaning slightly.

"You're still thinking of that man," she said. "You shouldn't. He died at once, the papers say."

She lifted his arm from his eyes and bent over him.

"But there must have been a moment, Isobel, a split second, when the pain . . . That shaft, driving through his body, smashing through the flesh and the tissue . . . So delicate, you see, and that brutal shaft, that was me, *driving* through. . . ."

"It's over now."

First to the left, then to the right, then back to the left again, she kissed his eyes until the horror left them.

About the same time as Isobel was kissing Mark in Dorsetshire, Somerset Lloyd-James received a telephone call in Gower Street.

"It's me, dear," said Maisie's voice, strained.

Although Maisie had instructions on no account to ring Somerset at his office, he did not waste time and make matters worse by reminding her of this. He simply said nothing, which conveyed his displeasure far more effectively.

"Can you hear me, dear?"

"Perfectly."

"I'm sorry. I know that you — Look," she said, and there was something desperate in her voice which pierced even Somerset's carapace of self-esteem. "You must come round. Please."

"This evening."

"Now."

Somerset had known Maisie for several years but he had never known her rattled or importunate. Now she was both. More; she was afraid and she was pleading. Trouble, thought Somerset: keep out of it. She's only a public whore, let her settle her own affairs, she's got no claim here: don't get involved.

"Can you hear me, Somerset?"

"This evening, I said."

"No, no, now."

If he rang off, she would only ring again. This was what came of being – well – distinguished. Sooner or later, however little you told them, people like Maisie saw your photograph in the paper, found out what you did, where you worked. You felt flattered, of course, but you told them not to take advantage, never to ring up, they agreed, and then – this. You should have changed your whore, he told himself, as soon as she found out who you were. Or had you yourself told her, late one night, boasting? He couldn't remember, it made no difference anyway, because . . .

"Somerset," shrilled the telephone, "*Somerset.*"

"I'm coming," he said.

Oh God, he prayed, as he walked down Gower Street searching for a taxi, if this is something the other side's thought up, some come back of Sir Edwin's (who could have told him about Maisie? Tom? but did Tom know? perhaps), then make me strong in cunning.

"Curzon Street. Near the cinema."

Presence of mind, O Lord, that's what I need. God damn the woman – sorry, Lord. Of course one should have foregone such childish pleasures long ago, but the flesh is weak, the member unruly, one had to think (Lord) of one's health. But if this turns out to be all right, a false alarm, just some bill she can't pay, then I promise that from now on – I'll get married, that's the best way. Whom shall I marry? He thought with mounting distaste of the three or four girls whom his father had from time to time recommended, tipped the driver two-pence ("Thanks for sod all, Guv"), rang Maisie's bell, and lifted his brown bowler hat to Maisie.

"Please be brief," he said as she closed the door behind him; "I've got a long morning's work."

She nodded, smiled nervously, led the way through to her sitting-room. He had never been in her flat during the morning before. It felt all wrong, cold and exposed. And yet the electric fire was burning, imitation log and all (Maisie knew he felt the cold, even in summer), the curtains were drawn, the corners of the room were in shadow, it might just as well have been afternoon or evening, so why this discomfiture? It was no longer irritation at being disturbed, not even curiosity, but a feeling of being out of place, worse, of being in an element wholly alien. Not a hostile element, exactly, because hostility he understood and this atmosphere was something which he could not understand, for all the cosy curtains, the familiar fire. No, this was worse than hostile: it was indifferent. It neither recognised him nor cared for him nor hated him nor understood him, any more than he understood it; but for some reason it had need of him. Was this how whores were when one did not bring money to pay for attention? Utterly indifferent, without sympathy or understanding of any kind? And yet, Maisie had always seemed a good-natured girl quite apart from the offices of her trade; and after all, it was she that had summoned him, apparently wanted his help, so she ought to make an effort to put him at ease, to dispel this . . . this fog of anonymity which flooded the room.

"Please be brief," he repeated.

"Gladly," said a man's voice.

Maisie smiled – weakly, guiltily, rather affectionately – and left the room.

"Jude Holbrook," the voice went on. "You remember me?"

"Yes."

But the name did nothing to restore normality. Even when the squat, remembered figure moved out of the shadow and stood in front of the electric fire, there was still total indifference in the room, the same impossibility of communication.

"Not that it matters," Holbrook was saying, "whether you remember me or not. What concerns us is . . . isolated. Nothing to do with past or the future. Just something that must happen . . . now."

"The sooner the better," said Somerset sincerely. "I'm a busy man."

"I must have that letter," Holbrook said, in a bored, courteous, reasonable voice.

"What letter?" said Somerset, bored, courteous, and reasonable in his turn.

"The one you bought from Lewson."

Somerset looked carefully at Holbrook and did not bother with denials or evasions.

"It isn't for sale," he said equably.

"I didn't suppose it was," said Holbrook in equable exchange. "All the same I must have it."

"What do you propose?"

"I propose that you hand it over to me. I don't want any . . . childishness."

"You've changed," said Somerset. "You are altogether less crude."

"The past is not at issue, as I've already told you. Such comparisons are irrelevant."

"Interesting though . . . if only one were at leisure. Good morning, Jude."

But the door was locked.

"You mustn't blame Maisie. I frightened her, you see."

He took a small bottle from his pocket.

"A little of this in her face and she'd be out of business," he said: "for good."

"My livelihood," said Somerset (Lord, give me strength), "is not so precarious."

Holbrook stepped softly up to Somerset, whipped his glasses off his face with the speed of a conjuror, and placed them carefully on the sofa behind him.

"I don't suppose you can see much now," he said casually: "your livelihood is more precarious than you think."

Somerset blinked and made a mild, deprecating movement with one hand.

"I suppose it's just possible," Holbrook was saying, "that a blind man might be elected to Parliament despite all the difficulties. But a blind editor. . . ."

He unscrewed a stopper from the little bottle, then, keeping the bottle vertical with the most delicate attention, raised it until it was just under Somerset's nose.

"How did you find out?" Somerset said.

"The usual way. I was given a strong scent and I used my nose to follow it. But let me repeat: we're not concerned with the past, only with what's happening now."

Now, Lord, now. Somerset lowered his head and butted. He felt a sickening pain in his bald scalp. He put both his hands over it, clasped them to make a helmet, butted again at nothing, and crashed to the floor.

"It will make a nasty blister on that pate of yours which will look very silly. And that was only a quick dab with the stopper. I did say I didn't want any childishness."

Somerset lay still.

"You can't cope with this sort of behaviour," said Holbrook affably. "You're clever enough and crooked enough to cope with almost anything – provided you can take plenty of time and proceed in your own way. The intellectual's way. But physical action . . . no. You don't understand it. You're not a coward – you've shown that. You're just incompetent."

He kicked Somerset carefully in the groin.

"That hurt," said Holbrook, "but not much, and it'll do no permanent damage. Any more than that blister on your bonce." He bent down and talked straight into Somerset's face. "It was much more difficult," he said, "just to raise a blister than to blind you. But I could do it because I have a talent. You have a talent too. You're as good at teasing, torturing, if necessary destroying, as I am – in your own abstract and cerebral way. But here, in this room, that way's no good. Mine's the way that counts."

He kicked Somerset with gentle precision at the base of the spine. Somerset's whole body stiffened as if in ecstasy. His hand shot out towards Holbrook's ankle.

"No, no, no," said Holbrook briskly.

He ground Somerset's hand with his heel.

"This just isn't your thing. As a rational man, you must see that."

He held the bottle over Somerset's face and began to tilt it.

"Very well," said Somerset, breathing heavily, "you shall have the letter. But I'd be interested to know what you want with it."

"That is for those who employ me to decide."

"If you say so. Pass me my glasses, if you would."

"With pleasure. Tell me, where is it hidden?"

"In my office. In the *Oxford Companion to Classical Literature*. Not a volume people refer to these days."

"Then let's be off. . . . You needn't be ashamed, you know," said Holbrook, solicitously dusting down Somerset's coat. "Only fanatics and morons are capable of resisting pain indefinitely, and if one's going to give in anyway, one may as well do so at once and save a lot of trouble."

They left together discussing this proposition in general terms. Some sort of relationship, after all, had been established by what had passed.

"Good of you to come," said Rupert Percival.

"Good of you to see me," smiled Sir Edwin, wearing his humility like an ill-fitting set of false teeth.

Percival led the way on to his terrace. As they sat down, the Minister hummed a few bars from Lilac Time, his favourite music when his spirits were low. For most of the time he kept them up very well without Novello's assistance; but the events of the last two days had been somewhat lowering, and the interview now in prospect was going to be the more difficult as he had no lever with which to prise Percival in the desired direction. Sir Edwin liked to have leverage. He liked to be in a position to propose a deal, or, failing that, he had no objection to having a deal proposed to him. What he did not care for was occasions, like this one, on which there was no proper basis for negotiation. He would have to *ask*, and of all things he hated asking. If only there had been something which Percival wanted for himself. . . . But Percival, as Dixon had told him, wanted nothing – a piece of intelligence borne out by the placid gaze with which he was now examining the Quantocks. He did not even seem curious to hear what Sir Edwin would say; at all events he made no effort to get him started.

"This election," said the Minister with all the resolution he could muster.

"Yes?"

"I gather you're not choosing your candidate until next month."

"The selection committee meets on July the thirtieth," Percival deposed. "Can I get you a drink?"

"No, thank you." He took a toffee from his pocket, unwrapped it and hustled it into his mouth. "What does Dixon think about it?" he said.

"He thinks," said Percival blandly, "that the committee will choose one of the five candidates on the short list."

"Five? But surely – ?"

" – Five."

This was getting Sir Edwin nowhere. He had been told, of course, that theoretically there were five men for the Bishop's Cross committee to choose from; but as he understood the case, everyone in the know acknowledged that in truth the choice lay between Lloyd-James and Morrison. To be treated as if he were not in the know was aggravating. He fumbled in his pocket for another toffee.

"I am going to take you into my confidence," he said, seignorially unwrapping his sweet.

Percival inclined his head politely.

"We need more ability in the House. To be candid, we're a bit low on intelligence just now."

Once more, Percival inclined his head.

"When it comes to intelligence, of the applicants for the candidature here two stand out."

"That had occurred to me," Percival said.

"I," said Edwin, sucking hard, "that is to say we, that is to say . . . well, no doubt you know who I mean?"

"Roughly," Percival replied.

"Well. We . . . would find young Morrison . . . an embarrassment."

"Indeed?"

"Yes. Indeed. Some years back he made a lot of trouble through that Young England Group of his, and we reckon he means to do it again. If he comes back."

"If he comes back."

"Well, will he? I'm asking you."

"That," said Percival, "is for the committee to decide."

Full stop. Percival turned his eyes back to the Quantocks.

"Look," Sir Edwin said. "At five o'clock this evening I have to attend a Cabinet Meeting, at which I must report on an important new proposal to do with the constitution of the Upper House. Instead of preparing what I shall say, I am sitting here talking to you. What does that suggest?"

"That you want something."

"*We* want something. To be precise, Somerset Lloyd-James returned at the General Election. And don't tell me it's for your committee to decide, because we both know better."

"Why do you want Lloyd-James?"

"I've told you. We want someone intelligent, and the only other intelligent chap you could choose is Morrison, and Morrison will be a bloody nuisance. I'm appealing to you for the good of the party."

The Minister sat back, fixing Percival with what he secretly thought of as his "Dunkirk" expression.

"Perhaps," said Percival, "it would be for the good of the party, in the wider view, to be made to accommodate a bloody nuisance."

"Not as bloody as this one," said the Minister between his teeth.

"I see." said Percival. And he did see. From the start he had thought it odd that a senior Minister should be paying him court in person; and now, watching Sir Edwin as he gritted his teeth and sucked the life out of a third toffee, he realised, very broadly, what was afoot. Quite accidentally, he had become involved in a big game; without knowing why or how, the quiet country solicitor had been set down in a seat at the Centre Table where there was no limit – none at all – to the stakes. For some reason, the Minister was trying to pretend that it was still an everyday, friendly affair, and the chips were only marked at a fraction of their real value – presumably to prevent him, Rupert Percival, from knowing the true amount of his winnings and claiming them in full. Alastair Dixon had been right when he said there was nothing which Percival wanted for himself; but this did not mean that Percival was prepared to sit back and be robbed. If they asked him to join their game, then, as a matter of equity, he must be told the real terms of reckoning and, as a matter of principle, he must be paid out in full. In short, the one thing which Rupert Percival did want was a proper degree of respect.

"Let's pretend we're starting again at the beginning," he said pleasantly, "and that when you say 'confidence' you mean it. Even we provincial lawyers have our pride."

The Minister smacked his lips as if relishing this rebuke. It seemed that Percival had a price after all: the truth. How very singular. Hoping for the best, he decided to go some way to meet it.

"Lloyd-James," he said, "is a crook. Therefore we would have settled for Morrison, nuisance value and all. But unfortunately Lloyd-James is too good a crook. He's got hold of something that could smash us to pieces, and he wants Bishop's Cross in return for holding his tongue."

"What has he got hold off?"

"Some regrettable facts about Suez. Which reflect on several gentlemen still in office."

"He can prove them?"

"On balance, yes."

This was enough for Rupert Percival. Although a lawyer's instinct is to ask for chapter and verse, Percival had always been a lax lawyer and preferred to deal in generalities. Again, by issuing a general confession of wrong-doing Sir Edwin had shown him sufficient regard; gentlemen need not concern themselves with details.

"The thing is quite simple," Percival said: "Lloyd-James must have his way."

"I was hoping you'd say that."

"Then why didn't you tell me the truth at the beginning?"

"I suppose I thought you'd be shocked."

"I," said Percival, "am a pragmatist. Like everyone else, I always suspected there was something fishy about Suez. But what is past is inevitable. Recrimination, retribution will not mend it. A good recovery has been made. Why ruin the party's prospects for a dead issue?"

"Some people would say it was still very much a live one."

"Moralists."

"So . . . Lloyd-James will be chosen?"

"Yes."

"Your . . . loyalty . . . will not go unnoticed."

Percival nodded. He did not particularly want his loyalty to be noticed, but it was only fitting that it should be.

"Don't let me detain you," he said rising. "You'll want to be starting for London. I hope you have a satisfactory Cabinet Meeting. And I should say how much I sympathise with you over this sad affair of your daughter."

"Like you," said Sir Edwin, who had been much heartened by the outcome of the discussion, "I take a pragmatic view. Once a thing has happened, one should regard it as inevitable. That way there is comfort both for heart and head."

When Somerset handed over the des Moulins letter, Holbrook said casually:

"Don't tell anyone that you've given it to me, will you? We don't want any more childishness."

By way of reminder, he struck Somerset in the small of the back with the edge of his open palm. Although the blow was light and the pain small, it seemed to Somerset to jar his very bowels, slyly hinting at an immensity of possible anguish.

"You see?"

"You needn't worry," Somerset gasped at him. Lord, can this be happening to me, your servant?

Holbrook nodded. "There's a good boy," he said.

When Holbrook left Somerset, he returned to Maisie's flat and used her telephone to put through a call to Venice. While the exchange made the connection, Maisie said:

"You realise you've just lost me one of my best clients?"

"Can't be helped. It was Salvadori's idea to use your flat. It was just bad luck that the chap we wanted was a customer of yours."

"You tell Salvadori to think of some other place for his dirty work."

"You tell him," said Holbrook, grinning.

"I've never met him. I've only – "

But at this point the exchange rang to say that Venice was on the line. Holbrook waved Maisie out of her sitting-room, and then listened for some minutes to the instructions, which were given him in a simple code, for his return.

After this he gave Maisie some money, which cheered her up a bit, and took a taxi to Buttock's Hotel, where he packed his two small suitcases. He had paid his bill in advance and had no mind to hang around saying good-byes; but as it happened he ran into Fielding Gray on his way out.

"Just off?"

It was the first time that either had spoken to the other.

"Yes, London is getting too hot."

"It's certainly been an exceptional summer," Fielding conceded. "Already the grass in the parks is drying up."

"Yes. High time to leave."

He walked urgently into the Cromwell Road and hailed a taxi.

"Ill-mannered tyke," said Tessie that evening: "going off without saying anything."

"Tom did warn you," Fielding reminded her, "that he wasn't much of a chap."

"Poor Tom," Tessie said. "Fancy that little madam choosing his wedding day to run off. It says in the paper that the honeymoon's been indefinitely postponed."

"I expect he's busy helping Sir Edwin clear up the mess."

"The more fool him. He was always too soft-hearted. If he's not careful that Turbot lot 'll drink the life's blood out of his body."

In Tiverton, two days later, Mark Lewson said good night to Isobel, who would be sleeping in a youth hostel, walked back to his hotel, and went into the bar for a drink.

"And now," said a cheery, unctuous voice from the television set, "Wessex Line-Up. Local news and views from Salisbury to the Dart."

"My fiancé was on Wessex Line-Up once," said the middle-aged barmaid to Mark: "he belonged to some funny religious lot who thought the world was going to end."

"Oh?" said Mark politely, thinking of Isobel and the lonely night ahead.

"Yes. So one day they all went up a hill, waiting for the Son of Light to come and find them there, and the Telly got to hear of it first. My fiancé broke it all off because I laughed at him about it later, what a lot of right fools they all looked praying away in their white nighties in front of this telly camera, and nothing to show for it. It was bad of me really." She snivelled. "I shouldn't have laughed like that. I shouldn't have, should I?"

"Perhaps not."

Mark, judging that he had heard the more amusing portion of this story, shut her off by turning to watch the television set.

". . . Her Royal Highness," the unctuous voice said, "had a particular word for ex-Sergeant-Major Cruxtable, the Camp Physical Fitness Officer."

Her Royal Highness appeared grinning toothily up the nostrils of an obese but otherwise presentable man in a track suit. The ex-Sergeant-Major seemed about to say something, when Her Royal Highness was whisked smoothly away by a determined-looking man with a bruiser's nose and a bowler hat.

"The Marquis Canteloupe, Parliamentary Secretary for the Development of British Recreational Resources, showed Her Royal Highness round the rest of the Westward Ho! Caravan Site."

Lord Canteloupe and another man, identified by the commentator as Camp Commandant Hookeby, helped H.R.H. into a gleaming caravan, from which she emerged two seconds later with gestures of enthusiasm.

"After the party had visited the nursery-crêche (picture of a fully accoutred but questionably sober matron recovering from a curtsey), the delightful modern-style dinette, the discussion room and the Maison Bingo, the Princess welcomed the first arrivals."

Two coaches came up a track, and Lord Canteloupe stepped forward with Hookeby and Cruxtable to help the campers out. This went well, for Canteloupe showed undeniable panache and the picture of Cruxtable carrying a baby revealed only his top half, so that the viewers could not see him aim a vicious kick at a puppy. H.R.H. simpered and waved by the gate; some sturdy and wholesome family groups moved past her with cheerful deference; the Matron appeared, walking with commendable steadiness, to make a fuss of a pregnant woman; and a man in peaked hat and spotless white coat (the refuse man with the haemorrhoids, if only the audience had known) started to distribute ice-creams among the children.

"Aaaaaah," went the barmaid.

"Westward Ho!, first site of many planned, is in the un-spoiled Quantock Hills, a holiday-makers' paradise. Let's hear what Lord Canteloupe had to say in his address of thanks to Her Royal Highness at the end of this proud and happy day."

Canteloupe appeared on the steps of the Maison Bingo; he looked strained but was plainly still well under control.

"Your Royal Highness's gracious presence at this opening" – gruffly, chivalrously, rather movingly the old scoundrel repeated what Carton Weir had written for him – "has, among so many other values, a symbolic one. Your youth and beauty (a quick shot of H.R.H.'s splendiferous teeth) remind us that this camp exists, above all, to bring the glow of health and happiness into the fair cheeks of our young. And not only the young in years but also the young in heart. ('That's modern English for senile,' Weir had explained. 'For Christ's sake don't leave it out. "The old folk" are all the rage just now.') Yes, for the young in spirit as well as for the young in strength there is an honest welcome here. Come one, come all . . . to Westward Ho!"

"That's what I like," the barmaid said: "not forgetting the old folk."

But Mark wasn't listening. He had had an idea: if Isobel and he hired separate caravans on Canteloupe's site, they would be together and yet seemingly apart. They could "meet" in the natural course of events without anyone's knowing of their prior connection. And what better hiding place than among a crowd of lower-class holiday-makers? They need wander no more: they would go to the Quantocks the very next day and there bide out time until Sir Edwin's surrender appeared in the Personal Columns of *The Times*.

It was Max de Freville's custom to hold a special gambling party in late July or early August every year in order to mark the end of the season. This year he had announced the party for much earlier, for the end of June. When the guests arrived they found, instead of the usual sumptuous canapés of caviar and foie gras, slices of dry bread covered with cheddar cheese; instead of champagne, bottled beer; instead of a properly appointed Chemmy cloth, a plain kitchen table on which lay two packs of greasy cards. However, since Max's prestige was immense and since this evening he moved easily among them talking in his usual manner, they were reassured after a time and imagined that he was playing some kind of joke. Perhaps he had devised a transformation scene to amuse them: the cheese and beer would suddenly disappear through the floor, to be replaced by refreshments even more succulent than usual; the splintering surface of the kitchen table would somehow be metamorphosed, at the touch of a switch, into luscious green baize. . . .

And so, when Max announced, as he shuffled the greasy cards, that this evening they would be playing Slippery Sam for threepenny stakes, there was a good-humoured laugh all round.

"I mean it," he said.

This time the laugh was rather awkward.

"Threepenny stakes," he shouted. "*Cash*."

All his energy left him then. He let the cards fall to the table and sagged back into his chair.

At this stage his guests at last realised something of what had happened. With low murmurs of deprecation they moved off into the night: sooner or later, they told each other, the end had been bound to come; Max had had a sensational career, but it was over now, and they must look for someone else to fill his place. As Jonathan Gamp summed it up for them, "He made more money than was decent, my dears, and now God's being puritanical about it."

Of the guests, only Captain Detterling, who had watched Max rise all the way from scabby poker games and post-dated cheques to undisputed pre-eminence, remained behind to comfort him; and this he did more out of curiosity than affection, though there was affection too.

"What's all this about?" he said.

"An idea I cribbed from Shakespeare. 'Timon of Athens'."

"Has everything gone?"

"Oh no," said Max lightly. "But things were beginning to break up. People weren't paying – they thought I had so much that it didn't matter. And besides, I was bored."

That makes sense, thought Detterling; but all the same there's something disastrously wrong. His eyes.

"So I've deposited a nice little sum," said Max, still speaking lightly but staring straight before him, "in France. Thank God Angela persuaded me in time. I shall go to her now and settle with her there in Menton."

"You always said she couldn't be a permanent thing."

"I can give it a try. Move on if it's no good."

Silence. Fascinated, Detterling watched the eyes bulge, as if they were about to explode out of their sockets.

"How much I achieved," Max suddenly shouted. "Nobody achieved as much as I did."

He put his head down on the bare wooden table and started to weep.

"You were the most famous gambler in Europe," said Detterling, soothing him.

Max raised his head and brushed the tears away. His eyes subsided, deflated and wizened balloons, back into his head.

"You don't understand," he choked. "It isn't that I'm proud of. It's the other thing. Given time, money," he blubbered, "my network would have encompassed the whole world . . . the *universe*."

"You did very well as it was."

"Yes, you could say that. There just wasn't enough money. Mind you," he said, with a temporary return to calm and rational discourse, "I'd been neglecting my business, letting the debts go, not bothering to attend the games myself. The accountant warned me but I wouldn't listen . . . because, you see, I was so absorbed in the other thing. Every day, letters, cables, phone calls, messages by hand . . . from all over Europe. I was really beginning to see the pattern behind it all. But it's useless now."

His eyes began to swell again. I must get him to a hospital, Detterling thought; he can't go off to France like this. But once again Max's eyes subsided.

"Where was I?" he said.

"You were neglecting your business interests . . . in favour of your very expensive private correspondence. So the money was running down?"

"So the money was running down. But there wouldn't have been enough anyway. There wasn't enough money in the whole kingdom to pay for all I wanted to know."

"How much did you know, Max?"

For hour after hour Max told him. He told of facts established, connections proved, of policies and plots uncovered; of men made wealthy overnight, of men who lay down in the fullness of power and woke with a prison cell for their only empire. Much of it was speculation, much fantasy and much sheer madness. But here and there Detterling recognised a fragment of probable truth; and one such fragment, explaining several odd things which had lately been brought to his notice, was the story of the des Moulins letter and its sale by Lewson to Somerset Lloyd-James.

For Max, this crazy outpouring of what he knew or thought he knew acted as a kind of purgation. Despite the insanity of much of what he was saying, his manner was now consistently calm, his eyes no longer dilated at short intervals. Even so, Detterling judged that he should be given into medical custody; but before he could do anything about this, Max was gone. Perhaps he had anticipated Detterling's purpose. At all events, he had excused himself on the ground of wanting a pee; and when, fifteen minutes later, Detterling went to look for him, the house was empty and Max's car no longer parked in the square outside.

So Detterling shrugged his shoulders and walked home in the light blue dawn to his chambers in Albany, reflecting with some interest on what he had heard that night and on what might now be done to prevent Somerset Lloyd-James from using the new weapon which had come into his hand.

Although Alfie Schroeder had been prompt to respond to Tom's telegram, he had pleaded commitments for the next few days. In the end they met, on the day after Westward Ho! had opened, in Bath, which seemed as good a base as any for the search. The trouble was that there was nothing to go on. Isobel and her companion had driven off, as Alfie had put it at the wedding, "in the rough direction of Bristol." They might be anywhere in England by now. Tom's only hope was that suggested by Sir Edwin's briefing: he must put himself in Lewson's place. But before anything else was begun, Alfie must be brought up to date. So Tom had explained, as he drove Alfie from the station, that the hit and run driver was identifiable, by the letter he had left, as Mark Lewson; he then told Alfie what Lewson had said in the letter, what little more he himself knew about the man, and finally the reasons which Sir Edwin alleged for protecting him.

"So what it comes to," said Alfie, "is that you've to find Miss Isobel and bring her home to Daddy – having first swept this Lewson chappie safely under the mat."

"That's it."

"And why have you called me in?" said Alfie sourly.

"In case something nasty turns up."

"Something already has. A man's dead, if you remember."

"That's just it. A man's dead and my father-in-law is trying to protect the man that killed him. Why, Alfie?"

"Why ask me?" Alfie took off his enormous trilby and fanned himself. "Christ, this summer," he moaned. And then, "Why drag me in? Suppose there is something smelly in the closet. Do you think I want to be there when you find it? I'm your friend; I don't want to be the one to dish up the dirt about your father-in-law."

"Someone may have to."

The car stopped.

"Five star job, eh?" said Alfie, surveying the hotel. "You wouldn't have stayed at a place like this when I first knew you."

"I've come up in the world."

"You could still start sinking."

"Too true I could. For God's sake have a drink and stop grouching."

When Alfie had worked his way morosely through two large Tom Collinses, Tom began again.

"Alfie. . . . You must help me. Patricia and I – we'll have

no peace, no honeymoon, nothing, till all this is cleared up. You remember what you said about your honeymoon," Tom went on shamelessly, "how it was the one good thing that ever happened? I'm still waiting for mine to start, Alfie."

Alfie sighed, almost sentimentally.

"Same again, laddie," he said.

The drink came and Alfie fondled it thoughtfully.

"How are you supposed to start looking?" he said at last. Tom told him.

"Jesus Christ," Alfie said, "the ideas educated people get. Put yourself in the other chap's place! That's Dornford Yates, laddie, back in the nursery. Don't people like Sir Edwin ever grow up?"

"If you'll take time off from being so bloody superior, just what do you suggest?"

"Elementary. You say Lewson's letter instructed Sir Edwin to put an 'all is forgiven' notice in *The Times*?"

"What of it?"

"Most people who read *The Times* have a regular order. Casual buyers in the provinces are rare and therefore conspicuous. And they are often disappointed, in which case they get irritated and make themselves even more conspicuous. When they have recovered themselves, they ask to be directed to other newspaper shops; by which time," Alfie said, "they are positively memorable. Now then." He opened a Racing Diary at a road map of the West Country. "Let us assume, as we must to have any hope, that they are still in this part of the world. Small towns and villages are our best bet. Where do you think we should start?"

"So if you'll allow me to sum it all up," said Captain Detterling, crisp and authoritative, "the position is as follows."

They were all in Gregory Stern's office – Stern, Morrison, Fielding Gray, and Detterling who had summoned the convention. Of those present, Stern and Fielding Gray were both in doubt as to why they should have been asked, but Detterling had undertaken to explain that later.

"If we are to believe Max de Freville," Detterling said, "and I for one am prepared to, then we must conclude:

"One. Mark Lewson has got hold of a genuine document which incriminates Sir Edwin Turbot and other members of the Cabinet.

"Two. Lewson, in return for a sum of money, has passed the document to Somerset Lloyd-James. And three; both Lewson and Lloyd-James, as partners, are now using its existence to put pressure on Sir Edwin.

"Four. In Lloyd-James's case, he requires Sir Edwin to persuade Rupert Percival that Lloyd-James rather than Peter here should be adopted as conservative candidate for Bishop's Cross.

"And five. As for Lewson, he is the unknown man whom the police want for manslaughter and who eloped with Isobel Turbot. This is proved by the farewell letter which Isobel sent Max from Blandford. What Lewson wants from Sir Edwin is consent to a marriage and a comfortable dollop of cash to support it."

There was a thoughtful silence.

"Any questions?" said Detterling in the approved military manner.

"Yes," said Fielding. "Why are you telling *me* this?"

"And me?" said Stern.

"I was coming to that. Now, my object and Peter's is to see that Peter gets back into Parliament this autumn. This means some kind of show-down about this letter. In the course of the show-down almost anything might happen, including the letter's publication. This would bring total disgrace on Sir Edwin, cunning as he may be at finding ways out, and Tom Llewyllyn, as a member of his family, would be involved in this. So I wanted you, Fielding, and you, Gregory, to be here as friends of Tom's and representatives of his interests."

"You and Peter . . . you're Tom's friends too."

"But we have other interests . . . which might well conflict with Tom's."

"I'm sure," said Stern, "that Tom would be the last person to want anything covered up."

"Think again," said Detterling. "He might not care whether or not his father-in-law was exposed, but he'll want to protect his new wife. The shock would half kill her."

"She might be tougher than you think," said Fielding.

"Anyway, a sense of public duty – " Stern began.

"We'll let Tom decide about his duty," said Detterling. "You and Fielding are in on this to see he gets a proper chance."

"How are we to do that?" snapped Stern.

"By acting as umpires?" hazarded Fielding.

"Right."

"And by helping you," Fielding persisted, "to reach the right choice."

"Choice?" said Stern.

"Yes. The choice will be a very awkward one. Between destroying the letter for the sake of peace and making it public for the sake of purity."

"Nicely put," said Detterling.

"Is there not a third way?" said Peter Morrison, speaking for the first time.

Detterling gave him an odd, enquiring look.

"I mean . . . perhaps we ourselves might undertake . . . to hold it in trust."

"Why would we do that?" said Stern. The look in Peter's face at once gave him his answer; Stern flushed scarlet with shame for the human race and squeezed his Old Etonian tie into a knot the size of a garden pea.

"You all seem to forget," said Detterling, who was eyeing Peter with wary amusement, "that before we can choose what to do with the letter, we've got to get hold of it. That's what we're here to discuss."

"You can count me out of that," said Fielding. "I'll willingly hold Tom's hand when the time comes, but meanwhile I've got my work." He nodded at Stern, who nodded back. "Let me know when I'm wanted again," he said, and rose to go.

"Sit down," said Detterling, briskly but without heat. "You had the curiosity to come here, and now you can see it through."

"My work —"

" — Can wait a day or two." Detterling looked at him gravely. " '*Res unius, res omnium*'. Remember?"

Fielding winced and sat down.

"Well then," said Detterling blandly. "The letter. The document. We must and will possess it. How?"

"Lloyd-James has it, you say . . . according to de Freville's account."

"I've been to see Lloyd-James. He says not."

Detterling allowed this to sink in.

"You believe him?" said Morrison at length.

"I don't know. He says it's been stolen."

"Then we can forget it," said Morrison. "If he no longer has it, he can't use it."

"Perhaps not. But is he telling the truth? And if he is, someone else may pop up with it at any minute and start making a nuisance of himself. It is essential, one might almost say for the national good, that the document be finally found and disposed of one way or the other. In any case," Detterling went on, "according to Lloyd-James the thief must have been his partner, Lewson — because he was the only person who knew where it was hidden. Lloyd-James deposes that Lewson must have taken it before absconding with the wretched Isobel — he soon guessed *that* was Lewson's work — as a handy weapon in case papa proved difficult. If this is true, then the letter is still held by the Lewson/Lloyd-James combine, and Lloyd-James is still to be reckoned with. It all leaves us just where we were: we must find the letter."

"Well," said Stern, taking an analytical interest, "there are only two assumptions you can act on. Either Lewson's got it or Lloyd-James is lying and still has it himself. If anyone else has it, you might just as well go home."

"Precisely. Only two assumptions we can act on, so we shall act on both. Two parties – one player and one umpire, so to speak, in each. I know the West Country, so I thought Gregory and I might hunt for Lewson and see what he's got to say for himself, while you, Peter – "

" – But how will you search? It's hopeless," Morrison said. "After all, the police have been looking, and if they've got nowhere – "

" – The police only know one of the people they're looking for. We shall have a double target. Anyway, that's our worry. You and Fielding will have your own job to concentrate on here – keeping an eye on Lloyd-James."

"It doesn't sound a very positive line of action," Fielding said.

"No," said Detterling. And then, with the faintest hint of contempt,

"Peter doesn't care for positive lines of action. In any case there's none open. If Somerset *has* still got the letter, he'll have hidden it far too carefully for you to find. We'd have to . . . coax it out of him later on."

"And meanwhile?"

"Watch him, to see if he does anything out of the way. Like making strange contacts. Visiting unlikely places. Anything," Detterling said, "that may give us a line on what cards he's really holding in his hand."

But Somerset Lloyd-James made no strange contacts. He visited no unlikely places. He was acutely conscious that he now held no card at all in his hand. The best that he could do was to pretend that the card was currently held by his partner, Lewson; for while people still thought this, they would probably regard him with some respect. In no case at all, even to a trusted ally, did he wish to disclose how he had fared with Jude Holbrook; for, quite apart from anything else, he was humiliated by the memory, not of the speed with which he had surrendered, but of the gross outrage offered to his person.

However, it now seemed only a matter of time before someone found Lewson. Once this was done, a number of things might happen, all of them to his disadvantage; because all alike must end in the arrival of someone or other on his doorstep to demand the original document, and in his own confession, which could not be avoided for long, that he did not have it. Whether he was compelled to make this confession to a policeman or to Detterling, it would amount to the same: the end of the power with which possession, or supposed possession, endowed him.

After much thought and some hours of prayer, Somerset went to see his loyal supporter, Carton Weir and for the first time made him privy to the summer's secrets. Weir, as he had expected, was both pleased and amused by the tale of the des Moulins letter. But, Somerset went on, the letter had now been stolen; he did not know where it was; and for the time being he was only holding his own by giving out that it was with Lewson. This might be true, Somerset said, or it might not; either way it was essential, if Somerset was to be sure of Bishop's Cross, that they should find Lewson before anybody else did. Since Weir desired Somerset's election, since he had the ideal excuse (Westward Ho!) for taking time out of Parliament and visiting the West Country, and since Somerset himself was exceedingly busy with his editing, let Weir get on with the search – and the quicker the better.

When Weir opened his mouth to protest against being sent on this expedition, Somerset sharply reminded him to whom he owed his place on the Board of *Strix*. When Weir seemed unimpressed by this argument, Somerset efficiently recited a few choice facts from Weir's private life which Weir had supposed to be secret, and the discussion closed.

So as June gave place to July and the grass in the Royal Parks of London turned slowly to dust, three different parties set out to hunt for Mark Lewson. Tom and Alfie, with a family mission to fulfil, much uneasy curiosity to quieten, and as yet ill-defined duties (to the nation? to the press?) beyond; Captain Detterling and Gregory Stern, searching, on behalf of a friend, for five sheets of paper which Lewson did not have; and the lone, reluctant Carton Weir, who was beginning to see that he had allowed Somerset to bluff him, and was now meditating a little scheme of his own.

9

THE CHASE

For some days Tom and Alfie had no joy at all. No one in Bath, Trowbridge, Frome, Shepton Mallet or Glastonbury had any recollection that anyone out of the ordinary had tried to buy *The Times*. Alfie began to be restive. As a long-established and trusted employee of the Billingsgate Press, he was allowed some latitude as to where and how he spent his time, provided he gave assurance that there might be a story at the end of it. On this occasion he had given the usual assurance ("Line on the Turbot girl"), but he had done so with considerable misgiving as he knew that his friendship for Tom might require him to be less than candid about whatever might transpire. He had left London under false pretences, in fact; and even if his mission had been wholly genuine, it would not excuse his indefinite absence. Four days after he had arrived in Bath, as they were driving through a faultless summer morning to pursue their enquiries round Bridgwater, he put the difficulty to Tom.

"If we don't come up with something," he said, "I must leave tonight."

"Just two more days," Tom begged: "today and two more."

"Can't be done, laddie. They're already spitting down the 'phone."

"Alfie. . . . I can't manage this alone."

In Bridgwater, Taunton and Longport they discovered nothing at all.

"That settles it," Alfie said. "I'll take the night train."

"It's your system that's let us down," said Tom petulantly.

"Granted. But could you think of a better?"

"Alfie. . . . Two more days. Please."

"Sorry, son."

"There must be something else you could report on round here. Something . . . anything . . . to keep them happy in London."

"Sorry."

"Don't you understand, Alfie? I'm being played along . . . blackmailed in a sense . . . by my own wife. I can't cope and I need your help."

"We're all of us blackmailed by our wives."

"You've had time to get used to it. I was only married last week, Alfie. That's what makes it all so desperate."

"God, I hate it when you whine," said Alfie. "Stop the car."

"What – ?"

" – Just do as I say. Now."

Tom stopped.

"Get out," said Alfie.

He led the way to a small public house. There was a little river, Tom noticed, and a bridge. Flat meadows, marsh and bat-willow; and beyond them, in the east, low, black clouds. Perhaps the weather was going to break at last.

"Get me a whisky."

Alfie went to a coin box in the corner of the bar. Tom bought two large whiskies and carried them over.

". . . Just till tomorrow night," Alfie was saying. "Yes, tomorrow. I don't think anything'll come of the Turbot business, but while I'm here there's something else I want to look at. . . . This new Caravan Camp in the Quantocks. There was something not quite right about the opening. . . . Yes, I know it was on television, that's what gave me the idea. There was something a bit fake. . . . Night train tomorrow. 'Bye."

He put down the receiver and took his drink without thanks.

"One more day," he said. "You know why? Because I can't bear to go away and remember you whining. I'll need a day to wipe out the memory. So for God's sake, when I go tomorrow, shout or foam at the mouth, but don't whine."

"All right. Do we really have to go to this caravan place?"

"Why not?" said Alfie. "It won't take a moment and we may as well look at that part of the country as anywhere else."

Captain Detterling was of sanguine disposition. Gregory Stern was not.

"A needle in a haystack," he said, irritated into cliché by the expense of time and trouble now in prospect.

"Two needles," Detterling remarked: "Sharp, bright needles at that. Bound to have pricked somebody's consciousness by now."

With this hope in mind; he carried Stern away to the west, where they would stay with his distant cousin, Lord Canteloupe, ostensibly in order to have a closer look, as potential publishers, at Canteloupe's father's memoirs.

"I saw them when I was there in the Spring," Detterling said to Stern, "And they're a complete dead loss. But they'll make a handy excuse now."

"I dare say. But they'll hardly help us find this Lewson creature."

Detterling, who was not only sanguine but sane, had given some thought to that. He had one undoubted advantage: he knew where to start. Max de Freville, on the night before he disappeared to join Angela Tuck, had told him that Isobel's last letter had referred to a village near Blandford; and Blandford was an easy drive from Canteloupe's pile in Wiltshire. Two days of enquiry, first in Blandford itself, then in villages around, then in Sherborne, Yeovil and Crewkerne, revealed a gradual progress to the north-west, not indeed of Lewson, but of someone who might well be Isobel. She had been travelling alone, apparently, in trains and buses; though someone had once seen her getting out of a grey Morris Traveller whose number plate bore the arresting letters – hence his memory of the incident – YOB. The Morris had immediately driven off, it seemed, and Detterling's informant had not caught sight of the driver.

Detterling wondered how much of this was known to the police, but reminded himself once more that the police did not know where to start, indeed were probably active only in the Bristol area, towards which the infamous blue and white sports car had last been seen heading. There was, in any case, nothing he could do about that. From Crewkerne his enquiries had led him and Stern, who was still sceptical but was now taking an interest in what he termed "the theory of the human spoor", to Chard. There Isobel's trail was lost, but in answer to a lucky question at a garage they were told by a mechanic that a dark-haired and excitable young man in a grey Morris Traveller had asked to be put on the road to Tiverton some days before.

"Very careless," commented Stern in scholarly fashion, "for someone who lives by his wits."

And now, on a cloudy evening – the same evening on which Alfie rang up London from the lonely inn among the bat willows – Detterling and Stern were driving slowly along beneath the Quantocks, whither the scent had drawn them earlier that day.

"Tonight," said Detterling, "we won't go back to Wiltshire. We'll sleep somewhere round here and get an early start."

"No luggage," said Stern, who liked to do things in an orderly way.

"We can buy a tootbrush and a razor."

"I need a clean shirt."

"We can buy that too."

Stern, thinking of the neat pile of clean silk shirts which

awaited him in his bedroom at Canteloupe's, gave a little mew of protest.

"Don't whine, Gregory," Detterling said.

"I don't see why we have to be so *Spartan* all of a sudden."

They passed a notice which said:

Two Hundred Yards Turn Left
For the First Canteloupe
Caravan Site and Country Culture Camp
WESTWARD HO !

"The next thing," Stern went moaning on, "you'll suggest we hire one of your cousin's beastly caravans for the night."

"That," said Captain Detterling, "would be going altogether too far."

"God, what a dump," Mark Lewson said; "but it's certainly handy for us."

"Home is where you find it," murmured Isobel, tickling his palm with her finger nail.

Every day the Caravan Site became dirtier and emptier. The morning after the opening the bulk of the "campers" had taken their fee for the television masquerade and left by special coach. The few genuine holiday-makers, puzzled and distressed by this desertion, had sniffed the air suspiciously but then, having paid in advance, had decided to give the place a fair trial. By the time Mark and Isobel arrived, however, few even of these were left. The almost total failure of the plumbing for two and half days; the indifference of Commandant Hookeby and the insolent manners of his wife; the vile language of Sergeant-Major Cruxtable; the two occasions on which the Matron had got crying drunk; the absence of the refuse man with a resurgent batch of "haemorrhoids": all this had made for a lack of refinement which members of the British proletariat were not prepared to tolerate.

But it suited Mark and Isobel down to the ground. Officially installed in separate trailers to maintain the impression that they had arrived independently of each other, they spent all of every night and most of every day together, and even while apart were enclosed in the same rainbow bubble of bliss. What was it to them that the Maison Bingo had closed its doors, probably for ever, that the dinette had succumbed to a plague of cockroaches, that Sergeant-Major Cruxtable had ruptured himself in his brief and sole attempt to teach three small children to play basket-ball? They had a bigger and more thrilling gamble on hand than any which a Bingo card could show them; for their meals they drove to a charming little hotel which they had discovered a few miles away; and for their physical activities they did not need the assistance of Sergeant-Major Cruxtable. A larger crowd, on which Mark had originally relied, might have given them more effective concealment; but as it was, their fellow-campers were too preoccupied with their own miseries to give anyone else a second thought. Nowhere is it easier to escape remark, however conspicuous one might otherwise be, than in a run-down city or a foundering ship: low morale inhibits curiosity. Furthermore, there was something in the air of desolation, they found, which was very nutritive of romance.

So Mark and Isobel were happy amid the growing piles of filth and broken glass. To complain of these gave a zest to love; as did the sullen clouds which were now gathering in the evening sky, for the threat of storm when shelter is near always stirs a delicious thrill of mock anxiety in the stomach, and to lovers rain is one more hostile element that gives greater value to the cosy, impregnable huddle into which, at will, they may retreat.

"It's going to *pour*," said Isobel, with a shiver of pleasure.

"First time in weeks. What a wonderful summer it's been."

"It's not over yet," she said, and went on tickling his palm.

"It's going to rain," said Canteloupe, looking happily down

from his window at the Amusement Arcade which he had lately erected in place of the formal rose garden. "And about time," he added, thinking of the trippers who would now be compelled to stop frigging about in the park and seek shelter in the Arcade.

"Yes indeed," said Carton Weir politely. "And what do you think about what I've just told you?"

He had arrived in Wiltshire to see his superior that afternoon and had spent most of it telling him everything that he had recently learned from Somerset Lloyd-James. For Carton Weir had a new ambition. He was tired of being grateful to Lloyd-James for his place on the Board of *Strix*, tired of accepting Lloyd-James's suggestions as to his manipulation of the Young England Group, tired of being dependent on Lloyd-James for his continued leadership. There were now, he told himself, fatter fish to fry: Lloyd-James's information had put fame and power within his reach; all he had to do was to initiate a public and sensational scourge among high persons. He would fire the fuse to scandal and dance round the flames, the acknowledged author of the conflagration. But he felt the need of an ally; someone who carried weight with the government and the country at large. There was one such to hand: Canteloupe. True, until the preceding April Canteloupe had been regarded, by serious people, as a mere figure of fun; but the general public had not so seen him, and now even serious people had reluctantly begun to revise their estimate, not least because of the recently published encomia of the man and his policies in *Strix*. Careerist and patrician united, thought Carton Weir, he and Canteloupe would make a mighty team; he would put up the brains, Canteloupe would provide the credit; and tradition would march hand in hand with progress, while the sword of purity was brandished and the angry war cry – "Who shall guard the guardians?" – rang against the battlements of Westminster Palace like the trumpets outside Jericho.

And if Somerset again tries to blackmail me, Weir thought, into playing it his way, I've got the perfect comeback: he's guilty of suppressing information which concerns the security of the realm. And now what's the matter with Canteloupe? Cat got his tongue?

"What do you think, sir," he said again, "about what I've been saying?"

"I think," said Canteloupe, "what I always thought. Lloyd-James is a shit." He gazed at the clouds and almost heard the coins as they tinkled into his new slot-machines. Could he get permission for penny roulette?

"Then you agree with me that the whole affair should be uncovered?"

"First," said Canteloupe carefully, "we must make sure of the truth and be able to prove it. Now, this man . . . Lewson . . . the one you're meant to be looking for . . ."

"He's very small beer. And he may not even have the letter. My idea was to confront Sir Edwin and the rest – "

" – First things first, boy." Penny roulette? Perhaps something like Boule would be better. "We don't want to rush round making fools of ourselves. This chap Lewson may or may not have the confounded letter, but he'll be able to tell us the story."

"Lloyd-James has already done that, sir. That's enough. With a man of your public eminence to take the lead – "

" – Drink?" asked Canteloupe curtly.

"Thank you."

Canteloupe poured two colossal whiskies.

"Public eminence, you say?"

He drank half his whisky in one swallow.

"I do, sir."

"Well, boy, I shouldn't count on it for too long. I've just had some very awkward reports about the new camp of ours out in the Quantocks. Unless something is done . . . quickly . . . they'll be howling for our heads. So we'd better put our own house in order before we go banging into somebody else's. You'll stay the night, if you please, and tomorrow we'll drive down to Westward Ho! and see what that infernal fellow Hookeby thinks he's up to."

Some days before all this was happening in Wiltshire and Somerset, Fielding Gray had consulted with Peter Morrison. As Fielding saw it, they had been left on duty in London in a supporting role: they were to watch for possible trouble from Lloyd-James while their allies made an active sortie into the west. Since the whole campaign had been undertaken for Peter's benefit, Fielding expected to find him helpfully disposed. Quite the contrary. Peter was vague, uninterested had no idea what either of them should do, made it plain, between bouts of irritable shrugging, that he found any notion of positive action distasteful if not indecent.

"So you're not going to make any effort?" Fielding said at last.

"Not this kind of effort."

"You'll just leave it all to your friends?"

"It's to oblige them," said Peter complacently, "that I've consented to come back at all."

"You don't want to come back?"

"I want to meet their wishes . . . if they think it's the best thing for the party. But that's not saying I'm going to take part in a running fight with cheap crooks. Anyway, I'm not sure they're handling this right."

"Look," said Fielding. "What your friends are trying to do, as I understand it, is to get you this seat without causing too big a bust-up or letting things go altogether to pot. Correct me if I'm wrong, but it seems that you don't care if everything does go to pot so long as you get the seat."

"Not quite that. But I can't undertake to involve myself with the wilful crimes and follies of other people. These must take their course and reach their destined end."

"After which you come marching out through the corpses in a nice, clean uniform and volunteer to take everything over? 'I'm sorry about the mess,' you can say, 'but it wasn't my fault, and I'll make a good job of cleaning it up'."

"Someone has to."

"And here and now? What do you mean to do about Lloyd-James?"

"Wait for him to become one of the corpses. He's carrying a powerful bomb about, and with any luck it'll go off in his face."

To hell with him, Fielding had thought. If that's the way he wants to play it, if he's just going to stand clear until the shooting's done, then I'm damned if I'll do anything to help. I've enough work of my own. So let him skulk away behind the lines, and serve him right if he stops a stray bullet.

But despite this reaction, and despite his fascination with the task of converting his youthful journal into the sumptuous novel for which Stern hoped, Fielding could not altogether lose interest in the *affaire Lewson*, and this interest was quickened, several days after his talk with Morrison, by a chance revelation of Maisie's.

One evening, as he was just about to leave her, Maisie had beckoned him to the bedroom window.

"Have a look at this, love," she said. "That chap hanging about in the street. Something went a bit wrong one day, and he swore he'd never come back, but he's been sniffing round ever since. Wondering whether to sink his pride and ring the bell."

In the street, lurking guiltily, was Somerset.

"I know him," said Fielding, relaxed to the point of casual indiscretion.

"Then you'd better wait till he goes."

"He might ring the bell after all."

"I don't think so," said Maisie: "he was rather badly put off."

"Come, come, dear. Professional secrets and all that."

"Nothing to do with me, love. I'd no idea what was going on. In fact, if you know him, perhaps you can tell me."

"I doubt it. What happened?"

"I've a correspondent . . . an Italian . . . who sends me little things from time to time. One day an agent of his turned up, one I hadn't seen before, and said he wanted to use my flat for a meeting. He was going to pay me well, and anyway there were . . . reasons . . . why I couldn't refuse, so I said yes. Then he said, would I ring the man he wanted to meet, because this man would recognise his voice and he wanted the meeting to be a surprise. So I said yes again, and the next thing I knew I found it was Somerset Lloyd-James I'd got to ring up, one of my oldest regulars, love, so was my face red."

"Maisie," said Fielding, grabbing her, "who was this agent and what did he want with Somerset?"

"The agent was called Holbrook," said Maisie, puzzled by Fielding's sudden excitement but anxious to please. "Bute or Jute Holbrook, something funny like that. I said to myself, how odd, what funny names these agents always have, because the usual one's called Burke Lawrence, which is pretty pec – "

"What did Holbrook want?"

"I couldn't hear very well. Some letter, I think."

"And Somerset agreed?"

"He agreed all right, love. This Jute or Bute was fair poison, I can tell you."

"You don't need to."

"You know him too?"

"Yes. Maisie, I'll tell you the whole story, I promise you, when there's time. But just now you must tell me: who is this Italian who sent Holbrook?"

A look of fear and distress appeared on Maisie's face.

"Sorry, love," she whispered; "I'd like to please you, but not that. Please not that."

"All right, not that. Then what about this other agent you mentioned? The usual one, you said. Burke something. Where can I get hold of him?"

"You promise you won't say I told you? He's all right, Burke, but others might get to hear I'd sent you and then – "

" – I promise."

"Burke Lawrence, love. If he's in London, which he often isn't, you'll find him at the Infantry Club. Funny place to stay, but he says it's cheap. Thirty-five bob a night with your own bathroom."

"Angel. . . . Has Somerset gone?"

"He's gone, love. You'll take care?" said Maisie, who had become very fond of Fielding.

"Only having one eye," said Fielding, "makes a man very circumspect."

After Fielding left Maisie he had telephoned the Infantry Club. Yes, Mr. Lawrence was staying at the club but he was out. So Fielding had eaten a quiet dinner in a small Greek restaurant in Charlotte Street (he had a taste for Greek food which his sad experience in Cyprus had not diminished) and then gone to the Infantry Club in person. Yes, Mr. Lawrence was now in the club; the porter would let him know. After about fifteen minutes,

"Mr. Lawrence, sir," the porter said at last.

A young man of his own age, Fielding noted, watching a figure come unsteadily down the stairs: vulgar good looks, oiled hair, a frightened expression, which was briefly replaced, when the eyes focused on Fielding, by one of undisguised repulsion.

"I'm sorry to disturb you," Fielding said.

"Who are you?"

"I gave my name. Fielding Gray."

"Can you identify yourself?"

"Why should I?"

"Because I'm not going to answer any questions until you do."

Clearly there was a misapprehension here; equally clearly Lawrence was very drunk. In which case it might be easier to exploit his mistake than to explain it. Fielding showed him an ordinary Army Officers' Identity Card which, through oversight, had not been withdrawn when he was invalided out.

"Major Gray," muttered Lawrence. "So they're bringing the Army in." He gave a little cackle of laughter. "At least one's dealing with officers and gentlemen."

"Shall we go upstairs? Or outside?"

"Out."

Together they walked down Pall Mall, Lawrence staggering at every third or fourth step. Fielding took his arm and piloted him down the Duke of York's steps, across the Mall and to safe anchorage on a park bench.

"Well, Major Gray?"

"Does the name Holbrook mean anything to you?"

"Yes. I had a girl friend called that. Penelope."

"I'm enquiring after a man. Jude Holbrook."

"Her husband. Or was. They were divorced some time ago."

"And more recently?"

"He survived," said Lawrence.

"Where is he now?"

"In Venice. Or rather, getting out of it, I imagine, as fast as his bandy little legs will carry him. If they let him."

"They?"

"For Christ's sake. You've come to pick me up. Can't we cut out all the crap about Holbrook? The wops will deal with him."

Fielding said nothing. Lawrence leant over the back of the bench and emitted a spurt of vomit. Then he turned again and said confidentially,

"You know, I couldn't believe it. No warning. Nothing on the grape-vine. And then to read about it, just like that, in an inside column of the evening paper."

Fielding still said nothing.

"Salvadori arrested. And dozens more of them. After all this time. And so bloody silly. Beating up that nice little Greek gambler who never did anyone any harm. Sheer spite."

"Salvadori," said Fielding, carefully groping his way, "is a big man. Too big for that, one would have thought."

"Salvadori never beat up anyone," said Lawrence with the grave conviction of counsel for the defence. "It was Holbrook. Must have been – before he left Italy for this last trip here. He's a mean bastard, Holbrook. I can just see it. He went to Lykiadopoulos to ask him what he wanted to know, and Lyki made some difficulty, and so Holbrook got impatient. That'd be it."

"He always seemed a very patient man to me."

"Yes, but mean. If there's one thing he can't stand it's the sight of a happy man, and that little Lykiadopoulos was a happy man if ever I saw one. So then, when Lyki held out a bit, Holbrook got impatient, couldn't resist it. . . ."

"It all seems highly conjectural."

"He was beaten to pieces, poor little sod. If that's what you call conjectural. Acid used on him. Bloody near killed. And so then the wop police came in, and this and that and t'other, and the next thing is they've got back to Salvadori. After all this time."

"Tell me," said Fielding. "If Holbrook gets out of Venice ahead of the police, where will he go?"

"Dunno. Or do I? I hadn't seen him in years, and no more had Penelope. Then, only a few weeks ago, I was told that someone was coming to England, and I must meet him and give him any help he wants, and it turns out to be Holbrook. The old bad penny. We saw quite a lot of him, me and Penelope, because she was curious about her ex. Took rather a fancy to him again – you know how it is after a long interval. So perhaps," said Lawrence, his drunken logic rambling to its conclusion, "he'll shack up with her. She's been through a lot of men since him, so she might be ready for a second time round. And she's a good liar, if people like you come poking their noses in."

"You think he'd come back to England?"

"As safe as anywhere. He hasn't committed any crimes here – or nothing like that foul business with poor little Lyki-thing."

"Where do we find. . . . Mrs. Jude Holbrook?"

"Just round the corner. Victoria. Carlisle Mansions. What are you going to do about me?"

"You can come too. Can you make it to Trafalgar Square?"

"Get a taxi here."

"Taxis," said Fielding sententiously, "may not pick up fares in the Royal Parks."

If, he thought in the taxi, Holbrook has managed to leave Italy, and if he is coming back to England, he'll be here by now. Salvadori – whoever he may be, the boss presumably, the one Maisie's so scared of – Salvadori must have been appre-hended this morning, since it was announced in the evening paper. So if Holbrook has escaped what sounds, from Lawrence's version of the news item, like a mass arrest, he must have left last night or early today.

"Look," he said to the slumped figure beside him: "when we're there just ring on the bell and ask. I'll keep out of sight."

"What are you going to do with me?"

"That's not for me to decide. But if you're helpful . . ."

"I get it. But I can't promise anything. Jude may have done a Gauguin for all I know."

With a great effort Lawrence lurched forward to tap the glass behind the driver.

"Just here . . . on the right."

Lawrence, followed by Fielding, tottered through an entrance hall into a dignified lift, which carried them to the second floor. About thirty yards along a corridor, Lawrence stopped and thundered on a door. Fielding flattened himself against the wall.

"Christ, you're reeking," said a shrewish voice.

"Jude been here?"

"Yes. But I didn't ask him to stay and I'm not asking you. You lot can bloody well keep out of the way till the row's over. I don't know you, see?"

"You had your share," mumbled Lawrence.

"The party's over now. So we'll all get quietly into our own little beds and go to sleep."

"Where's Jude?"

"He's gone running to Mummy. And brother, is he in a nasty temper."

"What's he going to do now?"

"Ask him yourself. I had enough to do keeping him out of here. Now git."

The door slammed and Lawrence got.

"He's gone to his mother," Lawrence said as they went down in the lift.

"Where's that?"

"I don't know. But I know who will. His old partner, Donald Salinger."

"Jesus," said Vanessa Salinger when Fielding rung up, "how in hell should I know?"

"Perhaps your husband. . . ."

"He's in the Princess Margaret Rose Hospital for Gentlefolk," she said in a prinking voice. "He thinks he's got a duodenal. If you ask me, it was the champagne at a wedding we went to. Enough to burn a hole in a rhinoceros."

"Perhaps . . . in his address book?"

"You sound nice. Come round and we'll see what we can find."

"I don't look nice."

He rang off, then consulted the directory and dialled for the Princess Margaret Rose Hospital.

"I'm Major Gray of Special Investigations," he said, rather enjoying the role which Lawrence had thrust upon him. "Kindly find out from your patient, Mr. Donald Salinger, the address of the mother of his former partner, Mr. Jude Holbrook."

"Mr. Salinger cannot be disturbed at this time of night. He has a stomach condition."

"So have I, baby," Fielding said. "Now get that address before I blow an ulcer."

Too strong a flavour of television? But no. The voice said it would see. After all, what could be more authoritative, in the television age, than the television idiom? Fielding wondered why more people hadn't realised this. Would it work on head waiters? Or tax inspectors? What effect would it have on Tessie Buttock? Or Somerset Lloyd-James?

"Mrs. Anthony J. Holbrook," the voice said, "The Ferns, Peddars' Way, Whitstable."

"Thanks, doll," he said, feeling quite skittish with triumph.

"Your friend's gone," said the taxi-driver when he came out of the telephone box.

"We don't need him any more." Should he? Yes, surely this was the television way.

"Drive to Whitstable," he said.

"Sweet bleeding Jesus, Guv. It'll cost you at least a tenner."

"Then start earning it."

He sat back and lit a cheroot. For the first time in what seemed years it started to rain. Nice and cosy in here, he thought, still warmed by the wine he had drunk at dinner; and what's a little rain to Major Gray of Special Investigations?

But when, an hour and half later, he arrived in Whitstable, Fielding's enthusiasm for the expedition had waned with the wine and he was bitterly regretting the expense. Peddars' Way turned out to be a long cart track, or little better, and by the time the taxi reached The Ferns at the very end of it he was feeling both empty and sick. But here he was and he must see it through.

"Wait," he told the driver, "or I'll never get away again."

"Very true, Guv," said the driver looking happily at the meter. He muttered something about adding 30 per cent for all journeys over five miles, but Fielding, gathering himself for a last effort, hardly heard. He went through the pouring rain to a low front door in a porch, could not see a light, could not find a bell, seized a knocker shaped like a lion's head, and knocked as if to summon the dead.

Almost immediately, a light went on and a sad, intelligent looking lady in a dressing-gown, her head surmounted by a neat bun, appeared at the door.

"Mrs. Anthony J. Holbrook?"

The bun bobbed assent.

"I'm sorry to disturb you."

"I was only reading."

"Even so. . . ." Come, come. Politeness to elderly ladies was no part of the new role. "My name's Major Gray." He decided against specifying his branch. "I must see your son."

"He's in bed."

"Nevertheless – "

" – Please show me your credentials," she said, calmly and sensibly, one hand on the door ready to swing it shut.

Fielding produced his identity card again. Mrs. Holbrook examined it carefully and passed it back.

"I don't know much of these things, but as far as I can see it's just an ordinary Army identity card. And I am reluctantly bound to observe that the photograph is one of a young man with regular features which bear no resemblance to your own."

Very slight Scottish accent, he noticed; with the tone, the

logic, the attitude, not of a shrilly protective mother, but of an intelligent man. Very well; treat her as such.

"Mrs. Holbrook. I can't make you admit me. But I should tell you that your son is in very bad trouble, and that it is probably in his interest, in so far as anything is, to hear what I have to say."

"Trouble?" said Mrs. Holbrook dispassionately.

"Trouble. Don't tell me you expected him here today. He's on the run."

"His visits are always sudden."

"Whenever he wants something, I suppose. Just now he wants refuge."

"And you? What do you want?"

"Simply to talk to him."

She looked at him quietly but sternly.

"Very well," she said, and drew aside to allow him to enter. "Please follow me."

She led him up a flight of stairs to a landing and knocked on a door.

"Jude. Someone to see you."

She gave Fielding another stern look and went down the stairs. Fielding opened the door. He found himself in a narrow bedroom decorated as a night nursery. Holbrook, fully dressed, lay smoking on a white bed. Above his head was a picture of a small bright boy, who might have been himself at the age of five or, to judge from the modern style of clothes, his son.

"I didn't expect to see you," Holbrook said. "You're a long way from Buttock's Hotel."

"The letter," said Fielding. "Did you give it to someone in Venice or have you still got it?"

"What's that to you?"

"Friends of mine . . . important friends . . . are anxious to know where it is."

"Indeed." Thoughtfully, Holbrook picked a strip of skin

from his thumb. "Well, I've no objection to their knowing. I've still got it, and as long as I'm left alone, no one will know what's in it. I suppose that's what they want?"

"Can I see it? I hate to appear mistrustful, but I must be able to give them proper assurance."

"Surely."

Holbrook opened a door in the little white cupboard by his bed. He took out some large folded sheets of paper and a small bottle.

"Now then," Holbrook said. "You can look at that letter for as long as you think necessary in order to assure yourself and your friends that it is the genuine article. While you look at it, I shall be holding this bottle." He unscrewed the stopper. "If you make the slightest suspicious movement, if you tear so much as half an inch of that paper, then you'll get a face full of acid." He gave the bottle a slight shake.

"Fair enough."

Holbrook passed the letter.

"Tell me," said Fielding as he looked over the first sheet, "why didn't you deliver it in Venice as planned?" Careful now. "To. . . . Salvadori?"

Make time.

"Salvadori was away, thank God. By the time he came back I knew there was something wrong. The police had been sniffing round ever since that little Greek was beaten up. . . ."

Make more time. How to get out of here with the letter and without receiving quarter of a pint of acid in the face?

"They tell me it was you that beat up the Greek. Not very prudent, surely?"

"Necessary. He wouldn't talk."

"Oh? I heard he was the sort of chap who'd be quite easy to persuade."

"He still wouldn't talk. I think he was going to. Then he stopped and gabbled something about protecting someone. It turned out later, when the job was almost done, that he didn't want to tell us about Lewson in case Lewson got hurt. He'd warned Lewson, when he gave him the letter, that sooner than get hurt himself he'd spill the beans right off, but when it came to the point . . . Funny man, Lykiadopoulos; sentimental."

Although none of this meant much to Fielding, it was providing him with time during which means of escape might occur to him.

"But surely," he said, "it wasn't Lewson you took the letter from. It was Somerset Lloyd-James."

"Yes. But I'd never have got on to him if I hadn't known about Lewson first. Lewson very nearly *did* get hurt – the Greek was right about that – but fortunately for him I found out that he no longer had the letter and what he'd done with it."

"How?"

Time. *Time.*

"Logic. A little luck. Lewson had been to see Lloyd-James and come away with a lot of money to spend. The answer wasn't difficult."

"What would . . . Salvadori have done with the letter if things had gone according to plan?"

TIME.

"I think he was going to use it to procure certain unofficial trading concessions for his own line of goods. He had legitimate interests as well, you know. Small arms. A word or two from one of the mandarins into an ear at the War Office might have been very helpful."

"But as it is . . . I wonder," said Fielding slowly, "that you left it so late to leave Venice. You knew Salvadori's time was running out. Yours too."

"I had other business to finish up. I always know," said Holbrook complacently, "just how long I've got. I'm the kind of man that always has a seat booked on the last train out. Have you finished with that letter?"

A bottle of acid. In the face. The face. *The face. Of course.* Why hadn't he thought of it before? Holbrook would very soon call the bluff, but even an extra second might make all the difference.

"I've finished reading it," he said. "I think I can assure my friends that it is genuine."

He folded the letter with care and moved closer to Holbrook, who held up the bottle.

"Careful," Holbrook said.

Fielding pointed to his face.

"Plastic surgery," he said, as he put the letter in his pocket. "I can't get any uglier and I shan't feel a thing."

Just for a moment Holbrook hesitated, and it was long enough.

"So the bottle was safely on the floor," Fielding told Peter Morrison in London two hours later, "and then there was a scuffle. He'd been well taught somewhere, but the dear old Army teaches you quite well too. Anyway, we hadn't been at it long before his mother came in and dressed us down like a couple of kids. Holbrook may be a killer but it seems he has a great respect for his mother. He just couldn't go on brawling while she was in the room. I fled . . . and that was it."

Peter crammed his hands fiercely into his dressing-gown pockets.

"Fielding," he said: "let me see that letter."

"I thought that you were not prepared to be involved in this kind of thing."

"If it comes to me . . . unsought . . ."

Fielding laughed. He sounded as if he were whinnying.

"I'm just an umpire," he said. "Remember? At this stage in the game I must consult my colleague. As you know, both Detterling and he are staying with Lord Canteloupe in Wiltshire, and I propose to go there straight away. If you want to

come too, you're welcome. You might like to drive us and
so save an impoverished ex-officer his train-fare."

He went to the window. His haste to see Stern and Detterling was prompted, as was this visit in the small hours to
Morrison, less by a sense of expediency than by desire for
congratulation. He was delighted and astounded by his own
performance.

"The weather's broken," he told Peter, "but it should be
an interesting drive. We can discuss the old days . . . and
consider how both our characters have deteriorated since."

"They're not here," said Canteloupe. "Detterling rang up
last night to say they were going to stay in some place near
the Quantocks."

"Oh," said Fielding, heavy with fatigue and disappointment. "Where?"

"Didn't say. But I suppose they'll be back this evening.
Spend the day here, if you like. There'll be some lunch. Stay
the night if it's important."

Canteloupe, as always when action was in prospect, was in
an expansive mood.

"Better still," he said. "Come with Weir and me. We're
going to the Quantocks to put my bloody caravan site to
rights. Might run across Detterling and his chum. Good day
out anyway. If only the rain lets up."

"That would be interesting," said Peter. Other things being
equal, he was always polite to men in office.

"I'd like to come," said Fielding; in his present mood,
tired though he was, any activity was better than none.

"So that's settled. We'll have a spot of breakfast first, and
we'll be at Westward Ho! by twelve."

"Right," said Alfie to Tom. "We should get to Westward
Ho! about twelve. I'll have a quick look, and then we'll have
the rest of the day to hunt for the love birds. And that's the

end of it for Alfie. If we've found nothing by five this afternoon, I'm off to London. Understood?"

"Understood."

"What's on today?" said Stern. "Not that I mind. Anything to get out of this unspeakable hotel."

"Usual procedure," said Detterling. "I thought we'd try up in the hills for a start."

"We can't start too soon for me. Did you see that look the waitress just gave us? Let's go before we get poisoned."

"Dreary day," said Mark to Isobel, as he looked out of her caravan window. "What would you like to do?"

"Be with you."

"Easy. Let's drive down to Weston-super-Mare and giggle at the people. And if the rain doesn't stop, let's come back here after lunch, and then – "

" – Yes please," said Isobel. "I shall enjoy that very much."

And so at about ten o'clock that morning, within a few minutes of each other, all four parties set out.

10

THE KILL

CANTELOUPE'S CAR was the first to reach Westward Ho! By this time the rain, which had been falling intermittently since ten o'clock the previous night, had become a heavy, continuous, absolutely vertical downpour, from a sky that was like an immense slab of filthy cotton wool which was being slowly lowered to stifle the earth. Not surprisingly, the caravan site looked appalling; but Canteloupe was quick to distinguish between the damage done by the elements and that done by man, and to find the latter even more deleterious than he had expected.

"Bloody great puddles are one thing," he said: "but when you can see dead dogs floating about on them, it's time to take action."

"Dead dogs" was an exaggeration; there was in fact only one dead puppy, the one which Cruxtable had kicked on the day of the opening and which, having fallen into a decline in consequence, had been deserted by its owners when they left the site. But one puppy was quite enough to make Canteloupe's point, and he now strode off through the mire, Carton Weir bringing up miserably behind him, to confront the Camp Commandant. Fielding and Peter, there being nothing else for it, sat in Canteloupe's Rolls having drinks from the miniature cocktail cabinet. They were just about to pour themselves a second round, when they saw Tom Llewyllyn's 1935 Mercedes, which was giving off dense fumes of protest after its struggle with the muddy uphill track, skid to a halt by the gate.

"Company," said Fielding, who found himself oddly un-surprised by this apparition. "Let's invite them over."

Canteloupe's chauffeur was despatched through the rain with the invitation. Tom accepted this, but Alfie, who was conscientious about his reporting, felt bound to undertake a tour of inspection; so he was fixed up by the chauffeur with a golfing umbrella and some galoshes, which Canteloupe had been too angry to bother with, and trudged away gallantly into the wet. The other three exchanged desultory chat over their drinks for a while and then, overwhelmed by the desolate aspect of Westward Ho!, by the total lack of human activity and by the constant drumming of rain on the roof of the Rolls, abandoned further social effort. Tom picked his nails; Fielding prepared the account he would give to Detter-ling of how he had outwitted Jude Holbrook; Peter sulked; and in front the chauffeur, who had fallen asleep, gently but persistently snored.

Mark and Isobel, having found nothing in Weston-super-Mare to giggle at on such a morning, and being still nervous of the police, decided to return to Westward Ho! even earlier than they had planned. There was a tin of something which they could eat for lunch in Isobel's caravan, and they would go out to the little hotel they had found for a proper dinner in the evening.

"If we can still get out," said Mark as they drove away from the sea front.

"The site's on a hill, darling. All the rain will be drained off."

"If it goes on like this, we'll find ourselves on an island. Like Noah and Co. on Ararat."

"Delicious," Isobel said, and started tickling the inside of his left thigh.

After a while Mark said:

"I found a *Times* in Weston. Still nothing from your old man."

"I don't mind. I like it as we are."

"Something's got to be settled sooner or later."

Isobel started to cry.

"Darling heart . . . what is it?"

"I don't want it to end," she sobbed. "I want it to go on like this. Even if Daddy did put a message in *The Times*, what could we do? We couldn't come out in the open, not with the police still looking for you."

"Perhaps your father could make it all right for me."

"He'd never do that. He's so upright, so hard. He won't understand about us. Sometimes I think this time in the caravans is the only time we shall ever have. In our own little world, because if ever we leave it there'll be some curse to break the spell."

They were both too preoccupied to notice a cerise Rover which was parked in a lay-by. The two men in the Rover were also preoccupied, as they had been quarrelling about where to go for lunch, but one of them gave the grey Morris Traveller a quick glance as it passed.

"YOB," said Detterling: "remember?"

He started the engine and dawdled along behind the Morris.

"Try to see who's in it," he said.

"I can't see anything in this rain," grumbled Stern. "I think there are two of them."

"Could be . . ."

"Could be the Queen and the Duke of Edinburgh. Just because Isobel Turbot was seen, days ago and miles away, getting out of a Morris numbered YOB . . ."

"It's worth trying."

Stern twitched.

"I want my lunch," he said, "and I want to ring up London. I'm meant to be running a business. Remember?"

Detterling nodded, then settled the Rover at a steady thirty-five miles an hour and about a hundred yards behind the Morris. As they neared the Quantocks, the black sky moved lower and lower, as though it must surely engulf them at any second.

"Yes, yes, yes," Lord Canteloupe was saying to Commandant Hookeby, "I understand your difficulties. But what I want to know is why there've been no new arrivals. Until yesterday the weather was perfect. For every one who moved out there should have been ten moving in."

Hookeby muttered something about teething troubles.

"You'd have got over those – if there was an atom of morale in the place. But because you've let things slide, let all the campers drift away, the staff have lost any guts they ever had." Canteloupe banged the office table with his fist; a tray of pencils clattered on to the floor; Hookeby began resentfully to pick them up. "But for all that," Canteloupe went on, "I still can't understand why no one else is coming. We could make everything all right – even now – if only people would come here. And God knows, we've run a wide enough advertising campaign."

"Salinger's have been going downhill," Weir remarked.

"It's nothing to do with Salinger's. They only print the stuff. It was good stuff – I saw to that."

"There never *were* any visitors worth talking of," said Hookeby, still scooping up pencils. "That opening – we had to hire most of them. You know that."

"That was just to get things off the ground. Of course people weren't going to come straight off. The holiday season hadn't really started, for one thing. But now . . . with that splash on television . . . they ought to be pouring in."

"The locals," said Hookeby, "have a story about this place."

"Story?"

"Legend. It seems that there was a wood on this spur before it was all cleared away."

Hookeby paused. Like many lazy men, he had a taste for local chatter, which he would absorb by the hour in the nearest pub. Uncritical by nature, he listened with placid interest to whatever he was told, little caring whether it was true or not; but it had now occured to him that Lord Cante-loupe might make a less tolerant audience.

"It's nothing really," he said.

"Go on, man."

"Well, it was a great place for lovers, this wood. Always had been from right back. So far back that it wasn't quite a joke. There was supposed to be some kind of . . . guardian, I suppose you'd say . . . who was very fussy about who came up here. Only real lovers could be happy. The rest found they weren't – well – welcome. Not that this guardian was hostile, exactly, he just didn't make them welcome. So what I mean is, perhaps none of us are wanted . . . if you get me."

Canteloupe did not. But he had no time to say so, because his chauffeur came into the room unannounced, dripping wet, and with a very funny look on his face.

"Please come at once, my lord," the chauffeur said.

Alfie Schroeder, sloshing round the caravan site, wondered whether there was a story in it. He'd seen the opening on television and he knew there had been something phoney about it; and now here was the camp, festering and derelict, looking for all the world as if it had been briefly occupied and then deserted by retreating troops – bored, unhappy, fright-ened men, who did not know where they were or where they were heading, only that they were passing through doomed wasteland in a foreign country, far from home. And yet . . . surely the place had been beautiful once?

Alfie looked at the dead puppy dog, then away to the blank windows of the Maison Bingo. He walked a hundred yards to the swimming pool; the outlet had been blocked, and scummy water lapped over the edges towards a shuttered ice-cream stall. He turned in among the caravans. One at least was inhabited, for the door, which had been left un-locked, swung open as he passed to reveal a gay little row of summer shoes and a bright cape hanging above them.

"Is anyone in?" called Alfie.

No one answered, so Alfie poked his head round the door. He saw the remains of breakfast for two, a lot of wine bottles both empty and full, and, at the end of the room, occupying the entire width of the caravan, a double bunk, unmade but somehow jolly and inviting, as though it expected people to leap back into it at any moment. So someone's having fun, thought Alfie, and his spirits lifted a little. But not for long. As he passed down the rows of lifeless trailers, most of which were supported by rusty iron bars or piles of brick, as he walked through the echoing toilets (his soles scraping on the dank and gritty floor), as he turned back again, through the obscenely dripping showers, out into the rain (surely it was even heavier) and down another row of soggy caravans, Alfie began to feel as low as he had ever felt in his life. A story? What story? Official incompetence? It seemed more like the wrath of Jehovah, who had apparently decided, by contrast with the quick, clean end which he had allotted Sodom, to destroy this place by gradual infection – to let it be slowly rotted to pieces by the spreading poisons of its own rain-diluted filth.

Well, thought Alfie, I'll tell them about it at Billingsgate House and see if they want something made of it. It all depends what line the old man's going to take on Canteloupe: the old man likes the idea of British Holiday Development, so he may want to give him a good, long chance; on the other hand, he won't like the idea of its being mishandled, so he may want to crunch him straight away. These galoshes are no sodding good and this umbrella weighs a ton. Only another fifty yards, Alfie boy, then into that steaming Rolls for a lovely goblet of fire-water.

But this was not to be. As Alfie emerged from the ranks of trailers and into view of the gate in the outer perimeter, he was greeted by an extraordinary spectacle. The door of the Rolls was wide open and three heads – Gray's, Morrison's, Tom's – were absurdly sticking out of it. The heads were all turned towards the gate, through which marched Captain Detterling, carrying a limp figure over his shoulder in a fireman's lift. Behind, twitching and gesticulating, stumbled Gregory Stern. And circling round them both, kicking up her heels behind her in a desperate, jerky trot, round and round and round, went Isobel Turbot, her mouth opening and shutting, like that of a ventriloquist's dummy, in a series of low howls which only just carried through the rain to Alfie:

"Eheu. Eheu. Eheu."

When Detterling was ten yards inside the gate he halted. Stern drew up to him and looked into his face, as if asking for instructions; while Isobel, whimpering, began to stroke the head which hung down by Detterling's left hip. From all sides people converged on this group: Alfie from the caravans; Canteloupe, Weir and the chauffeur from Hookeby's office; Tom, Peter and Fielding from the Rolls.

"I couldn't get the car up the hill," Detterling explained to no one in particular; "and she wouldn't let me leave him down there."

"What's wrong with him?"

One look at the dangling head which Isobel was caressing was enough to answer that.

"How . . . ?"

"For God's sake," said Canteloupe, "we must get out of this rain."

"Hookeby's office," Weir suggested.

"We'll leave Hookeby out of this."

Canteloupe looked round him, then walked straight through twenty yards of puddle and up the steps of the Maison Bingo. When the door wouldn't open, he put his shoulder to it and at the second heave sent it crashing inwards. One by one the rest trailed after him, except the chauffeur, who knew his place and went back to the Rolls.

Detterling took his burden to the far end of the Maison Bingo and laid it on the low stage. He pressed a switch on a panel in the wall, hoping to get some light, and got Harry Belafonte singing "Mary's Boychild" instead. Isobel, who had followed him to the stage, clapped her hands over her ears and ran towards the entrance.

"It was my fault," she squealed above Belafonte; "we were so happy and I knew it couldn't last, not after what he said, and I twisted the wheel."

Everyone turned towards her as she stood in the door. She looked back at them with hatred, opened her mouth as if to curse them, then turned and disappeared into the rain. Fielding made to follow her.

"Leave her," Canteloupe said. "Let her cool off."

"Born on Christmas Day," sang Belafonte, "Born on Christmas Day, Born on Christ – "

" – For Christ's sake turn that bloody thing off. What happened?"

"We were some way behind," said Stern in a high voice; "we couldn't see."

"Could it have been what she said?" asked Tom.

"I don't know," said Detterling. "They disappeared round a sharp bend. When we came round it, their car had left the road and run down an embankment . . . not very far. Could have skidded. There was nothing the matter with her except hysteria. He'd broken his neck."

"Who is he anyway?" said Canteloupe.

"Mark Lewson," said Tom.

They all turned towards the body on the stage, rather as if

Tom had uttered a summons and they expected to see the body acknowledge it. Instead of this they saw Peter Morrison with his hand in Lewson's breast pocket.

"What the hell are you doing?"

Detterling laughed. "He's taking action at last," he said. "Looking for the letter."

"What letter?" said Tom and Alfie, like a well trained chorus.

"No, I'm not," said Morrison, cringing slightly. "Fielding's got it. But I thought Lewson might have a copy, I thought it should be destroyed before anyone – "

" – *You've* got the letter?" said Detterling to Fielding.

"What letter?" repeated Tom and Alfie.

"I was right," said Peter. He held up some sheets of paper. "A photostat by the look of it."

"Let's have a look," said Weir soothingly.

"Give it to me," said Canteloupe.

Peter handed over the photostat copy. Canteloupe began to read.

"You see?" Weir kept prompting him.

Gregory Stern sat down on the floor, although there were at least twenty rows of chairs, and started to weep.

Tom, Detterling and Alfie crowded round Fielding, who shyly produced the original. He had been hoping to tell the full story of his ingenuity detail by detail, but this was not possible because of the incessant interruptions from Tom and Alfie. As Tom began to understand approximately what had happened and what was in the letter, his brow darkened and his eyes receded. He breathed deeply and muttered words like, "Treason . . . murderer . . . exposure." "Steady, laddie," Alfie kept saying, though he too looked quietly furious. Meanwhile, Fielding did his best to continue his tale of Holbrook to Detterling, who was not really listening as he was too busy instructing and observing Tom.

"So that was it," Alfie said at last. "Someone was putting pressure on the old man. Lewson."

"And Lloyd-James."

"But neither of them even had the bloody letter," said Tom. "That's good, that is."

"They did at first. Then Holbrook must have pinched it – "

" – And I," said Fielding fatuously, "got it back." He brandished it above his head. "For God's sake listen to me. . . . As I was saying, I found Burke Lawrence at the Infantry Club, and after I'd questioned him – he thought I was an authorised investigator, you see – after I'd quest – "

" – You shut up," said Lord Canteloupe, who was now standing on the stage by Lewson's body as if about to make a funeral oration, "and listen to me." He folded the photostat copy and put it in his pocket. "Now then. There's enough here" – he tapped his pocket – "to send several highly respected public men to the Tower of London for life and make a scandal to last a generation. If it's true. All I've seen is this copy." He tapped his pocket again. "It could be a fake, it could be a joke, it proves nothing at all – unless there's an original which will stand up to every test in the book. You apparently claim," he said to Fielding, "to have that original. You will be so good as to hand it over to me."

Fielding did not move.

"You heard. Give it to Lord Canteloupe," said Weir smugly.

"To the Leader of the Labour Party," said Tom.

"To the Director of Public Prosecutions," said Alfie.

"Keep it," said Peter Morrison. And then, when Detterling laughed, "*We* found it."

"And you stop blubbering," shouted Canteloupe to Stern, in order to have something to do while the squabble continued in the body of the hall.

"There has been a death," said Stern. "Have you not eyes to see and ears to hear?" He rocked slowly backwards and forwards and began to wail more vigorously than ever.

"It's quite obvious," said Weir, "that either Lord Cante-loupe, or myself as his representative in the Commons – "

" – Edwin Turbot must be publicly exposed – "

" – The nation has a right to the truth – "

" – We have a right to what we found," said Peter Morrison to Fielding. "We should take it into our own safe keeping."

"What shall I do?" said Fielding to Captain Detterling.

"You're the umpire."

Fielding looked at Tom Llewyllyn, who was silly with rancour; at Alfie Schroeder, who was bubbling with outrage; at Peter Morrison, who smiled with open, honest, boyish charm; at Lord Canteloupe, who stood splendid and pro-consular upon the boards; and then he looked at Detterling, who shook his head.

So Fielding walked over the Gregory Stern, where he sat cross-legged upon the floor, and dropped the letter into his lap.

"You're the other umpire," he said. "You decide."

"There is nothing to decide," said Stern. "This man" – he pointed up to Canteloupe – "represents government here. He must have it."

He rose to his feet, walked to the stage and passed the letter up to Canteloupe, who received it with a bow and stood examining it with care. Carton Weir executed a little dance of triumph. Stern went out into the rain. Canteloupe looked up from the letter and glared at his audience.

"What is there left," he said, "at the end of the day? A piece of paper which proves a debt. But it is not a debt owed to any of us here. Let the dead do their own dunning – if they still want to collect."

He stepped down off the stage and stalked towards the door. Nobody said anything or tried to stop him, though Carton Weir, for one, was writhing with frustration. But like the rest of them he silently followed Canteloupe, into the rain, down the steps of the Maison Bingo, past the dinette and the discussion centre, until they came to the camp incinerator.

But the camp incinerator had ceased to burn.

Still nobody said anything. They all followed Canteloupe back past the discussion centre and the dinette and the Maison Bingo; down a long row of caravans; past the caravan inside which Gregory Stern was comforting Isobel Turbot; past more caravans; past the showers, and into the toilets, where Lord Canteloupe tore the des Moulins letter into tiny shreds and then, with a great clanking of hardware, flushed them for ever down the drain.

I I

VERDICTS

"WELL?" SAID Tom to Alfie, as he drove him through the slowly brightening afternoon to pick up his luggage and catch his train.

"You've got your answer," said Alfie, "which is more than a lot of people get. You know what happened and why. So why not leave it at that?"

"You were as angry as I was."

"Certainly. But the proof's gone – halfway up the Bristol Channel by now. No good being angry if there isn't any proof. Simply makes you look a fool. Not much good being angry even if you have got proof: you only get ulcers and die young. What is there left," he said, in passable imitation of Canteloupe, "at the end of the day?"

"But whatever Alfie says," said Tom to Patricia that night, "I should do something. There's a duty here. What Canteloupe did was a conjuring trick, sleight of hand. I know I should do something."

"What?"

"Find a copy. Swear I'd seen the original before it was destroyed. Expose your father."

"They wouldn't believe you," Patricia said.

"I should still try."

"Why? Make us all unhappy, ruin yourself very likely, for something that happened years ago."

"A woman's attitude."

"A woman who loves you."

"There were bullets, bombs. Men died."

"Scandal won't bring them back."

"Canteloupe said something of the kind. But I hadn't expected you to be so complacent."

"A woman's attitude. If once things are right with her. . . ."

"And are they?"

"Now," she said. "The night, after the wedding, I was shocked. Not by any particular thing which had happened, but by . . . the farce of it all. Everything seemed to lack dignity. It had been . . . a festival of clowning and bad taste. But now . . ."

"Yes. Now?"

"I see how silly I was. None of it had anything to do with us. I should just have taken you in my arms and shut it all out. I think that's what Isobel was trying to do in her own disastrous way. . . . What will happen about Isobel?"

"Detterling and Stern are taking care of that. They'll quieten her down, and then she'll just tell the police that Lewson's car skidded on the corner. She probably imagined the other thing."

"I'm not sure. It's the sort of – "

" – Who's making trouble now? I wish I knew what to do . . . about your father. There's a duty."

"There's a duty owed to me," Patricia said. "Come to bed now." She came up behind him, put her arms round his neck, and kissed the curls at the back of his head. "I'm your first duty from now on. You can decide in the morning what to do about my father . . . my father and yours."

"I must say," said Sir Edwin the next morning, "everything seems to have fallen out very conveniently. Master Lewson was never any good. Poetic justice, you might say. And provided Isobel doesn't persist in saying his death was her fault . . . "

"She was hysterical. Nobody else saw what happened. There was a sharp bend, a wet road. . . . I think you'll find

Detterling and the police between them sort all that out without any trouble."

"Good. So. . . . I am to be grateful to you, Tom?"

"I told you what happened, sir. You'd better be grateful to Lord Canteloupe. And to Patricia."

"To Patricia?"

"She has had the last word over this.' You see, sir, I want her to be as happy as possible. There will be a lot to make her unhappy as time goes on, because she cannot understand that a writer's first love will always be his writing. I can't and won't alter over that; but I love her so much that I must concede something. Let's say that I'm making Patricia a wedding present of my moral conscience . . . for what it's worth."

"In return for which she will take second place to your writing?"

"Yes . . . though she doesn't yet know it."

"A very fair compromise," said Sir Edwin. "But I wonder whether you've got your priorities right?"

"I don't think that you of all people are qualified to judge."

"I'm not judging. I'm just wondering. Have a piece of butterscotch?"

"No thank you, sir. If it's all right with you, Patricia and I will leave for our honeymoon tomorrow."

"My dear boy. . . . But of course. And may all joy attend you."

"Thank you. Just one more thing," said Tom, "before I go."

"Yes?"

"Now that the letter is no longer a factor . . . now that there is no pressure . . . what will you do about Bishop's Cross?"

"You mean . . . I'm now free to let them choose Morrison?"

"Yes."

Sir Edwin began to feel the funny new kind of excitement

which had first come over him during the disastrous conclusion of the wedding and had reappeared several times since.

"Do you really mind which I choose?" he asked.

"As you know, I've always favoured Morrison," Tom said.

But then he frowned, remembering that Peter's behaviour at Westward Ho! had not been quite as he would have wished. There had been a degree of opportunism: Peter had made an oddly disagreeable impression . . . as of a man trying to sell places in the life-boat of a sinking ship? No, not quite that, because whatever Peter was up to, it had been in accordance with the rules. It was more as though Peter, given privileged notice of war or famine, had been quietly flying the country under pretence of a routine business trip.

"Well," said Sir Edwin, "I've been thinking about that. You know, it's not really for me to interfere. I shall leave Percival and his committee to get on with their own job."

Sir Edwin had spoken the truth to Tom; from now on he was going to leave Percival alone. But he did not mean by this quite what Tom thought he meant. To Peter Morrison, who had solicited an interview with him in London, Sir Edwin was more explicit.

"I suppose, sir," said Peter politely, "that now there are no more complications, I can consider myself sure of your support."

"No, you can't," the Minister had said. "I'm leaving it all to Rupert Percival. As I always should have done."

"It comes to the same thing," said Peter. "Rupert Percival has always been behind me."

"He isn't now. Before these . . . complications, as you call them, were finally dealt with, Percival had been instructed, and had agreed, to choose Lloyd-James. I don't propose to countermand the order."

Peter bit his lip.

"May one ask why not?"

"One may," said the Minister, feeling the thrill of excitement, of liberation, that had been affecting him more and more often over the past few days. "The answer is simply this: you're too damned wet. Lloyd-James is pretty foul, I grant you that. But he does things. He doesn't sit around moaning about his honour. He gets on with it."

Sir Edwin thought of what Lord Canteloupe had told him over dinner at White's the previous night. "I won't teach my grandmother to suck eggs," Canteloupe had said: "But remember this. When it comes down to brass tacks, one's better off working with shits. They'll kick you in the ghoulies as soon as look at you, but one knows that and can be ready for it. It's these chaps who have scruples that really kill you dead. They'll drop you in a sewer to drown when you least expect it, and then go round whining that it was their moral duty."

"It's the whining I can't stand," Sir Edwin now said to Morrison. "I've put up with so much of it for so long. Now I've come to a time of life when I won't put up with any more. I don't say I like Lloyd-James, but in one very important sense I know just where I stand with him: he's like Nature itself – he has few liberal sentiments and no moral ones. I find this singularly refreshing."

"He's a religious man," said Peter with insinuation, "a Roman Catholic."

"Exactly so. Of all religions, Catholicism is the least liberal and the least moral. I'm going to *enjoy* having Lloyd-James in the House. It'll be like having one of the Borgias. As for you Morrison," the Minister said, "you're a kind of social Bowdler. You take all the spice out of life. Give me that bald bastard from Gower Street any day of the week."

This last phrase was, of course, Canteloupe's, but Peter Morrison neither knew nor cared about that. Deeply hurt, he rose, bowed to Sir Edwin, and went off to spend the afternoon at Lord's. There he met Captain Detterling, who, when told what had happened, was less than sympathetic.

"You know your trouble?" Captain Detterling said. "You're like an officer in my regiment who could never have a crap when he was out in the field. You know why not?"

"No," said Peter miserably.

"Because he thought his men would cease to respect him if they found out he had an arsehole just like theirs."

"So it seems," said Somerset Lloyd-James to Carton Weir, "That everything's in order after all."

Carton Weir was not at all pleased with the way in which things had turned out. Canteloupe had thrown away a winning hand, and now he, Carton, was back in Square One – being, as ever, deferential to Lloyd-James. Still, things were as they were, and he had been in the game long enough to make the best of them with a good grace.

"If you ask me, my dear," he said, remembering what Vanessa Salinger had told him at the wedding, "Sir Edwin's going a bit funny. Change of life."

"Do you think that's why he's settled for me at Bishop's Cross? Out of sheer perversity?"

"One reason. And then Canteloupe's been pushing for you. Apparently he's very pleased with those bits you've written about him in *Strix*. He thinks you're the sort of man we need in Westminster these days. 'Someone who knows how to play it rough,' he told me: 'train us all up a bit to cope with the Ruskies'."

"I'm obliged to Canteloupe for his good opinion. He doesn't exactly play pat ball himself. I keep wondering why he destroyed that letter. I should have expected him to make use of it."

Weir suppressed a spasm of ill temper.

"Very simple, dear," he said. "He told me later. 'I like a rough game,' he told me, 'and even a foul one, but I won't risk having the entire stadium blown up'."

"A balanced view, on the whole. I think," said Somerset,

"that when Professor Constable leaves the board of *Strix* next month we might do a lot worse than Canteloupe. If we can square it with the Articles, of course."

"Come, come, sweetie," said Weir rather nastily: "you're not going to let those boring old Articles upset you? Why not take a lesson from Canteloupe and just tear them up?"

"I've told you before," said Somerset severely: "you will never attain to really responsible office until you suppress your taste for silly jokes."

"Cup of tea, love?"

"Thanks, Tessie," said Fielding Gray.

"Getting on well?"

"Not too bad. Stern's very pleased with what I've done so far."

"Is it true about Mr. Stern . . . that he's going to marry that Isobel Turbot?"

"Looks like it."

"Well, well. Next thing we'll have to find someone for you."

"I've got someone, Tessie."

He thought tenderly of Maisie. It now seemed certain, despite the Salvadori arrests, that she was going to be left alone. Maisie had been very marginal. As for Burke Lawrence and Jude Holbrook, God alone knew what had happened to them. . . .

"You know, love, you can always bring her here," Tessie was saying.

"I like going to her place, Tessie. I'm very happy here, but it makes a nice change to get out for a blow now and then."

"I suppose so, dear. What's her name?"

"Maisie."

"And her surname?"

"Do you know," said Fielding, "I've never thought to ask."

"So Mark Lewson's dead," said Angela Tuck to Max de

Freville in Menton. "Killed in a car crash, it says here."

"*Requiescat*," said Max. "He wouldn't have been happy with that Turbot girl for long."

"I don't see why not."

"He was like me. He enjoyed being unstable. People like Mark and me, we get tired sometimes and think we want to settle, but after a bit we find security unbearable. That's why I enjoyed being a gambler in the old days but got fed up with being a big-time organiser . . . just sitting there and taking the five per cents. It was a bore not being able to lose."

"So in the end you just didn't bother to collect. . . . When are you going to get bored with me, Max?"

"Pretty soon, I'm afraid. You were splendid for time out. But as a regular thing . . . no."

"Swine."

"Sorry. As a matter of fact, I'm thinking of going to Venice for a few weeks. There's been one hell of a stink about a chap called Salvadori, and I want to see what I can find out. It was one of the things on which none of my highly paid informants ever got a proper grip. It seems poor old Lykiadopoulos was badly beaten up by one of the henchmen – perhaps he'll be able to give me a line."

"Can I come?"

"No. You're my rest cure. I'm well again now."

"When will you be back?" Angela said.

"When I need another cure."

"I might not still be here."

"Women like you are two a penny," Max said: "frustrated mothers."

"You know, there's one big difference," said Angela bitterly, "between you and Mark. He was a man; when you'd been to bed with him, you knew it."

"Heigh-ho," sighed Max de Freville: "as good an epitaph as any, I suppose."